Part of
His Story

Part of His Story

Alfred Corn

Mid-List Press
Minneapolis

Published by Mid-List Press
4324-12th Avenue South
Minneapolis, Minnesota 55407-3218

Printed in the United States of America
00 99 98 97   5 4 3 2 1

Library of Congress Cataloging-in-Publication Data
Corn, Alfred, 1943–
Part of his story : a novel / by Alfred Corn.
p.   cm.
I. Title.
PS3553.0655P37   1997
813'.54--dc21   96–50021
ISBN 0-922811-29-6

Portions of this book appeared previously in
The Kenyon Review and *Evergreen Chronicles.*
Cover photo © British Museum.

♾ The paper used in this publication meets the minimum requirements
of the American National Standard for Information Sciences—
Permanence of Paper for Printed Library Materials, ANSI Z39.48–1984.

For Larry Wexler, hero of recovery

Acknowledgments

I would like to thank Adam Mars-Jones for reading a draft of this book and making useful suggestions, and also Edmund White, for his willingness to read it and offer encouragement. Many thanks go as well to Christopher Corwin, who helped me prepare the manuscript for publication.

Part I

One

The postcards picked up at a stall near Westminster Bridge lie scattered on the desk, bright bits of blue, red, and black color glazed over by lamplight into partial invisibility. Their aim is to interest everybody, and that's also their main drawback. I can see my own thumbprint imposed on the card nearest (a view of St. Paul's), as though I'm being booked for some crime, defacement of public monuments, say. Turning the card over and scribbling a blithe message signed "Avery" or "Avery Walsh" will simply renew the misdemeanor in different terms: *Dear missed friend—Here is London, I mean, my blunt impression of it.* Blunt, yes, but not concealing the need to keep in touch.

Certainly I don't plan to come off as broken down with bereavement and sorrow (but I am, I am!). Most of the addressees will reply, let's hope. We all like mail, especially intrepid, solitary adventurers doing our worst to feel actual in another country. Putting my own invisible estrangement next to the confident, English rootedness all around me is risky. The people who belong here embody an almost offensive existence in the round, making ghosts of anyone whose speech differs from theirs, whose clothes were bought on another continent, whose friends and lovers have never been seen by them. Deep down, we're never surprised when the orders for deportation arrive. They confirm what has already happened.

Actually, letters from home have come slipping through the mail slot even before being solicited. All of them put the same question: Why go far away from your friends, why leave New York, where you have a successful play running and any number of admirers, men and women? And if you must go, why to London, you could have some time to yourself in Connecticut, for example, or Provincetown, couldn't you? No one has taken seriously the unofficial broadcast outlining my project of doing a biography. Most have assumed it all actually is a way of dealing with the bereavement, while a few of the more blasé suspect that I am pursuing someone kept secret up till now, someone very interesting indeed.

A biography? Adele's frowning smile, an S-shaped wrinkle monogrammed in her forehead, and an indulgent irony in her eyes: that's the picture that comes to mind when I recall breaking the news to her. And the jungle telegraph moves quickly: within two days everyone I know had heard, but, so what, they didn't believe it; or felt threatened by it. No one less wants freedom for you than your friends; they want you just as you have always been, next to them, where they can keep an eye on you. That's the way love operates, take it or leave it.

Now friends, and myself as well, have to believe me: here I am in my furnished flat just off Regent's Park, with my admission card to the British Library, a stack of fresh red notebooks waiting to be filled, and an accordion file to help organize my chapters. Not to mention loneliness, as good a spur to action as anything. And bereavement? Those who told me I'd be better off working through it at home near people who cared about me, have plausibility on their side. Well, that had been my first plan. No way to remember at just which moment in the endlessly resumed mud-wrestle with pain stronger measures suggested themselves. If loneliness was going to be it, then why not double or nothing? Stop trying to ignore the fact that the person I was meant to live to a ripe, youthful old age with had ignored the script and slipped off with no warning. (But I'm making it sound intentional, and it wasn't.) My apartment on Twenty-third Street seemed enormously vacant and echoey, the pictures viewing me rather than I them. In London loneliness would fit, and the pictures would be different, obviously. Now I can alternate focus between the two separate kinds of estrangement—the survivor's and the expatriate's—just as you shift a heavy suitcase from the left hand to the right, a regular pendulum swing of pain that makes time pass.

Yesterday it was bereavement I decided to put out of mind by substituting an afternoon spent in public as a stranger. For about an hour, it worked. Like so many others, but with different reasons, I settled on Trafalgar Square, wandering around not in straight lines, with the conspicuous purposelessness of the tourist, looking at my counterparts salute the flocks of pigeons there. No bird was going to go hungry, not with so much feed and good will available. The boldest people and birds got physical. You would see a cheerful father of three being photographed with a dozen pigeons perched on his shoulders and arms, the temporary pets making expert stabs at proffered handfuls of seed. Amputee Lord Nelson high up on his column had a quartet of birds resting like cockades on his hat, an infringement of personal dignity the coolness of stone helped him ignore. And the rest, was he aware of it?—the muffled detonation of traffic down below, taxis black-gleaming in the sun as they hurtled up the Strand from Charing Cross, scarlet duplex buses wheeling around his piece of flagstoned territory guarded by sleepy bronze lions, twin fountains that juggled bright ropes of water irresistibly magnetizing vendors and strollers around themselves, and one small child as well, who ran teetertotter up to clots of pigeons as they exploded into the air like scattershot, casting speckled shadows on a solitary observer in sunglasses and blue windbreaker, gaze fixed on the stony Admiral as if hoping for a response, words more useful than, "England expects every man to do his duty."

I walked out of the square and up toward the perforated spire of St. Martin in the Fields, unusual among churches of England in that its doors stand always open. Street alcoholics come here as to one of their few safe harbors, so it's never entirely empty. The homeless, though, must settle themselves into counterfeit postures of devotion if they don't want to be invited outdoors again. As I slipped into a rear pew, I noticed two human casualties slumped forward in an attitude of deep penitence that could only be sleep. Also (respectably dressed), a husband and wife, both white-haired but intent and alert. They were looking toward the front of the church where a middle-aged man, in a not new but expensive jacket was speaking into a microphone. "… Clive had shown from the first that energy and resolution that became his trademark."

A talk was being given, but about what, and to what audience? The amplified voice reverberated from the vaults of the church. Further descriptions of Clive, and always in a persistent, ominous past tense. The voice turned ragged: "… an irreplaceable loss." So Clive was dead, and this was his eulogy. "I have memories of him as we sat and picnicked on the bank of the Cam, and then later of finding our house in St. John's Wood Road, and of the improvements he made to the garden there, and of many evenings spent pleasantly at the hearth." The fact that the speaker was the "life companion," as he said, of the deceased had to compete with the parallel recognition that no one had come to pay respects—or rather, no more than five people: a middle-aged couple, two homeless alcoholics, and myself.

I guess anybody would feel pity for this man, this survivor, but for me there was also the unhealed memory of Joshua's memorial service to unlock sympathy, fellow-feelings given a strange twist now by the fact that the elaborate one we gave him had overflowed with friends and relatives. Still, I had enough protective cynicism in me wonder what the problem with Clive was that he had so few friends to mourn him. But as the gray-haired speaker brought his carefully composed address to a close, I felt the unfairness of his situation and some of his grief as well, the pangs driven in even deeper, no doubt, by the British negative technique of reining everything in, never showing raw emotion, never performing an opera. Tears welled up in my eyes, though not to the point of spilling, not even at the memory of the least summarizable human being I will ever know. The sadness of middle-aged Clive's skimpy box-office appeal seemed to reconstitute in different terms the sadness of another unrelated dismemberment, Joshua's death in his early thirties. Normal tourist disorientation wasn't, this particular afternoon, going to screen out the glare of loss.

My fellow sufferer stood silently at the microphone folding the sheets of his eulogy. A clergyman in white clerical collar and not black but gray shirt-front strode discreetly from the rear of the church up to the microphone. "Excellent," he said. "I have one suggestion. When you get to the part about his military service, you want to *slow down* and pronounce the name of each decoration very distinctly...." Sympathetic tears suddenly congealed. The older middle-class couple were getting up to go, their curiosity satisfied, an occasion of vicarious grief tasted with no actual cost. We had been watching a rehearsal; like everything social, a memorial service is theater and must be run through at least once before the actual staging. Those big vases of flowers up around the altar weren't to be wasted; they had simply arrived early. Next day or the next, street people and tourists would have to share the church with flocks of mourners come to partake of a little handout of bereavement divided among survivors, survivors and friends who would never again be gathered together in this same mixture, representatives of the several worlds that the gentle speaker and his military companion had belonged to.

Two

When Adele telephones, I'm already in bed, propped on pillows, going through some notes on the Cibber family, the subject of my biography. File cards spill out into a fan on the floor as I reach for the telephone. Her excited "Avery!" and my excited "Adele!" tip headfirst into each other as we both struggle with the cramp of trying to speak naturally over transatlantic distances.

Then comes the purpose of the call: "I was over to the apartment today. You know, Joshua's things are still hanging in the closet. Should I give them to one of the charity outlets?

"I don't know."

"Did you have some special reason for keeping them?"

"If you want to take care of it, go ahead."

"Mothers get used to disposing of their sons' clothes when they outgrow them. Twenty years I did that."

"Do whatever's best," I said, silently conceding that Joshua had outgrown his clothes once and for all.

"Avery? I miss you."

"The bad part of being away from New York is that you're not here. I still wish you would come over."

"I know. I just can't. Anyway, not yet. If I don't wake up every day in my own bed I'm completely thrown."

"So you said. I don't find being here all that easy, either."

"Then why on earth don't you come back?"

"I will. But not yet. If that's OK." We listen to the faint frying noises of the connection.

"All right. I just wanted to remind you that I love you, darling, and miss you—and Joshua, too."

"Is everything OK? Are you all right?"

"Fine. Everyone says I look better. So, suppose I do something with those clothes."

"You do whatever you think is best."

"Talk to you in a couple of days?"

"I'll telephone you. It's cheaper from this end because I can call late."

"You won't forget?"

"Promise. I'm glad you went ahead. I miss you. Love you."

"You too. Bye for now."

I don't know why, exactly, but these conversations with Adele always leave me in a cold sweat. There are reasons, but the question is whether I want to go into them now. I know it was wrong to have come here and left her by herself—even though she gave me her "permission" by answering every one of the arguments I came up with to discourage myself from doing it. Maybe now she's sorry she didn't dissuade me. At some point in the future I will have to find a way to make this up. Even listening to her voice is hard, though, because it sounds so much like Joshua's. Seeing her is worse, given that they have the same thick brown hair (hers streaked with gray) and the same dark spaniel eyes. I'm completely hers and was from the moment we met seven years ago. But it's as though all the things we used to have in common have now been displaced by—Joshua's not being here.

If only that weren't true. I wish she and I could spend evenings together like old times, she telling her stories and pouring glasses of wine, showing us the new Moroccan shawl she bought today, or stirring cream and slivers of a white truffle she got at Dean & De Luca's into a dish of linguine. Therapeutic, almost, to think of back then, the Days Before. Clearing away after dinner, then settling in for a talkfest. She always used to ask me which new books to read, and, having read them, waited studiously to hear my opinions before framing her own, in a series of groans and openhanded gestures. What I thought seldom altered how she saw things, but she would always conclude with, "Of course I see your point." And she never had anything but praise for my plays— in fact, could be counted on to perform ritual shreddings of any unfavorable reviews they might happen to get. Sometimes when Joshua was away, we would spend evenings together, usually quieter in tone, as though she felt less obliged to be a show-stopper without Josh, who made her nervous, she loved him so much.

It may be I liked her best those evenings. A person who has spent some time on most of the squares of life's checkerboard, she is less dogmatic than anybody I know. "It could be," is one of her favorite replies. Sometimes she doesn't answer a question, but only gives me, particularly in candlelight, what we've come to refer to as her Simone Signoret smile. She knows a lot about men- or do I mean she knows a lot about men and women. (After the past seven years, she must know something about men and men as well). Living according to her particular rules of independence for so many years, she has a sturdy familiarity with loneliness, its ins and outs. Joe Lambert was her second husband, and, although she never remarried after his death (partly for Joshua's sake), I'm told there were long- and short-term replacements. By the time I knew her, she had almost entirely phased them out as real love affairs, but a few had remained friends, and these I did meet. One was an artist, of course, who, like Adele, made collages but also did paintings (which she has never done).

Another was a Swiss rug dealer who must at one time have been the source of some of Adele's beautiful Turkish carpets. She likes color and pattern, and, though she hasn't given a show for years, her collages have been collected and written about. I brought one of them with me to London—composed, she explained, entirely of bits of posters stripped from various walls in Paris during a stay there fifteen years ago, her last trip abroad.

It sits on the bureau, leaning against the Victorian wallpaper, some of whose colors it also contains. But where the wallpaper is all botany and birds, the collage is geometry and abstraction. I'm sure she was right to stay home, and I'm not, well, inconsolable that she did. Her call alone is enough to start me off again, rerunning the well-worn repertory of interior home movies. Sleep won't come easily tonight. Everything is charged, heavy, electric with meaning; the thick curtains opposite look as though they're about to stir and waver.... Adele's collage used to hang in our bedroom, and remembering that makes me feel a little afraid. Afraid of experience, which teaches that anything, however illogical and cruel, can happen. I see it almost as an allegory—*Experience*, a statue in weathered gray limestone, dressed in skillfully carved animal skins and bearing a loose scroll in its hand. This unwinds and conveys a different message to each viewer, some good news, sure, but more bad than good. Nobody gets off entirely unscathed.

My scroll begins with Joshua, or rather with the announcement of his departure. No matter that I can close my eyes and see him face-on and from every angle, outdoors and in, surrounded by friends or in solitude, no matter that I can remember exactly the way his skin felt or how his hair smelled of fresh tea, or how resiliently symmetrical the tendons at the base of his spine were, no matter that I can hear the low rumble of his voice and that I can see us both at the dinner table or sleeping or walking along the river: He will never ever come back, and I can't accept that, I can't and I won't—Joshua, please don't really be gone, I mean it, it's not fair, you....

WHEN I WAKE, the bedside lamp is still burning, and my watch says two a.m. Switching off the lamp is the best plan but guarantees nothing. On the other hand, if I'm not really sleepy, what does it matter? I don't really care whether turning over memories is Correct Bereavement Procedure or not, I have a self-indulgent side, not to mention a habit of rule-breaking. In the darkness I can see him very clearly—several hims, from the first to the last. Naturally, it's the earliest images that have the densest specific gravity, a personal cargo I will carry with me until ... carry with me always.

Toward the end of the seventies, men's hair was beginning to shorten again, but Joshua's was still longish, a sort of Renaissance fluff, very light and fine. He was the center of attention at the cafe table where he was sitting with a half dozen of his friends. I was alone in my corner, sneaking envious looks at that group, young to the point of arrogance, most of them dressed to show off their best features, and exhibiting gay amusement at everything that was being said. They all seemed predictable—except for him. The cafe was a sort of actor's hangout just off Sheridan Square. *Duval Street Blues* was still in rehearsal, and things were going so badly I just ducked out of the theater and went off to debate whether I should forget writing and sign on as a travel agent. Joshua at the center of that group was like the sun breaking through March clouds. To make the scene work, my own ordinary, supporting-role looks—medium build, thinning light-brown hair, and long-nosed, sincere (I hope) Celtic face—would have to be put under bright overhead lighting.

A friend of mine came in, saw me, said hello, saw their table, said hello to them, and then invited me to sit with them. I was given each of their names in turn, but it was only Joshua's that stuck, partly because I don't especially like that name. He was wearing an old blue T-shirt, stretched out of shape so that it showed the skin over the lower neck and down to the collarbone. I could see that if he stood up he would be very tall; he had one of those large-boned frames that suggest neither slenderness nor heaviness. His coloring, a photogenic blend of tan and pink, I found disturbing. I can still see him perfectly, slumped back a little in his chair, his left forearm extended on the table; it is strong and fine at once, with a light veiling of hair brushed smoothly across cords of muscle. From time to time he would lift his hand to his cleft chin, and you would notice how broad his jaw was, with an underlying blue-black tone where he had shaved. I kept centering on his eyes, black-shining under close-set dark brows modeled into very light scowl lines as nearly permanent as his constant habit of thought, which was their source. A funny, almost embarrassing silence crystallized around the table— partly because some of the group were aspiring actors and knew my name, but also because everyone, though possibly not Joshua, saw how interested I was. Just their luck: he was not an actor. I could be of no use to *him*—nor, apparently, to them either. One by one they got up and left, abandoning the field to the clear winner. Joshua and I lingered on behind; the traffic noises dimmed to a distant hush. We exchanged banalities for a while, then fell silent ourselves. I remember being disappointed in his speaking voice: it seemed adolescent, almost goofy, anyway not in keeping with a face that serious. You had to abstract, listen to *what* he said, not the pure sound of it, and that's not easy for a theater person.

I have never believed in letting opportunities slip past. By the time we stood to go, a date for dinner some six hours later was on.

When I think of Joshua now, I realize that something in his nature was always a little beyond my reach, that his particular combination of reticence and stubbornly independent reason made a lot of him inaccessible to me. It was as though he loved me but also liked eluding me. That very elusiveness, I think, accounts for some of my devotion to him. And I guess the attractiveness of difference worked both ways. For one thing, I was six years older, which might not have mattered much except that it was the watershed of Gay Liberation: he'd grown up at a time when you didn't necessarily have to hide your boyfriends—though, of course, as with most guys his age, there had also been girlfriends, too. Just that spring he'd finished his Ph.D. in Sanskrit at Columbia and was planning to take an assistant professorship the following year as the first step in the long pull to tenure. I had never met a "Sanskritist" before; actually, I had no close academic friends. It helped to hear that Joshua's interest had begun as nothing more forbidding than a teenage fascination with Eastern religion, drugs, George Harrison, saffron robes, all of that. Somehow his brain hadn't been spoiled, and he had discovered in himself a real passion for classical Sanskrit literature. He had fellowships all through graduate school, mostly nominal ones, since both his father and his grandfather Lambert had left him an income. His father was a French-speaking Canadian from Montreal but had lived for years as a resident alien in New York even before marrying Adele. Joshua used to reminisce about his childhood, which was apparently very happy—trips to the Bronx Zoo, Saturday movies, birthday dinners in the Rainbow Room. He told me he had never really accepted his father's death, in fact, always expected him to reappear as though it had all never happened.

At the very beginning, armchair psychology told me that what he must be seeing in me was a substitute father, given the age difference and the fact that I already had an acknowledged place in the artistic scheme of things in New York. I suppose you could say I was "tougher" than Joshua. That would have to have been true since I had materialized there in the late sixties, a skinny Bard graduate with only one friend to look up, my parents both killed in a car accident two years before. The smashup happened at a normally safe intersection in New Bedford, Massachusetts, my home town, about three blocks from the clothing store Dad owned. I have no siblings so the estate and some insurance money went to me alone, which allowed me to finish college with some left over to get started in New York.

My other resource was an apparently boundless interest in the theater. Like most actors who come to New York, I got only so far, but unlike them I discovered I could also write. During the time when I began to show one- and two-act plays to people doing Off-Off Broadway, there was actually a shortage of good scripts. It was held to be an era of transition and experiment, and formula was definitely out, even though few had any idea of what was meant to replace it. Some of those early efforts are funny to think about now—where are the *Darvon Comedy*, the *Passion Fruit Cocktail*, and *Coke Can* of yesteryear? But their very preposterousness helped them get staged. You have to think back to the years of the first Theater of the Ridiculous productions, Harry Kotoukas, The Open Theater, Ronald Tavel, Lanford Wilson—we were all in it together. Eventually, after I figured out what was what, productions Off Broadway were forthcoming, and now I even have an Obie on my mantel somebody has to keep dusted off. As for Broadway itself, I will be happy to be produced there as soon as I and the right producers can see the point of it, but not before. I'm not driven to change my "professional profile."

People have asked me about my plays, professional secrets, and so forth. I don't know. The only "theory" I have about it is that ever since I was little, my thinking has been like dialogue. Not only do I think in words, I think in conversations; there's always another person hearing me. And that habit has gone over naturally into play-writing. No doubt this mental quirk can be thought of as constituting a ghastly neurosis. Sometimes I long to be "unconscious," nonverbal, moving through an unlabeled world of images and indefinite emotions. Doesn't seem to be possible, and, when I came across Chesterton's pronouncement that "to be civilized is to be a conversation," I decided to be reassured and go ahead happily with both ends of the interior talk show.

Meanwhile, instead of a play, I've undertaken to write a biography, and of a subject as arcane as the Cibbers. Whether it's reasonable to aim at the level of classic biographies like those of Richard Ellmann or Walter Jackson Bate—no way of knowing, but maybe I can get some serious attention, not just in the newspapers, but in those learned journals of the kind Joshua was always poring over. Is this an absurd project? Maybe, but I've done wilder things. Theater is a various medium and most of those involved in it lead rather improvised lives. My résumé will never land me a job in corporate business, but I always had good schooling, and I've never stopped reading. In my circle of friends, I can always be counted on for some really jaw-breaking pedantry.

That was one of the reasons Joshua and I managed so well as a couple. We always had something to talk about. Though I never learned a word of the language, I did vet some of his scholarly translations of the Sanskrit plays and offered criticism of them, as texts in English. Meanwhile, Joshua was passionate about contemporary culture. I never had to coax him to go to the theater or opera with me and felt lucky to have available someone with all that classical learning at his disposal. He also knew Greek, Latin, and German, the whole philology discipline. My habit of larding conversation with oracular bits from earlier literature was helped along by his almost total recall of the classics: he supplied me with them.

He sometimes said he wished he practiced some kind of art or other, and he questioned how interested I could be in his "uncreative" mind. But he was wrong there. I don't actually seek out artist types for friends, and, as for creativity, so little that's being done really deserves the name, all these "happenings" cooked up extemporaneously by adding one part drug trip, two parts sci-fi, two parts Tokyo, and four parts *Götterdämmerung* at Bayreuth. Give me Joshua and his accurate references any day.

Three

The TV image deflates into a tiny ping of light and then vanishes. I've been listening to a news broadcast, better phrased than the ones back home, it must be said. 1986 turns out to be the year when the British public finally realizes the full extent of the disaster. In the States we've already become jaded to it (along with so much else). What topic can sustain interest under the onslaught of coverage? The very newsworthiness of AIDS is what will eventually make it hard for anybody to remain actively concerned and not succumb to "compassion fatigue." And who knows what methods people will have to devise to keep the subject vivid in public consciousness?

For the past four years, news media there have been saturated with medical descriptions of the illness, theories of infection, and distant hopes for a cure. With a mixture of agony, weariness, and irony I watch them recapitulate here the astonishments, surmises, and reactions that we've been through at home. Up till a few months ago the percentage of people affected in Britain was small, but the figures have begun to make startling leaps, and now—now there's an uproar. I notice how the speakers here have even more trouble than our CBS and ABC anchormen handling unsavory particulars. They visibly dislike saying the words "homosexual," and "intercourse"—but then, so do I, for different reasons. These are like verbal tongs to fasten unto an untouchable subject and hold it aloft for public inspection.

Once again the inexorable conclusions are reached: if people other than "minorities" (more tongs) and drug users are going to be susceptible, then obviously a real emergency is at hand, and Britannia will have to roll up her sleeves and deal with the unpleasantness, just as Uncle Sam has begun to do. Words outside the norms of gentility will be pronounced, and a pamphlet explaining the disease in clinical detail will be sent to every home in the United Kingdom, an information blitz that brings to mind the Doomsday Book, whose eight hundredth anniversary this is.

I've developed a carefully fabricated nonchalance about the whole topic, put together during long periods of having to control terror for the sake of another person. My method was to acquire "scientific" objectivity by studying everything I could get my hands on concerning the disease and try to achieve the reasonable patience urged on me by friends and professional counselors. There was also self-protective numbness, useful for survival, if not so good for keeping sensitive to other people's dilemmas. All of the professional cool I developed back then is still mine, though I recognize that it is probably only a thin crust over who knows how much unresolved turmoil. Nothing says I have to achieve peace on every floor of the psyche by the end of next week. If I'm at least unanxious for the moment, then let that do. Mourning is a lifetime project anyway, nobody has set up a deadline. Deadline: what a funny word....

There's no deadline for my biography, either, yet I would like to have a draft of it in hand, say, two years from now. I've done enough research already to know that, for the first part of it, facts are few. Does that make things easier or harder then? The project as a whole may turn out to be to be a little tricky because I'm doing three generations of the Cibbers—I want to write one of those family biographies that seem to be the newest approach to the genre. Nobody has ever said much about any of the Cibbers other than Colley Cibber, the second generation; but, actually, both his father and his children are powerful subjects on their own. True, it was Colley, the actor and fellow playwright, whose story drew me into the project at first. But there's something peculiarly contemporary about the Cibber children.... And then the old patriarch Caius Gabriel, still noted (well, to some degree) as a sculptor, makes an absorbing character study as the archetypal immigrant who makes a place for himself in the new society only to throw everything into jeopardy with a personal failing. (In this particular case, addiction to gambling, which got him into debtor's prison.)

The elder Cibber composed himself as carefully as one of his allegorical figures. I haven't been able to find much about his first years, beyond the fact that he was born in Schleswig in 1630 and decided at some point to become, not a cabinet-maker like his father, but instead a sculptor. Less clear is how he managed to make his artistic pilgrimage to Italy; the best guess is that it was done under the sponsorship of the King of Denmark. Something in the air of Italy made him change his name to Cibber. Before that it was probably Sieber or Sievert. Here you've got a good example of his chameleonic psychology, which dovetailed nicely with his business sense. I'll need to do some character analysis on this topic, but on the basis of annoyingly few facts. My theory is that the flaw—and there unmistakably is one—running through three generations of the Cibbers first shows itself in this tiny bit of deception.

Caius Gabriel seems to have changed his name to make it resemble that of the Cibó family of Rome, who were his patrons. It's established that the coat of arms he appropriated actually belonged to the Cibó nobility. Why he came to London is a mystery; when he arrived he brought with him an identity in some ways specious. The great problem will be to locate information about those first years in England. What is known is that he first worked as an apprentice in the Long Acre (not far from what would be his son's theater a half century later) and that he soon became his own master, with new patrons and commissions. Teutonic industriousness seems to have been second nature to him. With considerable practical sense, he tackled the problem of marriage and eventually turned up a woman moderately handsome in looks, moderately well provided for, and moderately noble. This was Jane Colley, only child of a family of Rutlandshire gentry; she brought with her a dowry of six thousand pounds. The Colley name was given to Caius Gabriel's first son, and it is verifiable fact that when the young man reached adulthood, he used a coat of arms that combined the Cibó and Colley emblems.

What will be interesting to do is to render the social and cultural background of the period, the curious amber-tinted half-light of the Stuart Restoration. I've been getting some good things from Pepys, and there's plenty of period detail to fill in—low-ceilinged interiors, heavy coffee-colored wood paneling, music for viols by Purcell, Dryden performed in candlelit theaters, the construction of the Wren churches, and a local tradition of sculpture whose most original examples were realized in wood. Perhaps I'll include a picture of something by Grinling Gibbons—garlands of leaves and fruit carved in linden and walnut, or the awkward but appealing pelican at the main altar of St. James, Picadilly. Close by my subject is the development of Restoration theater, and giving some sort of précis about the King's Players and their repertory should be easy for me. Meanwhile, throughout all these banquet decades of cavaliers in beards and lace and Peter

Lely-style beauties in blue brocade and pearls, Cibber Senior
was executing important commissions for public statuary. The
limestone Charles II in Soho Square is by him, as well as the
Phoenix on the facade of St. Paul's. More to my purpose is the
bas-relief panel at the base of the memorial raised as a sign of
hope after London's Great Fire, a work referred to simply as
"The Monument."

As part of my research, last week I went to see it. I'm not
even remotely an expert in baroque sculpture, but I thought
there was a chance I might patch together something
plausible about the technical and allegorical aspects. A friend
of mine who teaches art history at Columbia said that when
you're dealing with the form of bas-relief, one of the compar-
isons to make is to stage design and the blocking of scenes, the
problems of illusionism, perspective, and composition with
human figures being nearly the same. The Monument relief is
possibly Cibber's most "theatrical" work. But you have to get
fairly close to decipher his design. It's just above eye level at
the foot of a tall column standing in a small square right in the
heart of several modernist bank towers in the City, a weird old
survivor as baroque (in its own way) as some of the confused
street people who were wandering around the square the day
I found it.

Anyhow, Cibber put his scene together with quite a lot of
forethought. In the rectangle that constitutes his "proscenium," you see, stage right, an impressive rendering of Charles
II in Roman cuirass, tunic, and greaves, his pose recalling so
many statues of Augustus, but, instead of a boyish Roman
crop, wearing the outrageous peruke of poodle curls dictated
by seventeenth-century fashion. On the left is the recumbent
figure of a goddess, who in the allegory stands for London
prostrate in the post-fire destruction. A crowd of stiff-limbed
rebuilders stands by, and another allegorical figure (probably
Architecture) gestures toward a floating apotheosis overhead:

London as she will at last appear when restored to glory, a glowing assumption in soot-stained marble.

The inscription explains some of this and makes an allusion to the "martyrdom" of Charles I. (Looking up some of this background, I came across the fact that Charles actually has a day on the Anglican liturgical calendar.) Gradually the viewer comes to understand that the Great Fire itself is being assimilated to Charles I's execution and the Puritan abolition of monarchy. Restoration of the second Charles will have settled disorder and destruction for good, if we can see that. There I stood, piecing it all together, no doubt regarded by passersby as a better dressed representative of the homeless category, or possibly some drug-tripper swept up in the swirls and grooves of meaningless marble. Maybe they wouldn't be too far wrong.

The cake-icing in any long-term assignment comes largely from the "extras" you gather along the path, things that didn't play a role in the original intention. Poring over primary sources in the British Library and making reams of fascinating notes, I find that whole days can glide by in no time flat. Which is one way not to think about things that can't be changed.... And if the armchair psychoanalyst tells me that I'm trying to bring Joshua back to life by *becoming* him—a scholar, not a playwright—OK, I can accept that, not every word spoken from an armchair is false. But it won't stop me, if only because right now I've lost interest in the theater, I couldn't care less if I never wrote another play. And I have to do *something*. What I've seen is that having this project has given me a framework for my stay in London; it helps organize my day, my excursions, and, yes, it helps "interpret" the city in terms that mean something to me in the present.

Here's an example: Fire and religious strife are intensely Londonite themes—to which you could also add plague. The City has a record of surviving all three, one weathered

testimonial thereof being the Monument itself. The old land-
mark is dwarfed by surrounding high rises, implying that
those themes are now all safely historical, no threat to a world
built of concrete, steel, and glass, and founded on religious
indifference. All right. Is modernity then a form of large-scale
nonchalance also? Achieved by methods not much different
from my own in dealing with personal loss. But what exactly
is the loss that modernity wants to cover over in its perfect,
glass-smooth constructions, its hard-won serenity? The usual,
no doubt: the old unsolvable dilemma of fleshly suffering and
physical death.

As for plague, the theme has returned again this year, and
nonchalance is the last thing in evidence anywhere. Not even
the new architecture seems to be any use. Not the government, nor religious authorities, nor the private sector seems to
have achieved any calm concerning these new emergencies,
and maybe we'll get nothing but concealed panic until somebody solves the Riddle of the Virus. When they do, perhaps a
new monument will be put up to those who worked for a
solution and those who died while waiting for it. Cibber, Old
Phoenix, will they draw upon you as a source for the design
of the new relief at its base? Possibly, but first I have to get you
out of Marshalsea Prison, where you've been locked up for
your gambling debts. And I have to get your firstborn son further along in his upbringing, otherwise how can you hope to
have any worthy offspring, natural and otherwise? Your suc-
cessors will want hints from you in designing that new apotheosis: Londinium aloft on clouds of marble cream, her head
tilted back as at a theater, raptly gazing up at the bright con-
stellations that figure forth our destined arrivals and depar-
tures. Standing to go, we pause a moment to admire the aging
actress, then whisper a brief "I love you," to the friends we
leave behind in a gilded box.

Four

Is it because producers want the writers they've invested in to make influential friends that Robert, impresario extraordinaire, has been telephoning to ask who I've been seeing. Not just asking, but probing. He said, with his familiar profitable expansiveness, "Look, I really think you should be going out more, meet a few of their leading lights while you're over there." (He must be cogitating a London production of one of the plays. But would they travel?) He gave me the number of a woman friend of his here, saying I was certain to like her. With some reluctance, and only because being alone didn't seem to be getting me anywhere, last week I telephoned her. Her name is Gillian Fournier (a French name because she is a descendant, apparently, of one of the old London Huguenot families that came to England after Protestantism was outlawed in France). I had read one of her novels and knew she had also written a study of French immigrants to England in the seventeenth century. That, however, I had never even seen a copy of, despite its high reputation. Robert says she's one of the brightest young writers in

London, constantly reviewing and lecturing and appearing on television to discuss contemporary issues from a Left point of view. When I telephoned, I mentioned our in-common friend, and a genial, almost professional rapport was immediately established.

"Actually," she said, "I'm having some people to dinner on Thursday—including Corinne Waldman, whom you probably know in New York. Would you like to come? You've probably seen her already—."

"We've never met." I explained that writers in our over-populated home town didn't always know each other; and I would like to meet Corinne Waldman, it was always terrific to get to know people whose work you admired. This compliment, designed to range farther than its immediate object, seemed to warm the telephonic connection, and I was told to come at eight to an address in Belsize Park.

Punctuality is no fetish to me, but, thinking local custom might be strict, I climbed up the steps in front of a brown brick house with white-columned portico and rang the bell about one minute after the stroke of eight. A pause and then a rattle from the lock; the door swung open. Before me stood a hostess ever so slightly flustered; it was clear that no one was expected to be on time. "You're Avery," she laughed. "Come in." A gesture toward the rank of coat hooks by the door: "You can put your coat here."

She was younger than I had assumed, on the tallish side, with elfin features underneath medium-length blond hair fringed over the forehead. Speech-delivery was what I guess you call "sparkling," her voice intelligently highlighted with British upper-class falsetto. She waved me into the front room, where a small fire was burning. I said Robert had told me so much about her, and she asked for news of him. But I really had none. Robert's life is determinedly unvarying; instead of traveling, he telephones. I said as much, leaving us without a next steppingstone, and unfortunately there was no one else to herd into the conversation. Letting something in her inflection suggest that she didn't really like to probe, she asked what there was about London that made people want to come and live there for stretches of time. I explained about the biography.

"Oh, Corinne will want to hear about that. She's doing one of Gertrude Stein. It ought to be fascinating." Not a serve I could return—so I glanced around me and made some remark about the pictures on the walls. While these were being attributed to various friends of hers, a very tall youngish man ambled into the room, wearing a tie under a sweater, casual trousers, and only socks on his feet. "Oh here's Alun," she said. I didn't hear his last name clearly, but it was different from hers—not proof positive that they weren't married, and it seemed nicer somehow that they shouldn't be. (In fact, they are married.) Something mentioned as an aside let me know that Alun was involved in experimental film, as scenarist or cameraman or both, anyhow, a job that didn't require him to go to an office. At first I thought that Gillian was in charge of the household, as a feminist might well be, but then, as they spoke, I could see that Alun in subtle ways had the upper hand. Also, he clearly had no idea who I was and didn't particularly care—why should he?—at least, not enough to bother with launching into the hesitation waltz of lightly proffered leads and quickly drawn inferences that pave a path across the neutral territory of the dance floor, over toward the bar and deeper acquaintance. It was clearly Gillian's party; in the interests of marital teamwork he was willing to make an appearance, but the rest would just have to take care of itself.

The doorbell rang and here was Corinne Waldman, also a bit early. She was wearing zip-front trousers and a blue sweater. I remembered that she and Gillian had feminism in common, though Gillian tonight wore a dress (pale tan linen with a square white collar edged in lace). Corinne and I nodded and smiled when Gillian exchanged our names, and, we ritually admitted we had heard so much about each other.

"It takes coming to London to meet though," she said.

"A good argument for making the effort," I said. "Unless the point was to get *away* from people."

"Is this your first trip?"

"Third—no, wait, fourth. But I've never stayed longer than two weeks."

"Well, you're an old China hand by now."

"Gillian told me you were writing about Stein. Wouldn't Paris be the best place?"

"I was there already. The British Museum has quite a lot of material, turns out."

"The British Library?"

"Right. But actually most of the research is done now. I just thought I'd have a better chance to get down to the writing here. I like England, or at least London, don't you? You must or you wouldn't have come. "

"I haven't quite made up my mind. But it's easier, probably, to work here. Not that I've done that much so far." She nodded, glazed over, and then turned back to Gillian—who was going to answer the door, the other inviteds now at last beginning to appear. It was a distraction these still-tentative acquaintances welcomed as much as I did.

For Corinne's benefit, there were two other women biographers, one of them with her husband Julian De Compton (much older), who in the forties and fifties had made his own mandarin mark right along with Cyril Connolly, Peter Quennell, and Nancy Mitford. He doesn't seem to publish anything nowadays except for an occasional review. Actually, I was curious to talk to him but as the evening fell out, we never addressed a word directly to each other.

Possibly for my sake, Gillian had invited a young unmarried poet named David Hunt, who happened to teach at Westminster School where her son was enrolled, which would be another reason. Under his blazer he wore a scarlet V-necked sweater, a white shirt and a blue bow tie. He was bearded and spoke with a voice much like those produced by actors in revivals of Restoration comedy. The pitch drawled up and down, diphthongs were stretched out to reveal all their component phonemes, and "were" rhymed with "wear." When inaugurating a topic, he had a habit of placing his right hand lightly against his chest, as though fingering some heavy gold medallion so present to him it became just as solid and real to the rest of us. The fact crept out that he had published a volume or two of poetry, which of course I had never heard of. (Why is it as soon as people identify themselves as poets I get nervous and defensive? Unresolved guilt about being less literary, no doubt.) Dead certain he wouldn't know anything about Off Broadway, I steered conversation away from me; pretty quickly we got onto his teaching.

"If you're a poet, you must teach English."

"Greek and Latin, actually. They *wearen't* my favorite classical languages, but schools have no real need for the others."

"What are your favorites then?"

"Persian, for one. That began as an undergraduate enthusiasm for Hafiz. But of course once you begin climbing the branching tree of Indo-European language, there's no end to it. It wasn't long—." My stomach knotted up as I felt a premonitory fear of what he was going to say, and here it came: "... two years, I think, before I looked at Sanskrit, the grandaddy of them all. Endlessly fascinating. There's an extensive dramatic literature, actually, which perhaps you—." He had no idea why this answer should startle anyone and was startled himself. I sat frozen and wordless, looking not at him but through him. Why did it have to be Sanskrit? An image of Joshua bent over one last translation during the final months snapped into my mind and blotted out everything else. Seeing that I'd suddenly dematerialized, David Hunt mumbled a conclusion to his comment and then turned beseechingly to Gillian for rescue, who refilled his wineglass and drew him over toward the De Comptons.

I knew she must be beginning to regret the unselfish impulse of inviting a perfect stranger (less than perfect, as it happened) to her party. Here was that disaster, the guest who is off by himself talking to no one. I sat stock still in my armchair next to a basket of magazines, one of which I picked up and began leafing through with not very convincing absorption, the print and color photographs a blur before my eyes, now filling up with salt water. After a while, the other biographer, the unmarried one, came over and on some pretext I don't remember began to talk. She had no way of knowing who this person crumpled in his chair might be, but it was clear at least that I was a Yank, pre-middle-aged, and apparently unattached. What she brought over to my corner was a hearty manner and ready jokes, a style based on too many generous instincts to qualify as "good form"; but this was just what I needed, unreliable social being that I am. Not that there was really any question of disobeying the first law of social life: everyone must pull his oar, everyone must contribute comments, words, noise. And, if one of us no longer wished to participate, that was just too bad: he'd contracted to share a few hours of conversation with everyone present. As we strolled into the dining room I squared my shoulders and straightened my tie.

A piece of luck came when Gillian placed the unmarried biographer (her name was Henrietta) next to me at table. Then, on my right, was Vera De Compton, whose low-key self-presentation and Charlotte Brontë looks, for undiscoverable reasons, made me feel at ease. Meanwhile Julian De Compton was up at the other end of the table at Gillian's right hand, David Hunt, her son's teacher, at her left. Corinne sat at De Compton's right, next to Alun, midway down the table in the thick of things. I was at the bottom, in the Biography Corner. Where, soon, I felt a tickle, a light botanical flurry, around my ears; and noticed a houseplant sitting on a shelf just behind with long spears of pale green leaves extending down as though to place a mock laurel crown on my head. Hmmp.

"Gillian, mind if I move this?" She gestured into the air and said nothing but watched me set it down on a sideboard. I suddenly felt very American, unable to appear at some new venue without rearranging it. The low, imperturbable pizzicato of conversation continued on just below decipherability as I plumped down again and smiled at my dinner partners. Gillian managed to keep the conversational lead even while functioning as hostess and server. After the soup, our lamb with flageolet beans was served and handed around. Fragrant steam curling off the plates jarred pleasantly with the scent of freesias in a small bunch at the center of the table between twin silver candlesticks. As the chef took her seat again a small moment of silent appreciation was allowed to elapse until she picked up her fork, and several separate conversations began.

By then I was enough recovered (the prospect of food has a way of reviving me) to push off into the stream, eventually to the point of aiming something up to the head of the table, a gambit triggered by half a phrase I had heard Gillian deliver along with soft laughter on an ascending scale. "No, you're dead wrong," I said. "Gielgud's voice, just as a voice, isn't good at all. But he can do more with it than anyone alive." My comment (made by someone who until then had been taken by all present for an unfortunate, a deaf mute) was just enough on target to achieve unanimity around the table for a little while. The others watched and listened as Gillian and I exchanged a volley or two, with Henrietta eventually pitching in ("But Simon Callow, in comic roles …") to make a threesome. Lucky the subject was acting, which I can usually be convincing about. The point made, hands resting on the table, I leaned back in the chair and subsided, letting the waters of surrounding conversations close over my spotlit, twenty-five second number. Vera De Compton turned to me and asked how long I'd be staying, her eyes direct under soot-black lashes. I said I didn't know, but probably not as long as I would end up wanting to. Striding on, I said I assumed she was working on a book or something.

"Yes, I'm doing a study of the *récit*."

"Oh—now what is that exactly?"

"Well, obviously it's a French genre. A short novel told in the first person, with a lot of side comment and reflection on the action. Constant's *Adolphe* is one, and Camus's *The Stranger*. Most of Colette. And there's one by an American: Glenway Wescott's *The Pilgrim Hawk*."

"Odd, I didn't know that kind of novel had a name."

"Well, people don't, and that's why I thought it would be useful to write about it."

Gillian stood up and sent pudding around to each place, which reminded me that, like our dinner, the evening would gratefully come to an end. It had turned out not too awful, but I made a solemn resolution not to work up any social life in London; I wasn't ready yet.

Afterwards there was coffee and brandy, if people wanted either, in the living room. The low-burning fire or more likely our wine guzzling seemed to have given a soft-edged haze to the atmosphere. Quiet, unhurried comments mixed with the sound of tiny porcelain clacks of cups on saucers. Social deceleration left me to focus on the effect of warm lamplight as it momentarily transmuted a hand reaching for matches, or illuminated a garland of ormolu beads around a mirror, or suspended a gilded ellipse above an empty, almost invisible wineglass left on the carpet. I watched Gillian supervise the evening's last scene, erect and relaxed on the edge of her scarred Regency chair, both its front legs carved to terminate with a small lion's paw resting on a wooden orb. What emanated from her was the calm of someone aware that those around her, friends and almost friends, admire her and her attainments.

A series of topics followed. Possibly because of the presence of Americans, discussion turned to constitutional monarchy, Gillian stating a settled conviction in favor of republicanism: the royals really didn't do anything for Britain that justified the effort and expense.

"But don't you think," I said, "that the monarchy is intertwined pretty tightly with the national imagination? The English absolutely depend on having those figureheads. Who would they get to do those ribbon-cuttings? A terrible apathy would set in without all the pageantry. People wouldn't know how to set priorities for themselves."

"Some of us would," said Gillian.

"And some of us hardly know the royals exist, we never think about them. Which is why we don't bother to get rid of them," Alun added.

"Sure, but you're exceptions to the majority. I'm not saying three cheers for monarchy. But the British clearly do want to keep it. You'll always have royalty, just as your cars will always have the steering-wheel on the right."

"Why do *you* think monarchy's bad for us?"

"Because—like the peerage—it's hereditary. As long as law confirms differences based on birth, the class system will be impossible to dislodge. There will always be the conviction that 'breeding,' which is just a matter of doing and saying the best things, is really based on who your sire and dam were. It's the principle of horse and dog pedigrees applied to human society." Some of the listeners shifted in their chairs, but no one said anything so I pushed on. "Meanwhile anyone who's really determined can learn the approved habits and reflexes, there's nothing mystical about them. I won't even go into the question of whether those whose hereditary titles lead you to expect the best from them actually always come up with it. Evidence suggests that they don't, necessarily."

"Well, particularly if you're dealing with the Windsors," Henrietta said. "They're awfully middle-class."

"Yes, they don't really show well next to Tudors and Stuarts, do they?" Julian De Compton remarked. "But even with them, there's that old question of whether crown or peers are the paragon. It's probably true that the exercise of the royal function doesn't allow for the very best possibilities."

"Of course, that throws us back on the question of how 'the best' is to be defined," David Hunt reminded us.

"But that's *the* important question," I said. "Isn't 'the best' something that ought to be reconsidered time and again rather than assumed to be one thing forever?"

I didn't actually want to hammer home the point, as much from fatigue as a gut prejudice against making speeches. Yet I had been noticing just how much discussion English social life could include without strain. Comparing it with our counterpart back home—gossip-fests, exchange of information on real estate and book deals—should make me blush, I mean, if only I still could.

Gillian, who seemed genuinely interested in the topic, said, "Mmm, but it is wearing to keep *everything* provisional. We'd hate to have to paint our house a new shade each month, according to the latest thinking on color. Sometimes you just put up with things—but I don't include monarchy in this—when you realize that the promised happiness offered by a change wouldn't be worth the struggle and difficulty of transition." Her voice trailed off, but she drew herself upright with an intake of breath and began again. "That sounds more conservative than I am. But Americans strike us sometimes as so feverish. Am I being unfair, Corinne?"

"Well, remember that things are easier to change over there. You have no idea what I had to go through to have a new telephone number for the apartment I'm subletting. And the number of line-changes on the tube it took to get from St. John's Wood to the Belsize Park station—incredible. And don't say I should have taken a cab. Impossible to find one. In New York you just go to any corner and stick out your arm. I doubt people are going to spend a lot of time trying to abolish the monarchy, they're too busy trying to find a taxi. Now, you can't even get Mrs. Thatcher abolished." Everyone laughed.

"Yes, but there's hope there," Gillian said. "Elections are coming up, and things have reached a point where even the uninvolved see she has to go."

"Do you think Kinnock can get the votes? Do you like him?"

"I *quite* like him," Gillian answered, indicating distaste with one of those equivocal adverbs the English have a large supply of.

"Where does he go wrong, as you see it?" I asked.

"By not going far enough. He's not much of a libertarian, is he? Thirty years ago I doubt whether he could have been fit into the framework of Labour politics at all. I don't know that he has much chance to win, but he's the only one apart from Thatcher who *could* win, so there we are."

"There we are," the others echoed and glanced at their watches.

"Discussion to be continued on election night," Henrietta proposed. The De Comptons, with no particular hurry, got up from their chairs, and Gillian did also. They said in a caressing tone what fun they'd had, then everyone made light-as-air goodbyes to each other. For me, Corinne added a wink, maybe to suggest that nationality was thicker than water.

I thanked Gillian, discovering in the process that I actually felt grateful for her gesture of welcome toward a sight-unseen, just-off-the-boat stranger. She solicitously told me where to find a taxi. Instead, I decided to walk at least part of the way home as a way of working off accumulated nervous energy.

Damp pavement glowed faintly under lamps shedding circles of light that I moved into and then out of. Walking is a good way to do your Zen meditation on foot (joke). Meditate on what? Well, a very specific annoyance that had run through the entire evening: Given that Britain even under Conservative Party leadership has no legal prohibition against private relations between consenting adults, whatever the sexes involved, why is that topic unacceptable in company? Although English men are hard to sort out, I was almost certain that David Hunt was not now nor ever had been heterosexual. And yet he spent an entire evening without ever touching on any involvement he might ever have had with men, or about the attractiveness of men in the abstract. A blithe and explicit summary of his preferences would be unacceptable in Conservative gatherings, true, but apparently they were no more welcome among socialists. Certainly no avenues had been opened in that direction by anyone else. You could say I might have brought up these things myself; but I already felt like an interloper, a charity case who'd been shoehorned in at the last minute.

Part of me, actually, had wanted to shine and please, even within the framework of reigning conventions. That may have been a misguided wish to seem less boorish than most of the Americans they normally meet—but how did I know they considered Americans boorish? Gillian seemed to like Corinne. And how regrettable was it, really, that the evening had a formal gloss? The distance between private and public realms is only partly bridgeable. This wasn't a gathering of intimates; if it had been, I wouldn't have been invited. Doubtless there were venues in London where "taboo" topics were discussed at any length. What would have happened, though, if it had been that kind of gathering? I'd have been drawn out about my own attachments and would have had to explain about the death of the man I loved, forcing others either to feign sorrow for someone they didn't know or else brazen it out with frank indifference. Would I have been comfortable? That's the kind of impasse these conventions are designed to avoid. And then, after all, Julian De Compton was seventy-plus years old; his talented junior had gone to the trouble of arranging a few hours that he might enjoy, as consideration for his white hair required. Her first responsibility was to him and not to those invited as an afterthought. There was no known reason why I shouldn't fit in perfectly. She nor anyone else there could have had any idea what my last year had been and what I might be going through. If at some point she had turned and asked me point-blank what that was, would I have actually told her? I've never heard anybody at a dinner party answer the question as I would have had to do, unless I lied: "I'm alone. Entirely alone."

Five

Thinking back to that evening, I'm a little surprised at my reactions, even though feelings of every kind and in all situations have been unpredictable for a long time. I certainly never used to breathe fire or drape myself in the liberation banner. The political person in the family was Joshua, with me more as a supportive spectator. It's true that, as the crisis of the epidemic deepened, I felt myself begin to change. Not that there was immediate evidence of that in what I wrote. The ability to say something you care about, while still keeping the crazy balance of form—not to mention an inconvenient commitment to truth—is hindered by a million obstacles; adding one more can sometimes freeze the whole show. Still, I found myself beginning to invent characters and dialogue that had a certain edge to them, riffs that I would have revised out in the old days.

During those first years together, I was always grateful to Joshua for never pressuring me to make my plays fit the mold that his own activist politics might have demanded. Not in public, but in private I would justify myself by saying that having grown up during the pre-1969 Dark Ages, I was glad to have emerged as reasonably sane and productive, someone who didn't conceal that he lived with a person of the same sex, and who allowed liberationist arguments to have whatever effect on him they would. But as for moving to Fire Island, declaring it a gay homeland, and seceding from the Union, I just don't have it in me.

Joshua was always going to rallies and attending tactical planning meetings—with my approval but without my company. It seemed more appropriate somehow to have him come back and summarize what was being planned. How could it be otherwise, considering we're dealing here with one of the most domestic people in captivity? High-grade inducements have to be dangled in front of me before I stir from my living-room and study. One of my most persistent problems was finding subjects for plays outside of Joshua's and my quiet, homelike existence. Theater thrives on agony; we were mostly happy. It may well be that there are more people in our unflamboyant category (which lacks media glamour) than there are drag queens, gay people in prison, or sexual outlaws, but that isn't what theater audiences have been conditioned to buy tickets for. Whose fault is that?

The only thing remotely resembling drama that happened to us came in our second year together. Anyone could have seen trouble coming who'd stopped to consider the difference in our ages, and the fact that Joshua had never lived with a lover before. Like most people in their twenties (of whatever orientation) he'd been used to having short-term relationships with a series of partners. I don't suppose either of us asked ourselves whether the pink-champagne hallucination of that first year would ever end. There were moments (and I'm not a mystic) when I would see Joshua, his darkly tanned skin against the white shower curtain, the faint line of hair that ran from the center of his chest down to his navel and below the

bathing suit line to the powerfully totemic forms there—
moments when I would go up to him and hold him very lightly, in our little bathroom sanctuary, among the toothbrushes
and bars of soap, feeling a relaxed gratitude, along with an
irrational sense that "this had always been and always would
be." That in a way it had nothing to do with us in particular—
our beleaguered, statistical selves merely an opportunity for
some ideal paradigm of love to take bodily form in a specific
place during an actual run of numbered minutes; though no
one was counting. We were ourselves and more than ourselves. Even a news broadcast coming onto the FM in the next
room, putting an end to "The Air for G-String" or a Louis
Armstrong trumpet solo wouldn't spoil it. For those minutes
the fused pair that we were was safe, safe from marauders,
safe from the enemy—who often turns out, in fact, to be some
grimly judgmental fixture in our own psyches.

The first hint of trouble came one night after dinner, when
we were washing the dishes, or rather Joshua washing and I
drying them. I remember that he was wearing a rugby shirt,
with blue and red stripes. We never performed this joint
household chore without getting into involved discussions
about sundry subjects, this time, the impending divorce of a
married couple we knew. Suddenly Joshua said, "Do you
think we are *married*, in the same way that they are? I mean, is
what we have a *marriage*?"

"Well, as I remember they had a big church wedding. We
didn't. Nobody gave us a set of dinner plates or silverware.
We can't file joint income tax returns. So I guess we're not
actually married."

"But seriously. What would you say we were?"

"What's so great about labels? What do they give you?"

"Just because what we are isn't named doesn't mean it
isn't a category. Not naming it actually gives it more control
over what happens in the relationship. I mean, I keep thinking

that we're trying—unconsciously—to imitate heterosexual marriage, and, meanwhile, what's really at stake is a non-contractual relationship between *two men*. Which can't possibly be the same as a legally enforced bond between men and women, who will probably produce children."

"No argument there. But you sound like one of those day-time talk shows."

"I just wonder whether we're not in some ways cutting in on our freedom when there's no reason to do so. Given that we're not a married couple."

"Oh." A silence fell. "I don't ever remember telling you not to do anything that you felt you wanted to do." My voice had a funny hoarseness to it, which I tried to harrumph away. I could hear someone's adrenaline-soaked heart beating in my eardrums.

"I didn't say you had. It's more of an atmosphere that's been set up. Don't you ever get the feeling of being hemmed in? Of not doing and saying every important thing you want to?"

I dried the last dish and put it on the rack, noticing that the decorative gold ring around the rim was beginning to wear off, one of those irrelevant details that leap out at you those moments when your feelings go into overdrive. "Why don't you say what you want to right now." Of course I knew, in general, what the important thing was going to turn out to be. Which didn't mean that I was prepared to hear that someone had asked him out for that very night and that he wondered whether I would object. If I did, then he wouldn't go. The fact was, at one of his political meetings, he'd met somebody that he was sort of interested in, "physically," and he just didn't want to hide anything from me. What I didn't say is, Why *don't* you hide it from me? That's what wise people do. Haven't you read Colette? Instead, with all the therapist's maturity rap I could muster, I said I was glad he trusted me enough to talk about it because I knew he didn't think having secrets was healthy, and of course I didn't, either. (Fifty percent of me believed that.) I asked if this had been going on for a while. No? Then I didn't have to take it too seriously?

"Only to the extent that it's something I've been thinking about. I don't want you to feel threatened. It's probably just getting something out of my system."

"Then go ahead and get it out." Inside, I heard "maturity" crack in half. "But if you're worried about being a mere imitation of heterosexual marriage, this imitates it all too well, to judge by current statistics. We may just have to imitate heterosexual divorce while we're at it."

"I was hoping to work through this without anybody getting hurt."

"Hurt? I'm not hurt, I just see this as one of us being a little shortsighted."

"So you really do think of me as a piece of property that you own. Love for you is just a way of putting fences around someone else."

"This is absurd. You're free and twenty-one and have stronger muscles than I do. I don't have any way of putting barbed wire around your—freedom. At the same time, I'm not going to limit *myself* to the extent of not saying what I think about this."

He suddenly grabbed my shoulders and pulled me close to him. "Look. I love you. Try to love me. Me, not the person you *think* is me. Maybe I'm not as nice as you want me to be. I'm going now." He walked out of the kitchen, calling back, "Don't wait up. Talk to you tomorrow." Then he was gone.

After the door closed, I realized what an imbecile I'd been. Suppose I had driven him away forever. Why object to some silly instance of sexual curiosity, considering that *we* were something on another order and were always going to be together? I paced up and down. Come *on*, he was just trying to maintain the level of honesty that we'd always had by not hiding this from me. That proved he really loved me. Now what was I going to do? If he would just come back once more, I'd behave differently, I would show him how tolerant I could be. I must sit tight until the wave washed over. He said he would talk to me tomorrow. Look, he walked out without taking his jacket....

The "wave" didn't break and wash over for two months, two months during which I felt as though I was drowning. I was never able to appear as accepting and supportive as I tried to be. None of my acting skills came to my aid. We would sit for an interminable half hour together with leaden silences falling, Joshua's head sunk on his chest, mine prickling with questions I didn't dare ask. *What's so great about this boyfriend of yours? What's he got that I haven't? Why are you punishing me this way?* Of course all my secret self-doubts came roiling to the surface. Joshua was infinitely better-looking than I; how could I expect him to be content with this battered old tank when he could be having fun with a twenty-five-year-old gymnast? And of course he was right about my proprietary attitudes. I didn't want to share what I considered mine with anyone. So, on top of everything else, I wasn't even really a balanced person, instead, some sort of creepy miser, trying to hoard up a living, breathing human being in a casket that could only be opened by my key.

To be abandoned by those we love almost always means becoming a self-accuser as well. We come to think that being thrown over is fit punishment, really, and admire the person who left us for his perceptiveness and courage in detaching himself from a substandard partner. I wondered how I had ever imagined I could hold on to Joshua. To complete the lovely picture, I went through with some retaliatory motions, bringing home a pinch-hitter suitable in one way only—but soon realized I'd never be able to follow through with the plan. I wasn't really reassured about my own value and romantic viability; evening the score didn't do for me what it was supposed to. Between being alone in someone's company or alone by myself, I eventually chose the latter.

And yet something animal and stubborn in me refused to give in to the idea that Joshua would never come back. I really had no choice. He was staying at his new interest's apartment now, but he would stop by from time to time to pick up clothes or a book or whatever. I would simply drink him in, fastening on every shaving cut and frayed shirt collar, as if they were symbols of some secular sacrament, repeating silently to myself, I will not live in, and will not do dialogue from, a soap opera. I was never able to look at him directly for long. My eyes would settle on a bright gleam reflected from, say, the lip of a stainless-steel ashtray, and that little teardrop of light would become my principle of logic and steadiness.

Later Joshua told me these visits were most often just an excuse to see me and to keep the connection between us alive. I never dared to ask him if he thought he was teaching me a lesson, but, whether he intended it or not, I was learning things. For example, that for me he was worth whatever sacrifice might be required. I know loyalty to oneself comes first, but loyalty in this case demanded that he be part of my life, a life that would be incomplete and club-footed without him. I also learned not to try to make those idealizing moments we had experienced together any sort of daily standard for taking our measure. "Love," the greatest catchall word ever, was going to have to include much more (and no doubt a bit less) than its whole romantic press would have us believe. After Joshua came back, we made a point of being very much down to earth; from that location we could always sense the presence of the underground river of feeling beneath us, imperturbable and continuous. We had only to dowse for it, it was never not there.

Six

The letter from Adele that arrived this morning mentions that she has finished clearing out Joshua's clothes from our apartment. So the rugby shirt, and everything else, is gone. If I stop to reread the letter, it's simply to appreciate Adele's voice, the way she has of angling in on things, using the word "animated" for "exciting," as in "September is an animated month," or, when things please her, saying she is "jubilant." The letter has the feeling of a talisman, carried from room to room, until I finally settle in the study, which has a window on the back garden. A thick green limb of the rosebush cuts across the window, with backward-tilted thorns projecting down its length like shark fins. There is sun this morning and some wind, so that the branches of the trees toss up and down while birds flutter restlessly among them, but no species that I recognize. Balmy for October; and I remember that it was also warm that October three years ago in New York.

Things couldn't have been better for us. After our separation we had a long uninterrupted period of easy intimacy, with neither of us, so far as I know, feeling constrained or possessive or at all uncomfortable in living together. Joshua had gotten his departmental promotion and was at work on a study of late dramatic literature in Sanskrit. My new play, *You Had to Be There*, opened and it was clearly going to run for a while, maybe a year. I liked it, but I knew, in the way that writers can sometimes know, that the one I was working on would turn out to be even more the thing I was after. Joshua and I were always remarking to each other how lucky we were, with a stress on the word "lucky" to show how little deserving we felt ourselves to be and, no doubt, to ward off any abrupt end to that luck.

We had heard of—but just barely—the new, unexplained physical syndrome that was affecting hundreds of gay men, the loss of immunity to a huge array of life-threatening diseases. It was like answering the doorbell and seeing a hooded skeleton holding a scythe in one hand while the other bone pincers reached for your neck. When John, a friend of ours who worked in public television, suddenly came down with pneumonia, we were upset but didn't at first make any connection to the illness medical researchers had begun to call AIDS. He was quiet when we visited him in the hospital's intensive care unit; but wouldn't anyone that sick be? It was only after he was released that he told us that his particular kind of pneumonia was the one associated with the loss of normal immunity. We didn't know what to say, partly because of our ignorance about the illness.

Making up for that as best we could, we read what there was available—very little then—and talked to volunteers who answered at the AIDS Information number on the telephone. Checking with them about difficult points as these arose quickly became a familiar routine. I soon got to know the voices of the telephone answerers, each different in timbre and accent, but all alike in their rushed, almost angry delivery. It was like talking to the chief of an ambulance corps on a field telephone just to one side of combat.

We saw John through another bout of pneumonia, but within a few months of his discharge from New York Hospital, he was too weak to leave his room, emaciated, unable to eat, mostly confined to his bed. Possibly because of his snow-white sheets, I kept thinking of the cross-country skier who unexpectedly comes to a sharp downhill slope. You had the illusion of high-pitched, icy wind in your ears and a physical sensation of the skier's intent, wary crouch—easy to see in John's actual bent-knee position on his bed. During the visits Joshua and I made, we would listen as he talked with ravaged honesty about the approaching end of his life, from time to time throwing in a camp joke about going out in style, just to show he hadn't lost his sense of humor. We would grind out a fake laugh, but we also tried to hold out hope to him for the possibility of a cure. One afternoon he died, only a few hours after we had seen him, desperately thin underneath his blanket, his large gray-blue eyes bracketing back and forth between Joshua and me as we tried to talk, make noise, say anything at all to make things seem right.

There was the sensation of quicksand having reached chin level. Joshua heard about a study program of "homosexual males" being conducted up at Columbia; it was carried out anonymously and designed to collect as much information about the lives and sexual practice of a cross-section of New York's gay population, all in the interest of discovering how the syndrome was acquired. He decided that he should enroll, that it was the least he could do in what looked to be an unimaginable calamity. As so often before, I let him represent me in the study, thinking that the kind of data he had to offer would more or less be duplicated by my own "case history." He would come home from his sessions at the research institute and tell me about the proceedings and the counseling, which, all told, amounted to a form of special medical education, meant to be disseminated as widely as possible. It was a good bet that members of the study groups would spread the word about latest findings to their friends and serve as a sort of counter-epidemic, this one based on knowledge and determination.

Because of Joshua, I was one of the first to hear details about the discovery of HIV, a virus associated with the syndrome, and, not long after that, of the first test for antibodies stimulated by this previously unknown viral entity. I was never any good at science; he had to explain everything several times. I used to try to save face by saying he'd missed his calling as a doctor, but he let the comment ride. Actually, I think his long didactic sessions with me were rehearsals for the explaining he did to so many others, some of them close friends, some not. People were always dropping by, singly or in groups, to hear the latest. Our apartment was turning into an unofficial seminar. Privacy being what it is for some of us, I might have tried to put a stop to these weekly invasions, but too much was at stake here, I had to agree, for the usual rules to apply.

The real beginning of everything, as it comes back in memory, was that afternoon in late October, the angle of the sun slanting in differently now, and setting earlier—but still reflecting fiercely enough in the windows of the high rise opposite to leave an askew golden rectangle of light on the wall above Joshua's head where he sat in a chair across the room. I was sitting at the dining table cutting out scenes from my manuscript with a pair of all-purpose shears, splicing and taping rearranged parts to the page in the new order. Joshua was telling me how the day's session at the study group had gone. "And then," he said, "after the lecture, those who wanted to volunteer, took the test. You just give a little blood sample." He held out his arm to show me a little circular piece of tape at the inside crook of his arm. I looked at it and then at him.

"Hold on. *You* took the test? For AIDS?"

"Avery. It's not a test for AIDS, how many times do I have to tell you? It shows whether you have any antibodies to HIV in your system."

"Yes, yes, I know. But, of those who test positive, a high percentage will come down with AIDS. It is an indicator, right?"

"We don't know the percentage. That's why we have to test and get some sort of profile."

"And you volunteered to be a guinea pig. I'm sorry, you took me by surprise." I put down the scissors and moved the manuscript aside. "Now, what happens if you come out positive? Of course you won't, but ... I just wish we had discussed this first."

"Well, it's part of the study. Are you really upset?"

At first I didn't say anything, then decided to tell the truth. "Well, yes. For how long now have they all been urging us *not* to take it? And you realize that—that by taking it for yourself, you've also taken it for me?"

"Not necessarily. The best guess is that the receiver in sex is the one who's most at risk."

"*Most* at risk." We sat in silence for a minute.

"I didn't realize you'd be opposed. I guess I ought to have checked with you. Even so, as you say, it will probably be negative. It's not like we screw around, either one of us."

"Joshua, I haven't listened to you talk about this topic for nothing. They say the dormancy might be, what, ten years. That goes back to before we met. The point is, nobody knows." I picked up the scissors again and began cleaning a fingernail with them. "Even if that isn't true, remember, we did live apart for a couple of months, and that's only *one* year ago. I hate to bring all this up."

"Do you really? Look, let's try to keep the issues separate. OK, point one, I'm sorry I took it without checking with you first. Point two, if there's still some resentment about that thing last year, then we've got to deal with it. And point three, I took the test but I won't be given the results until ten days from now. If you don't want me to get them, then I won't. The main thing is that the figures be available for the study."

"Oh. Well, to begin with, if by some chance it turned out positive, you know your name has to go, by law, on some government list, don't you."

"No, Avery, this whole thing is done by number. They don't *have* my name. So that isn't a problem."

"They don't have it so far as you *know*."

"You're really paranoid."

"Somebody had better be." By now the sunset light was gone. Joshua stood up and switched on a lamp. He came over to me and put his hands on my shoulders.

"I really, really don't want to fight. I love you and I'll do what you say about this." He bent to seal his promise with a light, dry kiss. I was suddenly all compliance. We went to the sofa and sat down together.

I began again in a quieter tone. "So, there's really no need for you to pick up the results, is there? Unless—."

"Unless what?"

"Unless you have a strong reason."

"I don't. I don't, except that—I wasn't going to mention this, but, lately, I've noticed a little swelling right here." He touched both sides of his neck just below the ears.

"Oh, I get that all the time. It's just from breathing the polluted city air. That's nothing."

"I know. Just that, with all the focus on the epidemic these days…. It could even be hysteria. You can talk yourself into thinking you have cancer or TB or anything. But that's not usually my style."

"A friend of mine actually did get TB once in Europe," I said. A silence fell. Outside in the hallway, going in or out, one of our neighbors slammed the door to his apartment.

"You know what I could do? I could pick up the results myself and just never mention them to you. You wouldn't have to know one way or the other."

"You serious? I mean, they're going to turn out negative, right? You wouldn't tell me that?"

"Well, sure, I'd tell you if they were *negative*."

"In other words, if you said nothing, then I'd know you'd had bad news. That sort of takes us back to square one."

"True. Well then, I would just resolve not to tell you, even if it was good news."

"Think you could stick to that? It would be awfully tempting if it were good news. But this is crazy, anyway. Whatever you knew, I would want to know, obviously. Besides, if the news were bad, we'd have to make plans."

"If you think you would do things differently, you should do them differently even without getting test results. Everybody knows the percentages aren't in our favor. We're gay men living in New York. We belong to the highest risk category in the world.... If you got a positive, what would you do differently?"

"Well, for one thing, we were planning a trip to Asia next March. I'd cancel that right away."

"Why?"

"Because, what if we got sick during the trip?"

"Avery, you can't drop your whole life just because you get a positive test. It doesn't mean you're going to come down with AIDS. You have to go on as before."

"Sure. But don't most people in fact make a few changes? What would you do?"

"If I had no symptoms, I'd go ahead with my plans, whatever they were."

"Well, I wouldn't. I wouldn't make any major travel plans."

"That's a difference in our outlook."

"Yes, it is. I can't see myself in a hospital in Calcutta. I'm not sure they accept Blue Cross, and I wonder about their equipment."

"You talk like it's certain you would develop the disease if you tested positive. The doctors don't know as an absolute fact that HIV has anything to do with the syndrome. There's no proof."

"But there's a very, very strong probability."

"You really supervise your percentages carefully, don't you?"

"When I was bumming around in the East Village back in the sixties, a lot of my friends believed in doing your thing and going with the flow and taking whatever chemical concoction they were given, on the theory that any hallucination, even a horror show, is better than dull-normal reality. It struck me as risky, and I didn't always go along for the ride. Well, I'm here, and a lot of them aren't now. I think I was right."

"This isn't the same thing."

"True, but I still mean to proceed with caution and give myself the best shot." The word "shot" had a sinister ring and seemed to vibrate in the air a long time before I pushed on.

"Look. Let's get back to the topic. You don't have to worry about it. I definitely will not pick up the results. Don't change any of our plans."

"It would be nice if we could do that, and we probably could have if none of this had come up. At this point—well, for one thing, it's very easy for me to imagine you picking up the results and not telling me what they are."

"Well, if you're not going to trust me, why not just assume I'd pick them up, and then say they were negative, even if they weren't?"

"You might very well do just that."

"Wow, you really *don't* trust me."

I pulled out my sugar-sweetest tone and said, "It was you

who brought up the possibility of withholding information, darling."

"I didn't say I would lie, though. Do I have a record of lying? I get myself in trouble all the time by refusing to be dishonest."

"No, you don't lie, I didn't say you did. But this case is a little more complicated, considering life and death and the mental suffering of someone near and dear to you are involved. Almost anybody might consider lying justified under the circumstances." He looked at me with what I guess you'd call consternation.

"I just don't know what to say." Suddenly he was crying. I said uh-oh, put my arm around him, apologized, and said that we didn't have to talk about it any longer, today. He nodded mutely, and then we walked hand in hand to the bedroom, whose door I found myself closing behind me.

Anyone who lives in New York knows about the particular sensation that comes over the city at dusk, a mood that colors anything that takes place during that hour, and certainly lovemaking. I can't cry, but I can feel the sensations that go with being on the brink of tears. This time, in this particular city twilight, that sensation arose from the mixture of guilt at having quarreled with Joshua, and the secure comfort of making love with him, a ritual release where, not only emotion and tearfulness, but material and immaterial facts of all kinds echo back and forth into each other in a climbing spiral of urgency until a glistening forgetfulness overtakes us (despite the occasional dissonance of an elbow in the wrong spot or the pause for an abrupt shift of stance), and we no longer know whose hand this is, alive with nervous reverence, whose ear filled with jagged whispers of indrawn breath, or whose grateful, drawn-out shout of laughter twines with whose poured-out groan—vocal lines in casual counterpoint, each brought to full purpose and meaning only by the other.

And yet, try to avoid it as I would, the barest sensation of past-tenseness overlay that hour of putting an end to our quarrel, a sensation I assimilated to the half-light filtering through the window, which emphasized now the soft-lit contour of a forehead and now the dark hollow above a collarbone, all the impulsive, dancing involvement that the heat of the moment could release somehow reined in this time by *noticing*, an alertness not entirely distinct from fear. For how many people our age had this coming together in desire and love been the beginning of the end.... If sexuality and death are always blended into one at some level of the psyche, now their tandem was all too easy to feel, a hard, cold plateau just below the surface of thought.

My own hesitancy, which took the form of being overly expert and competent, might not have mattered at all except that it was also matched in Joshua, who was making efforts in the direction of pious reassurance, the repeated sounding of a celebratory note you might expect to hear at anniversary parties. By insisting on our full and unalloyed presence to each other, we subtly distanced ourselves and were made conscious of a tinge of doubt coloring the emotional ambient in which we floated side by side and apart.

The customary double-up shower afterwards dispelled some but not all of that subtle tension. As we stepped out onto the bath mat to towel ourselves dry, our eyes met inadvertently in the mirror with an awareness that quickly tried to veil itself in irony and carelessness. The problem about once having been perfectly attuned to another consciousness is that any dissonance ever to appear later, however small, is as unbearable as a grain of sand between two sensitive membranes. Joshua's smile, with dimples straining at the corners, struck me with an impact I was able to single out later as the first blow of the axe.

Seven

I've just returned from a visit to the Guild Hall Museum, where I saw, among other things, reproductions of Caius Gabriel Cibber's two most famous statues, *Melancholy Madness* and *Raving Madness*. They were commissioned to adorn, if that's the word, the gate to the new Hospital of St. Mary of Bethlehem. Its founding has to be seen as a step in the direction of enlightened treatment of mental illness, even though the name was later colloquially shortened to "Bedlam" and came to stand for unleashed aggregate insanity.

Cibber's statues, rescued when the building was demolished, were designed to perch on the curved surfaces of a broken arch over the main portal of the hospital. As he was developing his first ideas for the pair, Cibber recalled from his stay in Italy the Medici burial chapel in Florence, whose statues Michelangelo had conceived as reclining figures disposed on the arched top surfaces of the tombs. Using a curved instead of a flat base introduced a note of instability and disquiet into the composition. *Night* and *Day*, much brooded over by art historians and critics, suggest the approach of the world of gloom, dream, and nightmare that a part of humanity can never put aside even when dawn arrives with the sane light of the sun.

Of Cibber's pair, *Melancholy* is the more successful. Art, especially when the art is sculpture, doesn't accommodate raving very well; but melancholy has always been one of its keystones. In Cibber's version, we have an old man entirely bald, his legs extended lifelessly to the left, torso half lifted up and resting on his arms as he gazes forward intently, without, apparently, finding what he is looking for. His cheeks are deeply hollowed, his lips parted as though about to speak, and the aura of despair flickers through a chalk-white face that both the acids of knowledge and weather have ravaged.

I don't describe my own state of mind as Melancholy. What I have is melancholy's scientific younger sister, depression—clinically diagnosed and with a chemical remedy, if I want to avail myself of it. But I have never trusted medication for mental pain, and so I don't take the Elavil that has been prescribed. OK, I took it once, just as an experiment, and found myself on a sort of psychic roller coaster, thrust upward and upward on a rising track of intensity and then whirled down again as the dosage wore off. No thank you.

My own regimen involves revisiting the past, but not pulling it over my head; becoming acquainted with the extent of the pain but not stoking it. When I turn up a pleasurable memory, I hold on to it and let it light up my mind. The process is something like panning for gold, while still acknowledging each lump of lead as it appears. As a method for lightening depression, it hasn't worked wonders yet, but it's the best thing I can come up with.

After some more tossing back and forth of arguments, Joshua and I came to the conclusion that he must pick up the results of his test and not hide them, positive or negative. Furthermore, I must also take the test, and Joshua wouldn't pick up his results until I had mine. Whatever discovery we were going to make we were going to make at the same moment. I went so far as to have my doctor give the report to me in a sealed envelope, which I didn't open until I had gone with Joshua up to the office at Columbia where case histories were filed. I sat in the waiting room while he consulted with the medical assistant in charge of the test phase of the program. The long white legal envelope lay in my lap, glowing and trembling under fluorescent light. The door opened, and there was Joshua stepping out ahead of the assistant and thanking him. I stood up. He walked over to me and his eyes began to sparkle. "It's OK, I'm negative," he said with laughter beaming into his voice.

I hugged him as tight as I ever have, then said, "All right, let's have a look at this." I ripped open the envelope. A note inside said, "Dear Avery, Your results have come in and I am happy to inform you that you have no antibodies from HIV virus, according to this test. You may wish to submit to testing again, since there is a possibility of error. In any case, be sure that you take every precaution to keep yourself in good health. Sincerely, Milton Marks, Physician."

We looked at each other, stupefied with relief.

"Congratulations," Joshua said, shaking my hand. We left the office and, once on the street, went into the first bar we found (which happened to be a rather seedy Blarney Stone) to toast our good health and luck. In theory we were entirely out of place among the melancholy crew with bleary eyes and seamed faces, who half reclined on the bar among ashtrays and puddles of ale reflecting red neon beer signs above the bar, but in fact we felt deliriously at home there.

Joshua eventually asked me if I thought we should take the test a second time, you know, just to be sure? I gave a categoric no, saying we had put ourselves through enough and that the probability had never been high to begin with. This seemed to make sense. Why be morbid? I remember one night sitting at the table together over a plate of pasta and feeling a flood of gratitude overtake me just like the good old days. We had come through.

Of course we never mentioned having taken the test to our friends who hadn't done so. It wasn't supposed to be politically correct, nor did we want those who were living in the shadow of fear to think of us as being enviably out of danger and therefore not concerned with the plight of other people. Just the opposite. I had decided that, since I had been spared, I owed it to, to—something, to help those who hadn't been so lucky. There was a new volunteer organization (called the Gay Men's Health Crisis) with the purpose of providing personal assistance to those who had the AIDS syndrome, and I decided to do volunteer work for them. I don't need to have the superstitious side of this pointed out to me. Of course there was an element of warding off possible future tragedy in this, but some of my reasons might also count as "humane," though that can't matter to anyone besides me.

Duties weren't, in any case, too heavy. Three days a week I would telephone the person to whom I'd been assigned and see what he needed. Sometimes that involved grocery shopping or picking up medicines, sometimes a little straightening up around his apartment, and sometimes just listening to him. His name was Emory, and he had been given his diagnosis about eight months earlier when he'd suddenly come down with pneumonia. Joe, the person he'd been living with for several years had had the same pneumonia three months before that. Both had been so weak after hospitalization, they weren't able to take care of each other. Emory had no family except for distant cousins. Joe, whose condition was particularly acute, was flown down to Florida to stay with his parents so that he could be cared for. This left Emory by himself. He gradually got stronger, and he always kept in touch with

Joe by telephone; but he knew it was impossible for his life-companion to come back. Then one day he called only to find out that Joe had died. The family made it clear that Emory was anything but welcome to attend the funeral, and we wondered which had more to do with it, race (Emory was Black) or orientation; probably both in about equal measure. In any case, Emory was too weak to travel. He was left alone to do his mourning and to somehow square away his illness, with little to look forward to but days one by one crossed off the calendar.

There was also a financial problem in that Emory's rent was high, his disability payments very small, and the ugly fact that Joe's family had bullied *him*, in the confusion of his last days, into making a new will that took the life insurance and savings account away from Emory. Who told me that these people had plenty of money; but money always needs more money to insulate itself. Emory had met the parents—once—and wasn't surprised. He considered taking legal action, given that he had a copy of the previous will, but he didn't feel up to a court battle, nor could he afford to pay an attorney. Besides, he said, he knew the decisions always went in favor of the family in these circumstances.

My job was not to advise him but to listen to him. I used to take care of his banking, and, as the months passed, I watched the account sink lower and lower. At one point I stopped taking money from it and paid his bills out of my own pocket, even though the volunteer agency told us we weren't to give financial assistance to the people we were working with. One of the reasons that I never join things is that I'm no good at obeying rules.

One morning Emory told me he was having trouble breathing and would have to go into the hospital. I raced over, put him into a taxi, and took him to a downtown hospital where his doctor was in residence. We sat three hours in Reception (their misleading term for the waiting room), waiting until they could find us a bed. Cold drafts swept over us every time the door opened. A street person who had lesions that looked like Kaposi's sarcoma lay sprawled unconscious in one of the chairs. From time to time I would go to the desk and tell the attendant the patient needed a bed immediately. The answer, always the same, was that they were doing their best, but that nothing had come available yet. What eventually happened was that a gurney was wheeled into one of the rooms behind the main desk, and here Emory spent the next twenty-four hours until a room was vacated for him. When I walked back through the waiting room I saw the sick street person hadn't moved from where he had been before and for all I knew was quite dead, he was so still. I slunk home, exhausted and enraged, vowing to do something about the horrifying treatment of emergency patients.

There wasn't much to do, apart from writing blistering letters to hospital administrators (who had a fixed number of beds and no more) and to the editorial page of the *Times*. When I went to visit Emory, the next day he was under an oxygen tent, unconscious. I sat there feeling a big lump in my throat but not in fact crying. I don't manage extreme situations very well. At home, Joshua tried to make me feel better. He suggested that I might have gotten too involved and lost professional detachment. True enough, I said, but professional detachment wasn't everything. I knew what the risks were, but I was willing to take them.

When I telephoned the hospital next morning, they cut me off without giving any information. After several calls, I got through to the doctor, who said he was sorry to tell me that Emory hadn't survived this bout with pneumonia. He thanked me for helping his patient through the difficult last months and then said goodbye.

I decided to take a rest before signing on as helper with another client. Working with Emory and then having it all come to an end so suddenly had left internal bruises. I found myself listless and unable to work, or, more precisely, to care about working. About this time, Joshua and I heard that another friend of ours out in L.A. had just been diagnosed. Newspapers were saying that there was no sign of a cure anywhere. Joshua and I had been spared, I said to myself, but spared only to witness the extreme suffering of those around us, still without being able to understand them entirely. Part of the helplessness we experienced was this—the incapacity to place ourselves fully and absolutely in the mental state of those who were ill with no hope for a cure. We could never do enough because performing mindless little chores had to make up for not having the night sweats, the pneumonias, the lesions, the dysenteries, the loss of sight people we knew were suffering from. It's not that people have never died before, and that we're not all of us going to die one day; but that the form of death in this case is usually so drawn out, disfiguring, and painful; that it comes from a physical act of love, and, for gay people, one that has been the basis for a personal and political identity. Very few gay AIDS patients escape feeling, if only for a while, that they are being punished for who they are at the deepest level. Listening to them talk, I knew I couldn't entirely fathom the nightmare, but to the extent that I could, it was like having the blast-furnace door opened in your face and getting scorched with knowledge.

I wasn't surprised, that dark, rainy winter, when Joshua came down with a mild flu; I only wondered that I hadn't as well, my spirits were so low. He stayed home from work and I took care of him with some of the considerable expertise gained from working with Emory. Joshua wasn't in any real discomfort, but his fever didn't go down, and I insisted he stay in bed until he felt better.

One morning while I was still lying in bed, not really awake, I felt Joshua nudge me.

"Avery. I'm sick. I can't breathe."

Suddenly I was wide awake. "What do you mean? What is it?"

His voice was weak and pained. "I can't breathe." He labored for air and tried to sit up. I looked at him wide-eyed, feeling an icy current flow up my spine, and my own breathing speed up.

"Don't move. I'll call the doctor." Actually what I called was an ambulance and then a doctor. I jumped into some clothes, got Joshua into a bathrobe and slippers, feeling his bony frame through the thin cloth and prayed to keep calm as we waited for the ambulance. Joshua sat on the sofa in a stupor, his breath coming in short gasps. His eyes were trained on the floor, but just once they looked up and met mine with an expression of mixed bewilderment, sorrow, and love so searing I had to turn away for fear of what I might do or say.

JOSHUA'S CASE was not altogether typical. I believe his sufferings were less than many others' I had known and read about. Even so, I'm not able, now, to dwell on the facts of his decline, those I saw and those I couldn't see. It makes me sick. Adele and I used to sit holding each others' hands while we contemplated the frightening new order of things. Actually, we were trying to anchor ourselves to reality and practicality; to lose our heads would have made the disaster complete. We had to be available at every moment, to deal with each new crisis as it arose. What happened with Joshua is that his nervous system came under attack. He slowly began to lose motor control, and some time after that cortical functions began to be impaired. Still, until the last couple of months, he was fairly active and alert.

Adele and I dropped everything else to devote ourselves to his well-being. Now and then, feeling the threat of burnout, we would try to go off by ourselves for an afternoon, take a walk in the park, see a movie, or just stand by the Hudson and watch it trundle down to the sea. Thoughts of Joshua were never far from our minds, though, and we would rush back to him with a mixture of hope and fear that became horribly familiar. He might greet us at the door with that 500-watt grin of his. Or the friend who'd kept him company during the hours we were away might stand up as we walked in and aim at us a look of mixed guilt, concern, and accusation, and tell us that Joshua had fallen on his way to the bathroom and wrenched his arm. Times like those we would feel as though a load of bricks had been dropped on us. Excursions away from Joshua became fewer and fewer.

From time immemorial an ignoramus where science and biology were concerned, I suddenly became an expert on immunology and the AIDS syndrome. You have to imagine me poring over articles in *The Lancet* and *The New England Medical Journal*, talking to doctors about T-cell counts, and reading the week by week reportage in the gay press about AIDS research. It is amazing what you are willing to study when life depends on it. I was even prepared to explore the world of medical quackery, listening to theories on the macrobiotic diet, the use of homeopathy and holistic medicine, and even acupuncture. There was always the chance that conventional medicine had overlooked something helpful. I got friends who traveled in Mexico to buy Ribavirin and smuggle it back to us. Most doctors considered it ineffective and dangerous, but not all, and in those days there were no other tested and proven treatments to apply.

Joshua's bedside was crowded with bottles and cartons of food supplements, which, however, he could seldom bring himself to take, he had so little appetite. We knew he was losing weight but you can't coax someone to eat ad nauseam. He would shake his head and look at us with pleading eyes, and we'd just give up. He liked to read, though, and to listen to music, so at least his mind was being fed. I would see him deeply absorbed in books by Buber, Abraham Heschel, and other spiritual writers, and hope he was finding what he needed in them. When he was tired and bored, I would sit for hours at a stretch, holding on to him, in agonized happiness, grateful that this sensitive, warm being (too warm, of course, because he always had a little fever) was there to be held and coddled. I had made up my mind that somehow we would beat the rap, *somehow*.

Joshua's absentmindedness crept up like a new mental season. He forgot names and places, and he would stop in midsentence without being able to continue. Or he would add something that didn't really go with what had been said before. Even more oddly, he began to give the impression that he was *playing* at being ill—as though he weren't really in such bad shape but was trying to appear so in order to please all concerned, to fulfill the role expected of him. He would state his symptoms in an exaggerated way, and clap his hand to his forehead to emphasize what he was saying. Then he would smile and wink as if to say, But we're not fooled are we, this is all playacting, isn't it?

When Adele and I brought up this new behavior with the doctor, he explained that damage to neural functions could take strange forms and that we should be prepared for anything. There was a chance of convulsions, hallucinations, and even physical violence. Listening to this middle-aged white-jacketed professional outline possibilities and probabilities in his matter-of-fact voice, I was afraid I might have a violent reaction myself. Any adult is used to the built-in unfairness of life, but this was unfairness on an altogether different scale, beyond anything I knew.

In fact the worst-case scenario didn't turn out to apply to Joshua. I suppose that is unfairness again, with respect to others who weren't so lucky. And really I am grateful it wasn't one of those unbelievably horrendous stories; I don't know what I would have done. Instead what we got was an increasing sweetness of manner toward us, something childlike and unironic in his smiling speech, a way of taking our hand and saying something clearly meant to be funny, though the sense was lost on us. It was touching—and disturbing—to be addressed with this kind of tenderness and naïve charm; yet we kept thinking it was someone else's charm, not his. As Adele and I talked about the changes in Joshua we came to agree that it was important to know and recognize this new incarnation as part of his story—a painful but in its way revealing part—as well as the earlier more familiar person. The new Joshua might be drastically thinner than the old, and come up with some confusingly oracular-sounding comments at times, but our own he still was, and we wanted to hear what he had to say.

Later that winter he came down with a head cold, which terrified Adele and me until we learned that AIDS doesn't necessarily interfere with normal recovery from colds and flu; only certain other specific diseases can't be overcome. One night just after dinner, while he had the cold, we were sitting by his bed passing tissues to him for his sniffles, making odd comments as they occurred to us but not really expecting a focused response. The night table tensor lamp was burning, aiming a sharp white light at plates and cups on the dinner tray. Music from an old scratchy recording of Ella Fitzgerald singing Gershwin songs filtered in from the next room. When the record stopped playing, nobody stirred, and we sat for a minute or two in silence—as far as any moment in the city ever can be silent. Then Joshua looked up and began speaking much more coherently than we'd heard for a while. He told us that we weren't making enough plans, and that he was sorry to have taken up so much of our time. Nothing we said in protest seemed to budge him from this attitude. He assured us he was glad we had been there, but that we had to think about the future and ourselves.

"After all, neither of you has anybody else besides me. Except each other." He looked back and forth between us. "Now there's something you've got to think about. I don't want you to feel too much alone." He turned to Adele. "You don't have any family left, and I'm an only child. But you will have Avery, and that makes up for it." Then he turned to me. "You've been an orphan for a long time and you're supposedly used to it. But, remember, you've got, umm, not a mother-in-law, something better than that. And you can look after her in my place, just as you have been doing." He wiped his nose and blinked a few times. The rising panic I was feeling at his having made a sort of testamentary speech was suddenly deflected when he took our hands and said, "You realize that if you've got each other, you've got a good percentage of me."

I looked up at Adele who had clapped a hand over her mouth and was sitting very still, trying not to cry. The frail construction of our hopes was suddenly shown up as unreal and absurd. The food supplements and special medicines had been to treat Adele and me for despair, not Joshua for AIDS. He knew that he wouldn't be able to hold out much longer, and his knowledge had just been transferred to us. The space of time between now and that oncoming event had somehow to be passed through, but beyond that date I wouldn't think— though of course his assigning Adele to me and me to her was easy to accept, in fact, could be taken for granted. Adele was family, that was it, period.

Joshua asked us to help him sit up, please. Adele bent to rearrange the pillows as I lifted him from the armpits to a half-erect position. There we were, awkward and inefficient in our anxiety to make everything comfortable and to cover over the gravity of what had been said. A part of my mind glided out of my head and hovered above us, observing the tableau we made. There was the night table with its tray of empty cups and scattered bread crumbs. There was Adele in her blue smock, Avery in his red sweatshirt, and Joshua wrapped in his sheets, all of us linked together in the actions of pity, carried out here under a cloak of silence and the supervision of faces shaped by will. Will, for two of the participants, that love be a bond strong enough to hold to earth a body incurably ill and slowly being consumed—this third person drawn invisibly on, away and farther away, having done as much as he could to make his departure coincide with a compensating promise.

Six weeks later Joshua lost his sight because of damage to the optic nerve. Three weeks after that, his involuntary motor functions collapsed, and in a short time he died.

Eight

Last night England went off what they call "Summer Time," setting the clock back so that I have an extra hour today. The result is I feel I have too much time on my hands, especially considering that it's also Sunday. Traffic sounds rumble up from the street only at long intervals: few cities come to a halt the way London does on the day of rest. True, if I walk over to Camden High Street, I'll see them streaming out of the Underground, a hefty percentage of the disaffected youth of South England, on their way to the out-door markets around Camden Lock. Hard to believe so many people between ages fifteen and twenty-five are to be found in all of London, let alone this one out-of-the-way borough. Black is the favored color for jackets and jeans and skirts and even makeup. Hair arrangements cover the gamut from boiled-egg bald, to skinhead fuzz, to eraser-brush Mohawk, Rastafarian dreadlocks, Jesus-length tresses peroxided blond, or, finally, for the modest, a few green-tinted spikes cemented in place with hair gel. Whole tribes of hobgoblins flood into the streets, earphones secured in place so that portable radios can pour a vial of undiluted rock into the place it was designed for. Some have needle marks on their arms, not nearly as surprising as the occasional dewy aura of pure innocence that gazes up from beneath a polka-dot bandanna or emanates from a certain slouching fifteen-year-old way of walking. What explains the tenderness I feel for them?

Halloween comes with plenty of advance warning here. (I mean, to the extent that it isn't in perpetual session, given that youngsters posing as wicked spirits are the rule four seasons out of the year.) All of this past week children of actual child age have been gathering near the tube entrances next to a little homemade effigy of Guy Fawkes, whose day comes the first week of November. The kids, some of them not so young, actually, hold out their hand and say, "A penny for the Guy," though they expect something besides a penny. Few people refuse; obviously, more than Guy Fawkes is at stake. When the day begins to shorten and the year to darken, an old fear begins to make itself felt. If the sun can die, so can all those who walk by its light. Something or someone has to be appeased to fend off the approaching darkness, and so the Children's Season begins, when the regular forcing of the young into useful social molds relaxes, and they are allowed to step out of line and are offered special propitiatory presents—Guy Fawkes's penny, Halloween treats, and finally the orgy of Christmas and Santa Claus. One answer to death is children, and, besides, each adult is the product of the extinction of a child, secretly mourned forever after. The handing over of twenty pence to a small outstretched hand reminds us of that mourning, an almost helpless response to feelings stirred by seeing the little scarecrow figure of Guy Fawkes in his faded boy's blue jeans, slumped against the wall next to the entry of the Underground.

I called Adele earlier today. She says she has been thinking of coming to London after all. An old friend of hers, a woman well known as a photographer, is giving a show at a gallery near Bond Street, her first in fifteen years, and Adele thinks it might be fun to see it. She presented the possibility only very tentatively, though, and I could tell she was waiting for me to encourage or discourage her. I said of course she must come, and in fact I would look for a new apartment immediately, one with two bedrooms. This was rejected out of hand; if she came, she would definitely stay with her friend, all alone and comfortably fixed in a big house in Holland Park. In any case, nothing was definite yet, but she would let me know as soon as it was. She said she didn't like to make plans nowadays because her mind kept changing and she hated cancelling things at the last minute. I said how well I understood that.

When Joshua died, we both became demons of efficiency, refusing assistance from anyone, making funeral arrangements, and, later, putting together a memorial service up at Columbia. We knew even then that keeping busy was a way of handling what we weren't really ready to face. Eventually, though, after all of it was over, and Joshua's memory fixed in his friends' mind like the bright morning star, there was nothing more to do but get on with our lives. The froth of arrangements no longer stood between us and the loss.

People like us pride ourselves on our uniqueness, so it is always unpleasant to realize just how symptomatic our responses to large events like bereavement are. I have gone through the several phases of grief in almost textbook fashion—am still going through them. The first phase of keeping busy was followed by a period of frozen-fish numbness and, when that thawed out, by a period of rage. At first this took the form of snapping at my friends and occasionally at Adele. I even found myself thinking angry thoughts about Joshua—how dare he abandon me, and so forth. I was also angry *am* angry—about the HIV test, which had so badly misled us. Of course, I had known there was a margin for error, but that made no difference. I felt betrayed by it and became one of the most rabid opponents of testing ever.

Then for a while my anger crystallized around the person Joshua had had his affair with. One day it occurred to me to try to find out what I could about this offender's health. Discreet inquiries turned up nothing in particular. So far as anyone knew, he was perfectly well, showing no signs of weakened immunity. He went on being the sound-mixer for rock recordings he had always been, apparently without any problems. He had heard about Joshua and was aware of the prejudicial implications for himself, but had made what was considered the right choice (since there was no treatment) not to take the test and to go on as before. I was thrown back on my doubts about the source for Joshua's original infection, and I knew—though I could barely allow myself to think of this—that it might have come through me, even though I seemed to be in perfect health. Some researchers theorized that susceptibility to developing the syndrome varied among those exposed; heredity was very probably one of the deter-mining factors. When I eventually tried to get in touch with the person I'd been briefly involved with during Joshua's absence, I was told he had gone to California. No one had his address and no one had heard from him.

Not being able to determine the source of the virus turned out to be, I believe, a good thing. If I really knew where dur-ing the last ten years Joshua or I had contracted it, nothing would be any different than it is. On the other hand, if I did find out, I would be tempted to assign blame, and, where there was no intentionality, blame is irrelevant. No doubt there are sociopaths who know they are infected and go ahead and put others at risk with unsafe procedures. They belong with drunk drivers and people who knowingly sell appli-ances that are likely to explode. That wasn't the case with any of us. What happens from now on is a different question because we're aware of the risks. As for public attitudes, rather than arguing about who's to blame, a better channeling of collective energies would be toward discovering a treatment and a vaccine.

I know there is every possibility my test was a false negative, that I have the virus and will develop the syndrome some day. No doubt because of Joshua, I'm not really able to gauge the full impact of the threat, or at least not so far. I don't have any symptoms, and I suppose the basic animal confidence of a body apparently well works against full-throttle panic. No, it's still Joshua's death I think about, almost always returning to the unanswerable question: why.

When I exhaust that avenue, anger converges on a new target, the barbarism or indifference of a large segment of the public, whose representatives in Congress were slow to appropriate funds for research and for assistance to those already ill. Starting about a month after Joshua died, there was a long period of letter-writing to certain Congressmen, whose inertia I portrayed to them in less than glowing terms. There was also a series of small demonstrations at City Hall that Adele and I went down for, and both of us attended benefits and gave money to fund political action and AIDS research. At the very least this helped me simmer down a little, defusing anger to manageable levels. And, who knows, it may have been useful in bringing AIDS issues a little farther forward into public consciousness. I hadn't been quite restored to normal functioning, but these activities brought me intact through another stretch of mourning. I have to be careful not to return too much to that period, though, otherwise the rage flares up again. That way lies madness. If I begin to think, for example, about the drug companies who tested only those products from which they hoped to make a killing, or if I review statements made by religious leaders who have indulged in the pleasures of passing judgment on people whose sufferings they have never witnessed, I—but this is exactly what I must not do.

No, I really don't want to go into the possibility of imminent death. The thing is, sifting it all over and over again never yields anything—aside from cold sweat or the desire simply to give up, give in, the hell with it. Experts tell me that bereavement always involves a projected mourning of one's own eventual death. When the survivor is threatened by the same illness, the projection is intensified. Where does that leave me? I don't plan to take the test again. It would probably be positive this time, but so what? As Joshua says, even if it is positive, you continue living your life as before until otherwise informed. That is what I intend to do, test or no test. It's not as though we live forever, in any case. The clock is always running, for everybody. In a sense, every human being has "tested positive."

The sensation of thinking in circles. It's odd: last night I was soaking in the tub, staring down at a body slowly becoming aware of the forty years it has racked up, a thatch of dark hair floating on my chest, the bony knees as well as an outsize foot sticking up out of the water, in the gray haze of a hot bath. It suddenly seemed so arbitrary, having this particular body or existing as a physical being at all. What could be more accidental? There's no future in the body, and yet it's all we have to live in. More accurately, it has us. Sad to think of flesh as something potentially hostile to our very identities. It suddenly occurs to me that one of the things I have lost is the chance of, of, well, goodness. Because of Joshua, I had developed a kind of relaxed good cheer not really a part of my personality before him. That has gone now, and I see no way to get it back.

Anxiety is what I have instead, anxiety over every ache or twinge. You could say it's like a bass note underneath everything else, part of the mix of emotions felt when I discuss future plans with Adele, or take notes for the Cibber biography, or look at the young Londoners in their black witch and warlock costumes, or when I smile back at the snaggle-toothed boy standing next to his limp scarecrow outside the Camden Town Station, waiting for me to give him a penny for the Guy.... So easy to remember being his age, with fractions to do for homework, a pack of Lifesavers in my pocket, and a developing case of the mumps, the special acidic pain of which comes back vividly now when I reach up and touch the glands at my neck, swollen and painful from breathing the polluted air of one more dirty world capital.

Part II

One

The interval between ordering books and their arrival can seem long, so it's a good idea to remind myself that, all told, the British Library more than repays hours spent there. Think of it as a venerable hive for storage and distribution, the Reading Room dome poised over a swarm of worker bees below—though of course books, the deposits of nectar processed into honey, come to us, we don't come to them. Unless the patient attention we bring to them is, itself, a kind of nectar. Today the wait doesn't seem to bother me, staring up at the ceiling, ornamented with gold-leaf bands stretching up between the windows cut through it. Windows that show, this untypically bright November day, an untroubled sky beyond. Staring up there and daydreaming has become one of my favorite escapes, so that it sometimes doesn't seem to matter whether the books arrive or not. But here we are: after a quick glance at the number 22 over my part of the desk, the professionally disdainful book carrier sets down my leather-bound Colley Cibber tomes and passes by without a word.

Just opposite the title page of the *Plays* the editor has put an engraving based on the painting of Cibber by Vanloo: the laureate at ease, seated, worthy and comfortable in peruke and velvet coat. In his left hand, a sheet of paper; in his right, the identifying quill, a crisp, deft feather guided by what must be the young muse of dramatic poetry, bending around from behind, her left index finger lifted with tactful delicacy. The engraving shows us a Germanic face, full fleshed, nose slightly upturned; yet the eyes are English, thoughtful, forbearing, a little tired, maybe? A slight, satiric groove has worked its way into the corner of the mouth. The author is no doubt penning one of his "rational entertainments," as he called them, comedies whose stated purpose is to encourage good behavior and ridicule bad.

Some of these are still readable, actually, with moments of effective invention—the scene in *The Careless Husband* where Sir Charles Easy's wife discovers him and the chambermaid Edging asleep in each other's arms after an adulterous tussle. Forbearance: she takes the shawl from around her shoulders and drapes it lightly over her husband's head as he sleeps. When he wakes and finds it, everything that stands behind Lady Easy's non-verbal message shames him into putting a stop to reflexive dalliance and promising to do better, as the laws of religion demand as well as prudence in an age of (incurable in that era also) sexually transmitted disease.

The subject is close to Cibber's very first dramatic effort, *Love's Last Shift*, dating from the 1690s, when he was still a struggling actor in the Theatre Royal. Unable to land good parts, he wrote a play with a star-turn for himself and got it staged. The main character is a faithless husband who leaves his wife to lead a dissipated existence on the continent. At his return, she arranges an assignation with him in disguise. Next morning he awakes and, when the trick is revealed, acknowledges what a fool he has been, promising to reform, just as Sir

Charles does in *The Careless Husband*. One of Cibber's most popular plays, it was understood by viewers adept at decipherment as an allegory of England's relationship to monarchy before and after the Bloodless Revolution. James II's unacceptable alliance with Roman Catholicism and the Continent might have raised up another Cromwell. Instead a Protestant sovereign—or rather a happily married King and Queen—were set on the throne without civil war. *The Careless Husband* is what's called a comedy of sentiment, the first in English theater, but far from the last. Cibber's role in it was not the lead, though; he played Sir Novelty Fashion, an outrageous fop, but one with warm sympathies. By this time Cibber had realized his voice and body weren't right for leading-man roles, and so he began shaping his persona and performances for comic parts, those, at least, that require intelligence and subtlety.

There's an arresting incident from 1688 in his autobiography, the *Apology for the Life of Colley Cibber*. James's daughter Anne and her husband the Prince of Denmark had by that time severed ties with her father in order to ally themselves with William of Orange. She had left London in a coach and was fleeing toward Nottingham to overtake the Prince. Her companion was the already fabled Lady Sarah Churchill, later the Duchess of Marlborough. Cibber had enrolled (at age seventeen) in Lord Devonshire's service, and it happened that the Duke's troops were assigned to provide safe conduct for the two ladies. Cibber rode near the coach until they reached Nottingham, where the Duke commanded a celebratory banquet. The job of waiting on Lady Sarah during dinner was given to the young page, who fifty years later remembered the occasion in these words: "Being so near the table, you may ask me, what I might have heard to have passed in conversation at it? Which I should certainly tell you, had I attended to above two words that were uttered then, and those were, Some wine and water. These, I remember, came distinguished and observed to my ear because they came from the fair guest, whom I took such pleasure to wait on. Except at that single sound, all my senses were collected into my eyes, which during the whole entertainment wanted no better amusement than of stealing now and then the delight of gazing on the fair object so near me. If so clear an emanation of beauty, such a commanding grace of aspect struck me into a regard that had something softer than the most profound respect in it, I cannot see why I may not, without offense, remember it; since beauty, like the sun, must sometimes lose its power to chuse, and shine into equal warmth, the peasant and the courtier."

With his mixed parentage and compromised profession, Cibber must have seen himself as a blend of those two classes—a peasant-courtier who could, even so, act and write. It's fairly clear, I think, that he cared more about acting than writing. With the Lady Sarah passage, for example, one more draft would have helped. You don't have to be Dr. Johnson (who liked the *Apology* but said its grammar was poor) to see faults of style. The clumsy echo of "so near" and "so clear," for example, or the repetition of "came," or the "it"'s scattered about like bread-crumbs. Still, the paragraph keeps a nice balance and was probably judged good enough by an author whose concern to embody a Georgian gentleman's values precluded the appearance and fact of heavy exertions in the scribbling trade. Even after being made laureate, Cibber never claimed credit as anything more than an entertaining amateur whose plays offered licentious comedy only in order to end on the side of morality and good humor.

Notes, notes, notes: I must not be a Georgian gentleman, otherwise I wouldn't have spent the past three hours at desk 22, breathing book dust. An old wall clock above the shelves, by pointing to four o'clock, says, You may now go. A quick sweep of note cards into my file folder, dutiful return of books to the main desk, and I'll be on my way out into the early evening. A young librarian with longish hair and black-rimmed spectacles takes the leather goods from me and half smiles without looking me in the eye. Also returning books is a woman about my age, in sweater and trousers. But, wait, isn't this someone I know? Only when she turns to me and says hello do I recognize her as Corinne Waldman. Of course the light here is more direct than it was at Gillian Fournier's—probably why I didn't focus, that night, on Corinne's particular good looks. The silky, professionally streaked hair is cut short, with tawny swatches slipping down over her forehead. She tilts back her head, so that the strong chin and cheekbones become noticeable and her eyelids droop down. A nice light cinnamon freckling across the bridge of the nose. Aware that I am staring at her, she reaches up to scratch her right eyebrow with a long-nailed fourth finger and brushes the corner of her lips—pale, full, with nothing but a light gloss on them.

"Packing it in for today?" she asks brightly.

"All done," I say as we walk toward the door of the Reading Room together. I ask if she'd like to go for coffee somewhere.

She smiles and nods to the guard at the exit and says, "Oh, I can't today. How about another time? Listen, better than coffee, let's just meet for a drink. How about tomorrow?"

"Fine. Any place in particular? There's this bar on St. Martin's Lane—."

"No, I know a great place on Duke Street called, wait, Gold's Champagne Bar. It's just off Oxford Street on Duke. Want to meet there at six? OK, see you then. Gold's Champagne Bar." We've threaded our way through the tourists coming into the entry of the Museum, and, when I tell her I'm going to pick up some postcards in the shop, she waves goodbye and walks on toward the door, bumping into a tall, thin man in pinstriped suit and spectacles, who seems both shocked and thrilled by the encounter. An apology to him before she turns back to smile at me; then she perseveres on her way. One of the museum guards, light tan and probably West Indian, gazes after her as she glides down the stairs into the courtyard.

WHEN I PUSH through the door of the bar (inscribed GOLD'S in transparent letters on frosted glass) a chic barrage of sound and sight waits inside—the clatter and clink of glasses, plates and spoons, smears of light reflected from polished surfaces of all kinds in the yellow lamplight, and the little zoo symphony of voices, strident and seductive, that encourages the pub's dependable freedom of speech: no one can overhear anyone else except as supplementary noise. There is Corinne, seated at a little table of dark wood. She lifts her arm over her head and waves her hand from side to side.

I consider giving her a kiss, but then, we've only seen each other twice. She looks—pretty? handsome?—attractive in her loose silk blouse and thin gold earrings. A little on the plump side, which I like in women, actually. She bends forward, smiles, takes my hand, and says, "Hello, Avery."

Not knowing how to take the gesture, I formulaically ask if I'm late.

"No, I was returning something at Selfridge's and the lines—or should I say, the *queues*—weren't as horrific as I thought they'd be. I've already had a glass of champagne. Want one?" She holds up her glass and points to me at the waiter who has just come to the table. He gives a quick nod and sweeps off. "You should also try these," she says, "the local specialty." She is holding out a little plate with undersize boiled eggs slipping around on it. "They're gull eggs. Here. You dip them in this—it's celery salt. Delicious."

"Thanks." I dutifully take one and dip it as directed.

"Aren't they good?" She leans back in her chair. "I'm glad

you showed up. An unaccompanied female is considered dangerous stuff here. This is where all the businessmen meet their mistresses before they go home to their wives. See those two in back?" She gestures toward a pair in protective darkness far from the window, a man in gray tweed and a young model or dancer type in jeans and a loose, bulky sweater patterned in black, white, and pink. The model-dancer passes something to her man, who slips it into his suit pocket.

"How did you get to be so expert on London bars?"

"Because I like to go out and explore. Don't you ever do that?"

"Well, no, I don't, much. I've been working." Ostentatiously, to prove I also know how to enjoy myself, I take a big mouthful of stinging, misty bubbles.

"Right. You're doing a biography on that playwright you told me about, what was his name?"

"Colley Cibber. Actually it's also about his father and his children. Three generations. A family biography."

"Sounds fascinating, and it's not a subject you can say people have heard too much about already. If I see one more book on Bloomsbury—." She holds out the plate of eggs again and, when I refuse, takes one herself. "You know, my research here is almost done, finally. But I'm not anxious to get back to New York at all...." Her voice trails off and she looks down, shaking her head.

"Why not?"

"Because I like London and ..." she laughs, "because of the woman I've been seeing."

"Aha. Well, that's a good reason. She's English?"

"Um-hmmmmm." The hum on the last syllable is drawn out, to suggest luxuriant appreciation. "Her name's Susannah Kynaston. Works for the BBC, actually kind of high up on the shelf. Her father's one of these businessmen, the sort that comes here—though I don't think he's around today."

Corinne scans the bar and then turns back and smiles at me. "She brought me here the first time. But she isn't married."

This is all delivered with a champagne light touch, designed to pull me into the plot; and it works. Somehow I hadn't bothered before now to wonder whether Corinne was lesbian; but as revelations go, it's not exactly unprecedented and, I suppose, even has a reassuring side. "I envy you. You're obviously having a good time."

"'Live all you can,' said Henry James. But what about you? You're on your own, aren't you?"

"Just now I am." A pause: Should I push on. The room noises seem to get louder and at the same time more muffled. She looks at me with her intelligent cinnamon-colored eyes. "My lover died last spring. One of the reasons I'm here is to— for a change of scene."

"Oh, I'm sorry." She lets a moment pass without speaking. "Tell me about him."

An inert part of me doesn't want to talk; I make a false start and then settle again into silence. Corinne gets the waiter to bring us another drink and then asks several leading questions. She knows how to listen (knowing how, I guess, means wanting to). Most times it hasn't seemed worth the effort, but talking suddenly feels right. Even if Corinne's interest should turn out to be feigned. The prevailing traffic patterns of the pub go on indifferently around us, waiters swanning among the tables with uplifted trays, men and women making entrances and exits, slipping off coats or putting them on with practiced ease. "Reggie, dear!" a voice rings out before being drowned in the general hubbub. Incident by ragged incident, I piece together my past and present situation for Corinne. At some point I look up and see that she is brushing at the corners of her eyes. I reach out and touch her arm. "I'm sorry, I didn't mean to upset you."

"No, it's all right. Hearing you talk about your Joshua makes me think of my brother. My brother Rick. He got his diagnosis last year. He came down with that pneumonia. It's not the same, but—."

"How is he now?"

"Well, he's not under hospital care, but—not great." She pauses. "Interestingly enough, he isn't gay. It happened because of a car accident. He was out in L.A. and somebody slammed into him. They gave him a blood transfusion. After a year ... he eventually came down with the pneumonia. It didn't take long for it to develop. And then—. My funny brother. He was the bassist in his rock band. You wouldn't have heard of them. But he had to give it up. I miss him. I'll probably go back to see him for a week or two in the spring." She looks at me neutrally; sips at her drink. "Did he, your lover, have any family?"

When I tell her about Adele, she says, "Oh, *Adele* Lambert, I know her, in fact, she's a close friend of my mother's cousin. I haven't seen her for years, how is she?"

"She's doing well. Who's your mother's cousin?" The name she mentions I vaguely remember having heard, but I wonder whether in fact this cousin is a close friend of Adele's. Corinne asks me if Adele has ever introduced us.

"She's mentioned her, but we've never met. You know, Adele may be coming to London."

"Oh, please give her my telephone number. Here." She scribbles it on a paper napkin and hands it to me. "And listen, if you get tired of being by yourself, call me. Any time you'd like dinner or anything, I mean it. And if you don't, I'll just call you." She looks at me with a mixture of swagger and stage-door twinkles. I take her number, conscious of being under a pleasant spell. She stands and says she has to meet someone, Susannah, in fact, but this has been great, she's glad we got together, and I say I am too.

Outside, in darkness and mist, light drizzle is falling. A taxi swerves to the curb when we hail it, and this time I don't hesitate to give my new friend a kiss before she climbs inside.

The taxi growls off. A young woman and an older man duck inside Gold's as I trundle down to Oxford Street, continuing on foot past shop windows lit up with blue-gray fluorescent light, frozen mannequins in angular poses displaying the latest in ready-to-wear shock tactics. Now what about the rest of the evening? There is an Indian restaurant I know about in Soho, within walking distance, and where the dateless diner isn't conspicuous. Something about that place, probably the patterned cotton hangings on the walls, reminds me of Adele, of her rugs and paisleys. But she has never liked Indian cooking, can't stand food that "burns," she says. Maybe I'll take her to dinner with Corinne when she comes, something French or Italian.

A dazed feeling buzzes through my thoughts, probably champagne-induced and blended with guesswork images of Adele's upcoming visit, which will include all the frenzied tourist activity visitors expect. Of course we'll go to galleries, a couple of new written-up-in-*Vogue* cafes, and to the theater—in fact, there's a Congreve play (which one was it?) opening next week, we'll catch that. Everything'll be as Colley Cibberian as London of the 1980s allows for—anyhow, something to keep Joshua from weighing too heavily on our hours together.

Two

If the solitary sifter of experience finds himself attending a political rally in a country not his own, among people he doesn't know, and over an issue he probably has no power to affect, naturally he asks how he got himself into the situation. The answer, in this case is, Half blindly but willingly. I had planned to pick up tickets for a Shaw revival with Vanessa Redgrave and Ian McKellen at the Strand Theater; that, after catching an afternoon screening of a German film I'd wanted to see about Rosa Luxemburg. When it let out, I walked down St. Martin's Lane through Trafalgar Square on the way to the Strand for my tickets. It had occurred to me to invite Corinne, or, if she couldn't come, to substitute—I don't know who.

Overcast skies and cool temperatures, but no rain. I was waiting to cross at the corner where the William IV pub is, the one with that creepy mechanical effigy high up on the corner of the façade, a burly workman in rolled-up sleeves, who hammers pointlessly at the top of a keg, hour after hour, always without making a sound. I was thinking about the film: nicely edited but on the sentimental side and probably not strictly accurate in recording the facts. Which didn't mean I hadn't been stirred up by it at moments, particularly during the scene where Rosa Luxemburg is at work in her little prison garden; and the concluding footage where she is killed.

When the light changed, I crossed William IV Street and walked along the expanse of pavement in front of South Africa House. A knot of people huddled together in front of the building. Doing what? Closer, I could see that a demonstration was under way, maybe a dozen participants, all of them young, holding up yellow banners saying, "End Apartheid Now!" A young woman with dark hair came up to me and pressed a leaflet in my hand. She smiled when I took it and said, "Would you like to attend a rally tonight?"

"About South Africa?"

"Apartheid and racism. There are several speakers, two of them from South Africa. It's very important. Won't you help?"

"I'm awfully busy," I said, hoping the lie wasn't too obvious.

"Well, the address is marked here. St. Stephen's Church Hall in Camden Town."

"I do live in Camden Town, but I'm not sure where that church is, and—."

"You're American aren't you? I thought so. But you know, apartheid is a global issue. America has a lot of influence on what happens down there. The corporations—."

"I know. You're right." I looked at her spare, pretty features, her not-new clothes, and felt a warm gust of embarrassment. "But there isn't a lot to do about it, is there."

"Actually, there is. Listen, if you can make the meeting tonight at eight-thirty, come sit with me, and we'll talk afterwards. I have to give these out now." She smiled and turned to another passerby in a bowler hat. I looked at the yellow sheet printed with information, a sketch of a man spread-eagled against barbed wire, and several quotations. Gesturing with the leaflet at her and nodding, I started on my way again.

She waved and called out, "Do come." I nodded once more and held up the leaflet at her in my half-clenched fist. The other demonstrators chanted in unison, "Stop apartheid now!" while a pair of bobbies nearby watched without moving or commenting. Well, if I'm feeling adventurous after dinner, I thought, maybe I'll drop in and have a look. You never know where your next idea will appear. Sort of feel sorry for her, having to confront all of our middle-class reluctance. Does she really expect to do anything about South Africa? She does, and I wonder how she plans to go about it.

THAT WAS St. Stephen's Church, so this must be the Hall. Right, there's a leaflet on the door like the one she gave me this afternoon. I've purposely come early to avoid entering a big, institutional room filled with people I don't know staring at me as I try to find a seat. Actually, quite a few are here already, seated or standing around in cliquish groups. The drab room has been brightened up with instructive posters and lit with fluorescent light. Don't see my demonstrator, though. The best plan is to grab a chair in the back so that I can make a quick escape if necessary. But no sooner do I sit down than she comes striding up from behind and says, "Oh good, I thought you'd come." She smiles and holds out her hand as I stand up. "My name's Maeve Findlater. I'm glad you made it."

"Avery Walsh. I wasn't sure you'd recognize me. You must see a thousand people out there every day."

"Oh, but we don't have these every day. And I can't actually talk to all that many of them. Most people won't even take the leaflets."

"I'm not sure I'll be able to stay for the whole thing tonight."

A slight strain comes into her thin, sincere features. "Oh, do. It won't last very long. And if you like, we can go somewhere afterwards for a drink. The speakers won't cover everything you'll want to know, of course.... Oh, here's Derek," she says and with efficient herding gestures pulls toward us someone tall and good-looking with what looks like peroxided hair. "This is my brother Derek. Avery."

"Hullo," he says and takes my hand without much conviction. But he does look at me and smile. I sneak a deeper look at his eyes, leaf-green under light brown eyebrows that curve up into a final feathery crochet at the temple. The distinctness of his face has something to do with the hollowed-out cheeks and thin, carefully delineated mouth. And, yes, his hair is peroxided, to judge by a faint dark undershadow visible beneath the fine stiff fur of his buzz cut. We stare at each other for a moment.

"Might be a good idea to find seats for ourselves," Maeve says. "You don't want to sit back here where you can't see." She bullies us up toward the front and settles on a group of three folding chairs in second row center. Two long tables stand on either side of a podium, which is miked to speakers on either side. Four men are seated at the tables, three of them very dark-skinned, one wearing a clerical collar. The single white man stands and calls the assembly to order. He introduces himself as a member and organizer of the South Africa Congress for Political Equality, summarizes recent events negative and positive in the struggle for change. Beginning to warm to his subject, he pounds on the podium, making a loud boom in the P.A. system that threatens to develop into an amplified feedback scream. We listen as he makes his points and pounds harder. I think briefly of the mechanical figure over the William IV pub, but of course that one makes no noise. Both Derek and I have our arms crossed on our chests and throughout this preamble I have been conscious of contact between the jacket sleeves of our upper arms. I could shift position, of course, but under these public, even institutional circumstances there's something comforting about human touch, even if it's unintended and impersonal, mediated through layers of clothes.

Eventually the speaker turns the podium over to the Black clergyman, who proves to be an Anglican priest from Capetown. He begins by giving brief sharp summaries of what has been done to Black and Colored peoples in his diocese and mentions the names of several activists in prison, asking for our prayers and help for them. He describes Bishop Tutu's most recent tactics and future targets. Confidence and considered expansiveness come into his voice when he mentions his bishop. A moist glow radiates outward from his forehead. He says he is to return to South Africa in a short time and asks that our prayers go with him. Then he sits down. I feel Derek's arm shift its angle, while still remaining in contact.

The next two men speak a heavily accented and fragmentary English. They are recent exiles, escapees from prison, who talk about the human disaster of South Africa today and what its prisons are like. Especially awful is the contrast between the events described and the modest, matter-of-fact tone used to recount them. Both men say they plan to continue to fight in exile, and that they are glad to find brothers in the struggle even here in racist Britain. Warm applause follows. The White speaker stands and thanks everyone, speakers as well as audience, and announces a venue for the next two tactical meetings. Collection baskets will be sent around and new people are invited to leave name and address on a sheet that will be put out on the table up front. He leads the crowd in a final round of chants, "End apartheid now!" and the meeting is adjourned.

"Wasn't that wonderful?" Maeve asks. Her brother and I say yes, and then she tells us she wants to congratulate the speakers. We are left behind as she joins the crowd around the podium and tables.

"Are you a member of the organization?" I ask him.

"No, not really. But I go to some of the meetings. I'm against apartheid and that. I mean, it's hard lines if you happen to be a Black man in South Africa, really. But Maeve is more active than I am. She's very dedicated." There is a working-class lilt to his voice, plus something else I can't quite identify—and then he explains it. "Actually, I think it's from being Irish. Maeve is just as active in the Northern Ireland thing." As he says it, "thing" sounds almost like "fing," a peculiarity I've heard a lot on the street. And his "really"'s are pronounced "reely."

"Oh, you grew up in Northern Ireland?"

"We were born in Belfast, but Ma and Da got sick of it, so they moved to Liverpool. The house next door to us was bombed, and they got afraid. I don't blame them, really. England is mostly a kip, but Liverpool's not bad, from all the Irish people living there, and London's not bad, really. Do you like it? You're a Yank, aren't you.?"

"Yes. Yes, sure I like it, I mean, I'm getting to like it."

"Are you, em, on holiday or what?"

"I'm a writer. Working on a book."

"Really? I never met any writers. What's the book about?"

"It—it's a biography; about a person who lived in the eighteenth century." He blinks and I can see this disappoints him. "I haven't written one before now. I've only done plays."

"Oh that's brilliant, I love to go the theater. I used to do the pantos, you know."

"The pantos? Oh, the pantomime. Yes. Well, mine are stage plays. None of them have been performed over here yet." He nods sympathetically. But here's Maeve asking us if we're ready to go.

We leave the hall, forging out into the darkness, down and over to Chalk Farm Road, then to Inverness Street, where there is apparently a pub Maeve likes. Inverness is the one that runs from the tube station to my street and, as we come up to the pub ("The Harp"), I realize I've seen it any number of times—so many times as to stop seeing it at all—but have never been inside. "They have Irish music on weekends," Maeve says. "But not tonight." We walk in, finding relatively quiet but smoky premises lit up by little wall lamps in pink glass shades made to resemble ruffled cloth. One side of the room is mirrored. On some of the walls there are paintings grimed over into almost total obscurity, and unintentionally antique signs for Whitbread and Guinness near the bar, the overhead rack of which holds a hundred glasses suspended upside down. Maeve walks over to a red-faced older man at a small table in the corner, bends for a kiss, then returns to us. Derek gives our orders to the bartender—pints for Maeve and me, a Coke for him—and we find another table on the side of the room opposite the mirror. Maeve's red-faced friend eyes us from his table but, since she hasn't invited him, doesn't join us.

At first we simply sit without talking. Then Maeve asks me what I thought of the meeting. I say that it was powerful; seemed to make an impact on everyone there, certainly with me, but then who—who among people you would ever know—hasn't always been an opponent of apartheid? Not, unfortunately, that any opposition of mine was much use to Blacks in South Africa. "No, you're wrong about that," she says. "They need to know that the world community supports them, that's very important. The brunt of the struggle falls on them, but it helps them to know that pressure is being exerted on their government by other nationalities. And, needless to say, they need funds, which anyone," she looks at me levelly, "even those who aren't involved in the work directly, can contribute."

"By the way," I jump in, "Derek tells me you're also involved in the Northern Ireland question. How do you manage to find time for both?"

A gentle, smiling irritation comes into her voice. "Because it's my life. That's what I do. It doesn't take that much imagination to see some of the same forces at work in both situations. First, of all, look at the way Africans and Asians are treated in Britain. In effect we have apartheid here, it just isn't in the legal code. I'm not saying everyone is, but the majority of the English are racists. Same thing for the Protestants in the north of Ireland. Naturally I'm in favor of Britain just getting out and giving Ireland its land back, just as I'm in favor of South Africa recognizing its Black population as equal before the law. I might add," she said, sipping her pint, "that I'm in favor of equality for women as well."

"But there you've got more legal support."

"There aren't many legal restrictions as such, but that doesn't mean that prejudice against women isn't rampant. Just check the statistics about income. And the attitudes! It's absolutely horrifying. The law doesn't do beans. It's not just women, it's anyone who doesn't fit the mold, Blacks, Asians, whatever. Or take Derek. He's gay, and there's no law against his being. But do you think he can count on any sort of respect and more importantly any fairness in hiring and treatment from the middle class that runs everything?"

"Maeve, get off it, I'm not doing so bad," Derek says, shaking her arm. "Who gives a toss what they think, anyway?"

"No one, except when they fire you from your job, as they did at that money-mill where you were working. Anybody could see through the story they gave."

"They were just afraid I was going to give them AIDS."

"How did they know you were gay?"

"Because one of the secretaries and me got to be mates and I told her and she told the rest of the lot I was one of those lepers. I was also wearing a button on my jacket at the time that said "Hate Causes AIDS." He smiles. "With them, it worked the other way. Even though I, personally, didn't have it."

I swallow down a gulp of my pint. A sort of black mist overwhelms me and I choke out, "My lover died of AIDS." They sit very quietly. Mist subsides. "I'm sorry, I didn't mean to blurt like that."

"No, it's all right," Maeve says. "I'm sorry. We didn't know." She puts her hand on my jacket sleeve and lets it rest there.

At this moment a carnival contingent pushes through the door, with loud greetings for the collectivity inside, friends and unknown potential friends. I'm grateful for the interruption, since I've just brought us to a conversational switchoff. After the hearties have subsided and found places for themselves around the bar, we begin again on another foot. I run through again for Maeve what I'm doing in London and then ask her more about herself and her projects. I realize she's too fierce for real comfort but still feel magnetized by her small face with the skin drawn tightly over the cheekbones, her glistening black eyes, and her intense speech delivery. Facts: she is twenty-nine years old; is on the dole, but also cleans houses off the books; in fact, this is what they both do. Neither of them sees any immediate change of plans, though Derek likes music and would like to try something in the music business, he's not quite sure what. Maeve imagines that she might some day hold an important position in one of the freedom organizations, but that's not the case now, and it really doesn't matter.

"When I stop to think about it," she says, "and that isn't often, I realize that there's really no way that I *can* make plans like most people do. Because that would mean that I accepted the whole set-up as it exists now, and obviously I don't. The best I can do is survive and try to change minds. I don't have a crystal ball, and I can't read the future, so I don't attempt to."

"And you're happy, or rather, content."

"I'm surviving and I'm doing some work. Probably doesn't show, but I'm actually very patient. That's part of being Irish," she smiles and looks at Derek. "We just don't give up. Oh, I wish they were playing tonight. Those are the nicest times, when you just swim along with the music and don't think about what's wrong. But I can't, not all the time, and what's more, I shouldn't, until things are different." She sits for a moment and then, looking at her watch, says, "Derek, if we're to do Portia Brandon's house tomorrow morning, maybe we should think of going."

"Wait, before you go, let me have your telephone number."

"Of course. Here," she says, taking out a scrap of paper and scribbling a number on it. She hands it to Derek, who, more slowly, writes his underneath.

"You don't share a place?"

"No, I've got my own flat—I mean, it's more like an over-grown bed-sit. I couldn't bear not having a place of my own."

"Where are you?"

"Up in Kentish Town, near Tufnell Park Station.

"I'm down in Earl's Court," Derek adds. "Mine is just a bed-sit. But I'm not home that much." He half smiles at me, then brushes a hand across his face. "You might give us your number as well." I write out my address and telephone and give it to him. "Gloucester Crescent. That's just here, isn't it?" He turns to his sister and says, "If we lived there we'd be home."

"I almost am anyway," she says. "It's just two stations. But the tube slows down this time of night, so I'd better be on my way."

"Will you let me put you in a cab?" I ask.

She pauses and then, "Pay for it, you mean? All right, if you want to and have the cash reserves."

We walk to Parkway and almost immediately find a taxi. Suddenly I think of the meeting with Corinne, which ended the same way; and yet the two instances couldn't be more different. Derek gives Maeve a peck on the cheek and she rides off. I ask him if he would also like a taxi ride home.

"Thanks, no. I'm going to stay the night with a friend of mine near here. Maeve and I are supposed to meet tomorrow morning at this house by Camden Lock that we clean. I'm not going all the way down to Earl's Court and then come back again tomorrow." He pauses. "But I'll walk you home if that's where you're going."

We turn up to Arlington Street, then back across to Inverness. As we pass The Harp again, the same group of party animals spills out of it, rowdier than ever. One of them falls down and has to be hauled to his feet by the others. "Trouble ahead for that lot," Derek says, and then, "If they're lucky, they'll end up in the rooms."

"What do you mean?"

"Oh, nothing, I was just thinking out loud." We make our way up the hill on Gloucester Crescent and come to the little metal gate before my building.

"This is me," I say. "I'm on the ground floor."

Derek glances at the brick front of the house then back at me. "Listen, I'm sorry about your mate. I hope we didn't sound like stupid berks or anything." Again his "fing" for "thing."

"No, it's really all right. I was glad to have people to be with, seriously. It gets boring by yourself sometimes. We'll do something again maybe this weekend.... So, good night."

"Right. We'll do something." He bends forward quickly. There is the smell of soap and something citrusy as he gives me a brotherly kiss. "G'night." Then he goes off to the house of his friend, the sound of footsteps retreating down the street. As I turn and walk to my door, a picture materializes—the South African priest, talking about his prisoners, his dark brown eyes focusing on each of us in turn, and that taut glow on his forehead, almost like a spotlight, as he asked for our help in getting them out.

Three

We seldom give gray skies their due. No one really looks at them, or ever bothers to qualify their reputation for monotony. In England, opportunity for appraisal comes nearly every day, but, here as anywhere, it's against the rules to stare at the sky for more than a few seconds at a time. Whenever there is a chance, I do look up at what is, in fact, not a featureless ceiling, but a rounded, floating, tumbling cushion with more than a little light visible behind it and noticeable differences of color. All is in motion, shifting, regrouping, traveling, and drawing more cloud along behind. This quicksilvered, various enactment of the neutral tone is a good picture of English minds at their most characteristic. No lightning, but a steady lightening, moment by moment qualified or sent running backwards. Anger and stoicism, reason certainly, but no position held without a lot of tugging and churning, apparent to anyone who troubles to notice. Constable isn't pure English just for his lucid rendering of rural scenes along the Stour or the Wye, but also for his skies, the brushy, pewter-gray matter that trembles over his meadows, cattle, and cathedrals like an embattled conscience.

I've been taken over by daydreams for nearly a week now. Constable is in the foreground because I saw paintings of his yesterday at the Victoria and Albert. I'd gone to look at some maquettes of eighteenth-century stage design and, that done, decided to go up to the top floor where they have the English school. The windows here are large for a museum. Since it was an overcast day, I had an easy time of it checking painted skies against the real item outside the window. Also visible were domes and spires of the old institutions—not just the towers of the V. and A., but also those of the Natural History Museum, with its hemispherical observatory. Limestone, slate roofing, lead, and verdigris copper detailing. From windows at that height, nothing contemporary was visible, and it was easy to see what the Victorians saw, when London was a repository of the art, the biology and botany of an entire globe, not to mention ponderous telescopes every night aimed at realms even vaster.

One of the instructive spectacles in London today is watching all that traditional solidity and weight begin to erode. Mrs. Thatcher's generation won't live forever, and meanwhile a rising tide of youth is moving into vacated space, baby capitalists anxious for money and pleasure on the one hand, anarchic and outer-fringe types on the other. Derek and Maeve are examples I now know personally, but their counterparts, milder and much more extreme, are every-where, mingling if not blending with the young brokers and insurance executives who pour out into the streets of the City during lunch hour and plot economic development the rest of the day. Of course there is another group, a bit older and much brainier, with reliably socialist political views—univer-sity teachers, journalists, and writers; but their numbers are small and you don't see them swaying opinion far outside their own ranks.

This is not even to bring up the blocs of different national-ities who have come to find shelter here after the breakup of the Empire. Maeve is right about the Blacks and lighter-skinned peoples; they're here in force and not much liked. This time I've particularly focused on the Pakistanis, if only because they keep their grocery stores open on Sunday and are indispensable when you run out of milk or bread on that day. And they are so ... let-go. None of the shopkeeper's lower-middle-class earmarks—offended stares expressing deep-dyed disapproval of the customer, smug adherence to self-devised rules, and maddening strategic vagueness. No, with the Pakistanis you have black-brown, slightly bored almond-shaped eyes, physical relaxation in a hundred different leaning poses, the almost Mediterranean refusal to be hurried or bullied, the sense they give of "it all" being fairly ridiculous, just not quite funny enough to make them laugh outright.

Derek telephoned before twenty-four hours had gone by and made a date for last Thursday. He said he wanted to take me to one of his favorite places. Oh, and what was that? Madame Tussaud's. "It's strange, I've never been to a wax museum," I said, "and there's a reason why not." But finally he persuaded me. I had been planning to put in my three hours at the British Library, but he sounded so eager, and Corinne, who was going to have a drink with me afterwards had called that morning to cancel—there was an errand she had to do for her Susannah.

The weather was manageable—my nice gray skies, but no rain—so I set out through Regent's Park to meet Derek down in Marylebone. The wide stretch of green along the east side of the park makes an impression felt nowhere else in London. Vistas there have an almost American spaciousness to them, though of course the Regency pomp of Gloucester and Cumberland Terraces, with their pediments and cream-white columns, will let you know pretty quickly which side of the Atlantic you're on. A few obstacles appear at the southernmost end—a through road, a little pond with a bridge to cross—but these are minor. Then comes a swatch of Elizabeth Bowen territory, the neat terrace houses of the southern end. I keep meaning to find out exactly which of those establishments it was she lived in but haven't made a point of it yet.

Turning onto Marylebone Road, I saw the green dome of the planetarium and then the entrance to the wax museum. The crowds weren't too large to prevent scanning each face: but no Derek. A little flash of disappointment shot through me. Wait, over there, yes. I hadn't recognized him at first, in that particular outfit. He was leaning against a wall wearing a bulky denim jacket that had bright-colored appliqués sewn on the chest and sleeve. When he came up to me, I could see that a sort of tag on the chest was round, composed of green and yellow thread, with the word "Americanino" bent around the top of the circle and "Made in Europe" at the bottom. A little red and white rectangle on the sleeve said, "Fire Rescue Squad." Derek smiled at me, one of his front teeth just slightly longer than the other, and said, "Hi," as our interested gazes locked.

We pushed inside, got our ticket and walked up to the exhibit level. After a stroll through a darkened room with a few old spotlit standards in it—scenes from Shakespeare, the Brontë children, and some scantily clad French courtesan (Was it Madame DuBarry? on her bed asleep and hooked up somehow to a bellows that made her seem, almost, to be breathing, which must get the kinkier visitors really going)—we came into the contemporary room, a sort of courtyard, brightly lit, with white trellis fences and columns overgrown with artificial vines. Leaning against one of the columns, his hand propped lazily against it, was Paul McCartney, or his simulacrum. Not so contemporary, really, because they had him in a sixties Nehru jacket. Just opposite, Nastasia Kinski and Clint Eastwood. Wearing tennis whites and terry-cloth headband, Bjorn Borg bent over in midstroke.

Up a few steps, and more convincing than ever, Barry Humphries dressed as Dame Edna Everage, with mauve hair, a glittering organdy "creation," and pointed eyeglasses encrusted with rhinestones. "Looks as though she's about to offer us a cup of vodka and Bovril," I said to a guard standing by—who answered with stony or should I say waxen silence. (Yes, I was fooled.) Which Derek found hilarious; not to be a good sport about it, though, would have been an even bigger mistake.

"By the way, why did you bring me here?" I asked.

"Come on, the next room is brilliant."

This was the pop room, which features Dolly Parton, Michael Jackson, and Boy George. A spot shone on each of them in turn, synchronized with sound tracks playing a few bars of their music and then, from Boy George, a short recorded speech, which concluded with the statement, "You see, I think of myself as sitting under the tree like a sort of Christmas present to the British public." This was Derek's favorite, and we had to let the whole series run through twice so that I could get the full, kittenish effect of this important cultural figure.

A flight of stairs down takes you to the grand hallway with an array of historic figures like Henry VIII and his ("they were expendable") wives. Under a dais, in the place of honor, stand Elizabeth II and the other royal media figures, Princess Diana foremost among them. Meanwhile a herd of international notables all around, including a very convincing Stalin and Richard Nixon, a not so convincing Churchill and JFK. Some figures work out better in wax than others. I have to admit, it began to get more intriguing. Any person who regularly appears on TV would do well to visit this room and try to learn what to avoid—the wedding photograph poses, the glassy stares, toothpaste ad smiles, and pancake makeup complexions. Very instructive. And then, too, you gradually become aware of your own brand of implausibility, with your harum-scarum clothes, crude curiosity, lack of restraint, and general air of transience. The mobile starers might point and laugh at, say, Kemal Ataturk, but he wasn't laughing back— just so many cabbage butterflies to be glacially ignored.

Last stop is the dungeon. Downstairs and into a darkened room with a few spotlit exhibits in sinister half-light. I thought of the old carnival funhouses. First display: Marie-Antoinette's severed head; and the taste level of the other exhibits sank steadily downward from that point on. The upper floors had shown how lives could go right, and this one showed how they could go wrong—though, for that matter, many lives up above could qualify for the lower floor just as aptly. It's more a question of financial backing than actual deeds committed. Still, the occupants of Tussaud's "Inferno" were the best-sellers here. Public fascination with Jack the Ripper's victims strewn in the alleys of his little gas-lit diorama could be counted on. Not to mention unconfessed admiration for the "Bathtub Murderer" who, forty years ago, disencumbered himself of several wives by drowning them in the nearest container of water. It seems to have taken the police an awfully long time to become suspicious. The waxworks version shows him poised triumphantly over an old Victorian tub with claw feet as a livid nude exhales bubbles from under water.

"All they need is goldfish," Derek said, which still didn't quite dispel your basic queasiness before representations of ingenious murder.

"This is the last room?"

"The last one. I went bananas the first time I came here."

"When you were little?"

"I must have been twelve." We climbed up the stairs to the exit. There's food for thought anywhere, though, and I couldn't help thinking about Henry VIII on the *piano nobile*, as much a criminal as the bathtub murderer down in the basement. And who had been responsible for more deaths, Jack the Ripper or Lloyd George? "Reasons of state" is the great whitewash. A final guard, a woman in uniform, but in fact made of wax, sent us on our way. "All the world is a wax museum": point conceded.

Still, other points have an equal validity, and, as we walked out into the early darkness, there was a chance to make them. Post-five-o'clock traffic whizzed by us, headlights flashing in our eyes. I suggested walking down to Soho for an early dinner—it would take us a while to get there. We turned onto Marylebone High Street and threaded our way through steady streams of pedestrians trudging in the opposite direction, not talking much, but now and then glancing sideways at each other to see the other face lit up by the pale orange light of a street lamp, smiling slightly or simply gazing with bland curiosity at surrounding multitudes caught up in unguessable errands, all of us huddling forward along one particular street of one particular city in the late years of the century.

We paused at a crossing; farther down on my right was Manchester Square. Remembering that Duke Street runs down from there, I suddenly thought it might be fun to have a drink at Gold's Bar. A touch too posh for Derek, maybe, but so what. He immediately agreed, whether out of curiosity or simple cooperative habit I couldn't tell. A drizzle had begun to fall and the idea of a warm, dry interior sounded good.

We pushed through the doors with their etched glass windows and into the thick of it. After a rapid inspection, our waiter pointed out a table to us and led us there part way. I said, "The house specialty is champagne. That OK with you?"

"Em, actually, you know, I don't drink booze. I'll just have a Coke."

"You don't drink, ever?"

"Not for the last three years I haven't. I had my share, don't worry."

"Oh. Do you go to AA?"

"Yes. But to NA more often than AA."

"What's NA?"

"Narcotics Anonymous. I did a lot of drugs. Alcohol counts as a drug, actually."

"I don't know which sounds more impressive, drug addict or alcoholic. What made you stop?"

"I got sick of it. I was really sick. Then a friend of mine got into NA and told me it was brilliant. So I tried it and it worked."

"What does NA do?"

"You go, like, to meetings. Usually one person tells their story—how they got into drugs and how they stopped and how they feel now—and then the other people at the meeting talk a bit about what's bothering them and then the meeting breaks up and you stand around and have coffee and talk to everybody. All my best friends are in NA or AA now. A lot of the ones I used to drug with are dead."

"Does it bother you when other people around you drink?"

"No, not unless they get sloppy. I have a friend who's actually still an addict. But I think he'll probably end up in the rooms, he's been talking about going."

"What rooms?"

"You know, the meetings, the rooms where they have meetings."

"Where do they have them?"

"Oh, lots of places. The social halls of churches, mostly. Wherever they can find one available." He looked at me half as though he were afraid and half defiantly. "Does it bother you that I used to take drugs?"

"I've taken a few myself. You don't look any the worse for wear." He smiled and accepted the Coke the waiter had brought. Coke to champagne, we toasted the drug-free life.

"Although," I said, "there is one other complication these days. When you took drugs, did you use a needle?"

"Oh, you mean AIDS. Sure I used a needle. That was one of the reasons I had to get off it. I used to go down to the Dilly with two or three barbs of go in me and see whether I could get some more."

"What's the Dilly?"

"Picadilly—you know, with the statue. If it's sex and drugs you want, that's where you queue up." His eyes dropped. "I was lucky, though, really lucky. When I took the test, it was OK."

"Sometimes the results are false," I said, rather callously.

"I took it four times. They say it's almost a hundred percent accurate now. And my health is very good." He looked at me a little pleadingly.

"I'm glad you weren't exposed," I said.

"I know. But you—your lover died?"

"Yes."

At that moment I looked up and saw Corinne going out the door with another youngish woman in a long black coat. Could that be Susannah? At first it seemed like a strange coincidence, but then, not so surprising after all. I thought of jumping up and chasing after her but something made me hesitate. As far as I could summon up a reason, it had to do with not wanting to embarrass her, in case she might be embarrassed; but there was also something else, which I couldn't quite fasten on.

"There goes a friend of mine," I said to Derek, who turned his head and looked toward the door. Which had swung shut—they had already left. I suppose I might have dragged her back to the table; but I didn't know Derek all that well yet. Besides, there would always be a chance for them to meet later. For the next hour we sat and exchanged stories about Liverpool and New York. On his side there was the authoritarian father who beat him, on my side the ups and downs of making my way as a playwright. He talked about the youth scene in Britain. I told him something, though not much, about Joshua and Adele.

Eventually I asked him how old he was. When told me he was twenty-seven, I groaned inwardly and maybe even outwardly. "But I'm old for my age," he said encouragingly.

"Just like Boy George," I said. "It's time for dinner—what do you think?" As we were going out the door, it popped into my head that Joshua was twenty-seven when we met. But back then I was only thirty-one, thirty-two. And the situation was in every way different. Out into the half-light of the street lamps again. I looked at Derek and asked, "Now tell me really and truly, why did you want to take me to Madame Tussaud's?"

He hesitated and then: "I never took anybody there before. I used to go there when I was little with Ma and Da. When they put Boy George in, I went; a friend told me about it. And then you said you were writing a book about somebody from history. You just seemed like somebody who would know about all those statues."

"Yes, I probably look like one of them as well, to you."

Derek laughed. "Well, you don't look like Boy George."

"You don't either, thank God."

"You don't get him at all, do you?"

"He's fine for TV. I wouldn't know what to say to him."

"Yeh, he's a drug addict."

"Even if he weren't."

Derek turned somber and looked down at his feet. "I used to like him more than I do now. You get older and you get tired of the old things. I just don't know what else to like yet. I mean, it's fucking boring to just clean rooms and that."

I felt a slow swell of sympathy for him and a certain stinging irritation toward myself, a former fan of, well, Jefferson Airplane, and the Rolling Stones; and today something of a fat cat. Just that tiny glimpse into another life—the housecleaning, the bed-sit—was enough to make me see that I had been fencing myself in with grief almost to the point of smugness. Perhaps it was his "NA" or being Irish, but whatever it was, I was ready to count Derek as one of those people who, without especially trying to, could make you see yourself more clearly. I put my hand very lightly on his shoulder and pretended to lead him casually across the next street (the zebra stripes on the pavement glistening in lamplight) and down into Soho. Wish he was named something besides Derek, never liked that name.

Four

When Adele called to say she was definitely coming, excitement was the topmost layer of what I felt, but there were other things, too, including a certain edginess. She said she wasn't staying with her friend in Holland Park after all, but when I suggested bunking together at my place, she unhesitatingly said no, explaining that she'd reserved a room at the Connaught. Yes, I could meet her at Heathrow if I wanted to, though she was perfectly capable of getting into town on her own, dear. "Don't be silly," I said, "of course I'll meet you." She tried to conceal it but was clearly glad I insisted, not just because of the bags and unfamiliar ground, but also because, under that plan, we would be seeing each other an hour sooner than otherwise.

I stood in the crowd of those waiting outside the customs barrier, some of them holding up hand-written signs with the names of persons they were supposed to meet. We were all free to wonder who Mr. Tyson or Mr. Newsome was and what their business was with that tall man in spectacles and pinstripe suit, or that young woman wearing a denim jacket. I sketched out a cv for each of them, but then at last people began to throng forward from the exit, pushing their baggage carts with all the rabid efficiency of the tourist hellbent to get to monuments and entertainments. Something told me that Adele wouldn't be among this group but that even so she would follow soon after: yes, almost immediately there was Adele. (She has a way of gliding around obstacles still without hurrying.) I hailed her with a big, semaphoric wave as she broke out into a smile and strode through the gate, followed by a porter pushing her bags on a cart. She was wearing a black wool coat with blue frogging that I remembered from earlier years over a lavender-and-white sweater dress that looked new. She held out her arms and grabbed me close to her and planted a loud kiss: Ummhh! When we backed off a little to look at each other, I could see that her eyes were teary; we were both choked up and excited as could be.

"Oh, Avery, it's so *good* to see you, darling!" We exchanged endearments as we walked outside, she holding on to my upper arm with both hands as the porter followed behind. We kept our eyes on each other almost exclusively. It struck me that her hair was almost entirely gray now, caught up in a twist behind her head and fastened with a tortoise-shell comb. She looked a little less plump than before, and when I asked her about it, she said she'd been losing weight so as to look good for the trip. Diet-induced deflation might explain why there seemed to be more lines in her face. That's what I wanted to think in order not to feel partly responsible for them. Dealing with the Joshua issue would almost certainly have been easier for her if I'd stayed in New York. Just because she had gone through the process of deciding to come to London didn't mean she was perfectly at peace with everything and everybody. As I looked into her eyes searchingly, I saw or imagined seeing an answering glint of appraisal in return. Well, a shared calamity can strengthen personal ties but by the same token put new strains on what has been reinforced.

We climbed into the taxi waiting at the head of the queue and settled back for the long drive into town. Adele directed most of the talk, speaking in that smoky, pitch-varying voice I'd been missing. She filled in details about the trip, about her seatmate, an older London gentleman who'd been visiting his daughter in New York, and how glad the poor thing was to get away from that, as he said, *terrible* city. He didn't like his daughter living away from home and if she had to, why must it be in New York? Why would anyone want to live there? "I tried to explain, but you don't get anywhere with the English, do you? How do you manage with them? He was originally Viennese, but it doesn't seem to have made any difference." She aimed a skeptical look at me, one eye slightly narrowed, the other eyebrow raised.

"Actually, I don't see that many people. You know, I have my work to do."

"But, Avery, it isn't good to be by yourself all the time." She seemed genuinely distressed, not just meddlesome.

"I don't mind. And I have just made a new friend— American, though. She says she's met you. Corinne Waldman, do you know her?"

"Corinne Waldman? You've been seeing her? Oh, Avery, that's wonderful. She's a very bright girl. I don't know her all that well, but I hear she's very talented. She's a writer, isn't she?" I could see that Adele was pleasantly surprised, excited even, by this news, but was also clearly trying to appear calm. Not too hard to guess why. I felt sure that Adele wouldn't have said, if asked and given time to think, that she would like to see me happily married eventually; but being human means having certain human reflexes. Her fundamental wish was for my well-being, a wish that in this case had simply sparked a series of conventional reactions.

Partly wanting to save her from straying up a blind alley and partly out of an annoyed reflex of my own, I said, "Corinne seems to be having a good time here. There's an English girl she's involved with, but I haven't met her yet."

Adele hesitated and then, with cultivated unsurprise, said, "Oh really? How interesting. I didn't know she was gay. I wonder if her mother knows.... Arlene never mentioned it. But she isn't that close to Corinne's mother. Hmmp. Very interesting." Adele settled back and gazed out at the row upon row of brown brick houses riding past us. "I suppose this counts as their Queens, doesn't it?" she asked without expecting an answer.

But I said, "Or their Bronx. Anyway, something you'd say 'no thonx' to."

She looked around at me. "Oh, I don't know. They all seem to have pretty gardens. Never *saw* so many rose bushes." She gestured out to the prospect of brick-walled back gardens whizzing by, a display that could never have been found near New York. "It's funny the way they divide the houses right at the middle of the gable." She was talking about the practice followed by some, if not all, row-house owners—painting their walls a different color from their neighbor's, a line drawn ruler-straight down from the center of the shared gable and serving as a rough gauge of civic closeness or distance. Occasionally the color clashes glared almost malevolently.

"Now tell me about your friend's show," I said and took her hand in mine.

"It opens at a something called Seabright Gallery on Cork Street. Three days from now, no, wait, two days, I'm still on jet lag. She said it's right off Old Bond Street—or New Bond Street, one of them. She said you can get to it through the Burlington Arcade also."

"I think I have an idea where it is," I said. "Do you know what sort of photographs they are?"

"Only in a general way. What's she's done for the last ten years is go backstage at the theaters here and get shots of the whole process. Some of the actors but also of the technicians and prop people doing their work. I'm sure it will be fascinating. Fania's work was always good." Adele said this in a familiar melancholy-sounding intonation, giving a quick series of nods that I knew indicated real respect, respect that fell just short of envy. With the side of her index finger she reached up and touched the mole at the inner corner of her eye, a gesture that with her usually means she is turning over a problem in her mind.

Now we were in London proper, and Adele seemed too absorbed in the sights to want to talk. When we passed Marble Arch I told her what it was, but she said she recognized it, and wasn't that Speakers Corner of Hyde Park? Yes; but no speakers today, or ever, for that matter. "That's over with long ago, isn't it?" she asked. We glided down Park Lane and turned left at Grosvenor Street and then along the south side of the Square. "I know what that is," she said, "that's the American Embassy." I could see she was the kind of visitor that prefers to know about everything already rather than be told. We turned onto Carlos Place and pulled up at the Connaught. I asked Adele whether she'd stayed there before. "No, but Fania said I'd like it. And it's near the gallery. She also said to bring a few collages and she'd see about getting them sold. Otherwise, how am I going to pay for this hotel."

"Adele, if you're short of funds—."

"*Avery*, please, I was just kidding."

We walked into the lobby, embraced by the special quiet of "the good hotel." To the left was a room for tea. Near the muslined window there I saw two men, one mustached, the other thinner and older, arguably more distinguished, talking quietly but audibly over porcelain cups and a plate of little sandwiches. Adele was at the desk being checked in, a porter standing discreetly near her bags. I cast around for an adjective to characterize the place and came up with Jamesian—an ever so slightly faded gentility and determined avoidance of show that said hotel carpets should be almost invisibly patterned, not threadbare but slightly worn; that the wood of the desk should be massive, dark brown, and blindingly polished; and that there should be an old grandfather clock on the first landing of the stairs, its glowing brass pendulum swaying back and forth with the sort of gravity that establishes an appropriate tempo for the guests.

As Adele turned from the desk, an entourage of half a dozen notables swept in, including two men in turbans and several women in green, apricot, and mauve saris, the veils edged with gold embroidery. Adele stopped in her tracks. "I knew staying here was going to be worth it," she whispered to me.

I grinned and nodded. "Listen, would you like to go upstairs, and wash your hands and then come down for a pot of tea?" I gestured toward the adjoining room. "Or we could order lunch."

"What a marvelous idea, let me just—. On second thought, it might be better if I just took a nap and met you later for dinner. Does that make sense?" We agreed that I would come back at seven-thirty. Adele gave me one more hug and said how thrilled she was to be with me again. Then, with a mock-serious gesture toward the grandfather clock, she went up to her room.

Outside, a respectful taxi was waiting, just for my benefit, it let me imagine. Riding back to Gloucester Crescent, I reviewed feelings about Adele and our reunion. Everything seemed normal enough, and it was clear that in spite of this temporary separation we were, indissolubly, a two-person family. Stubbornly isolationist currents in me were grumpy about not being allowed uninterrupted solitude, but that was only part of the mix. Almost never do you, after a separation of nearly three months, instantly reestablish flawless communication. As I thought about Adele and me, two qualms, one new, one old, came into focus. First, that Joshua's name hadn't been mentioned the entire afternoon. Odd, but then, she might say she had come to see *me*. The second problem was something that had been hovering in the background for the last eight months: the issue of my own health. We had simply never talked about it. Adele knew that Joshua and I had both taken the test, with negative results. But we hadn't discussed the extent to which I saw my own future as standing under a shadow. My best guess was that she had left it up to me whether or not to raise the dread topic. Given that I hadn't brought it up, then would I never? Mostly I didn't want to— the whole avoidance of morbidity tactic—and, moreover, I had no symptoms yet. But if Adele was secretly troubled by the issue, wasn't it unfair of me not to open avenues toward discussion? (They wouldn't have to be melodramatic.) Because I work in the theater I cringe at theatricality in life; and needless complications. There has to be a way to bring up the subject, a natural way. My driver expertly nosed his way through a traffic snarl at Regent's Park Crescent and turned into Albany Street, which stretched pleasantly unobstructed before us. Well then: suppose I didn't make any plans about special revelations and just let the temper of the moment decide what we talked about. We would have a pleasant dinner tonight—maybe the Ritz, Adele being one of those who are receptive to manageable doses of swank. Then I thought about the fuss and fracas and decided on the Cafe Royale, former haunt of aesthetes like Oscar Wilde and Ronald Firbank. Yes, she'd be interested in all that.

THE WAITER in black tie and impeccable shirt front channels us to a table at one of the plush banquettes on the side. A light claret shade of red predominates here, with ormolu trim, and I remember Cocteau's description of theater-going as the "red and gold disease." From Covent Garden to the Cafe Royale is an almost effortless transition, though it isn't one that many people regularly make. A complacently unchic ambiance holds sway here, as Adele may or may not realize, but it makes no difference, she's enchanted and has begun introducing a few rather amazing duchessy touches in her comportment. The waiter has already been forced to understand that she is no ordinary client by her calf-length black organza dress trimmed with green piping at neck and sleeves. She tells me it is a Carolina Herrera bought at one of those stores where the rich discard designer originals after one or two wearings. A gold chain necklace and a bracelet made with what looks like a half-pound of gold—both old presents from Joe Lambert—complete the effect.

"I knew I'd get a chance some day to wear this stuff," she whispers to me and then rears back to give a gracious, close-mouthed smile to the waiter who has come to ask us what we would like as an aperitif. I tell him just to bring us a bottle of Moët, and his slight bow is a gentlemanly outward sign that he concurs with the wisdom of my choice. Adele glances around when she hears a ripple of low laughter from a table around which several Japanese businessmen in black suits stiffly sit, then turns back to me. "By the way, Avery, you haven't told me about your research for the biography. How's it coming?"

"Fine. There's as much material as I could possibly want on Colley Cibber, probably more than I can use, really, since the book is about his father and his children as well. I go to the British Library every day or so and take notes. There was a biography done about Colley Cibber already, one that's well written but out of date. And very little about his father and children. I'd say there was plenty of room for me."

"Colley Cibber—he's the playwright. Yes, that's what I remembered. You know, I keep saying I'll get one of his plays from the library and read it, but there's been so much to do lately. I will, though, when I go back. Which one should I start with?"

"You really think you want to? I mean, they're period pieces.

"Who isn't? No, I really want to read one."

"OK, you might try *Love's Last Shift*. It was his first success, probably because of the character of Sir Novelty Fashion—Cibber played the role himself, and in some ways it *was* himself. It was also the first really developed portrayal of foppery. Cibber was said to have perfected that." She looks as though she is actually interested, so I push on. "What few people realize is that Vanbrugh—you know, the architect who wrote plays—stole the character and made him into Lord Foppington in *The Relapse*, which I saw when I was in London back in 1967. That's probably where I first focused on Colley Cibber."

"OK, but isn't Cibber also the one that Pope made the hero of *The Dunciad*?"

"Yes, but I don't think I knew anything about Cibber when I first read Pope. It was just a name."

"I don't like *The Dunciad* very much. *The Rape of the Lock* is so much better. I've never been able to get through *The Dunciad*."

"Well, sure, I know what you mean." Our champagne arrives and is hosed gracefully into flutes that send up a bead chain of bubbles through the wine.

"Here's to Colley," Adele says. "Down with *The Dunciad*."

"Or you might try *The Careless Husband*," I say between sips. "It's when the first blush of Romanticism comes into English theater. The philandering husband reforms at the end, tears are shed—sort of like the last act of *The Marriage of Figaro* and any number of other plays. Cibber originated all that."

"Sounds sentimental."

"Maybe. But sentimentality was a new thing back then. He couldn't have known what an indispensable invention that was going to become. Let's see what else.... Oh really, Adele, don't bother with this. He's never performed. His plays aren't as good as *The Dunciad*, believe me."

"All right, I was just asking." She consults her menu, discusses choices with me, and lets me give our orders to the waiter when he returns. Conscious of trying to make our first evening together a small-scale bash, we keep the conversation strictly to light subjects breezily treated—news of friends back home, the exhibits Adele has seen, what her friend Fania has said to her about the gallery and the opening. Only after dessert, the ruins of pears, peaches, grapes, and cheese lying around the table, and while we are stirring our coffee with slow ruminative motions, does a silence fall. The Japanese businessmen have gone, and the tables near us are empty.

Adele looks up at me. Our eyes meet and exchange information for a long time. Eventually I say, very quietly, "Oh, Adele," and she looks down at her coffee cup.

"It's getting better," she says. She gropes for her purse and pulls out a handkerchief.

"Do you want to go? Let's." I gesture to the waiter, who bows and moves toward the table.

"No, no, let's finish our coffee."

"I'll get the check anyway. The bill, please." He bows and goes off. I turn back to Adele. "The first year is the hardest."

"Oh, sure. He hasn't even had his next birthday yet. I'll be glad when that's over."

"Well, it's only a month off. I just want to make sure that you have friends around when you need them."

"They're there if I want to see them. But that's not all the time."

I breathe in and say, "Adele, there's something on my mind. It's that—I should have stayed with you this year. I feel bad about it, I know I'm letting you down. You say it's getting better, and I think it is for me, too. And I *will* come back soon."

"Avery, really, it's all right. *I'm* all right. Of course I miss you and of course I want you back home, but that doesn't have to be right now. And anyway this is ridiculous because here we are, and we're having a lovely time." Mixed with the motherly reassurance, her voice has a certain edge, and her eyes give off little flashes of fire. I sit and look at her steadily; eventually she relaxes into a long sigh and settles back against the banquette. "The only thing I worry about is that you're over here where you don't know anybody—at least, no old friends—and I just think it must be hard for you."

"It would be hard for me anywhere. But I seem to need to be alone, and that's easier here. I just wish I could be more helpful to *you.*"

"Don't worry about me. You don't get to my age without developing a few resources." She takes a sip of coffee. "I've even been known to dose myself with whisky at times, but so far I haven't wound up at a drying-out farm so I must be doing OK."

This is a joke or at least the *wish* to be a joke. I take the escape offered and laugh. Adele smiles back and changes the subject. Our waiter brings a silver tray with the tally of our extravagance on it, which I cover with a sheaf of twenty-pound notes. Jet lag is weighing heavily on Adele, and, in spite of her determination to be on top of things, she looks tired. A rush of affection for her comes over me—gratitude, actually, for her presence. It's as though the conversation we've had was a necessary duty, tribute to be paid, something we've both been dreading and now have come through unharmed and free to enjoy each other's company. In the vestibule, as I help her into her coat, she turns and looks up at me, smiles, and reaches up to dust my cheek with a kiss. Her eyes muster the old sparkle. "Oh, Avery, it's so good to see you."

Five

Today's mail includes copies of reviews of the Seattle production of *You Had to Be There*, and I let their distant pink glow light up my prospects for a few minutes before going back into reality mode. Income from that run won't hurt and, with Chicago's *Through the Roof*, that makes for more than acceptable cash flow, something I'd prefer not to worry about while I'm here. It's while I'm mulling over all this that Maeve calls. She doesn't identify herself at first; only when she says something about Derek am I quite sure who is talking to me.

"He wonders why you haven't called this past week."

"Oh, well, my, um, a very close friend has been in town, and we've been going to the theater and museums. I think I told Derek about it. Really, there just hasn't been a chance to get in touch with you. Everything all right?"

"We're well. But now—your friend: how long will he be here?"

"She. Just one more day."

"Ah, she's a woman." The telephone went silent with guesswork.

"You remember I told you about my partner dying. This is his mother."

"Who's come to visit you. Perfect, I'm so glad. That will be good for you and for her. I'm sorry to have bothered you. Derek was worried and he wouldn't. So I just rang. I'll let you go. But we do want to see you soon. You'll ring us, won't you?"

"Of course. I should have done that already."

"No, no, no, we understand. Goodbye." She hung up.

Obviously the idea of some sort of relationship between Derek and me has crystallized not only in his mind but in Maeve's as well. The question is whether *I* think it has. Well, no, I don't. Defenses to the rescue. I took him to dinner after he invited me to Madame Tussaud's, that's all. I assumed we'd see each other again at some point, but I never imagined he thought any pact had been sworn. These peroxide-blond kids move fast.... On the other hand, nobody made me see him again after that first meeting. Was it anything more than an unformulated wish to spend time with a new (to me) personality type, someone young and attentive? Yes, he has pretty eyes and wears nicely cut jeans and talks with that appealing accent. But so what? I'm certainly in no condition to deal with hot and heavy situations, especially with someone his age, someone so different from me. Well, Joshua and I were contrasting personality types, granted. And I wonder what he would have made of Derek. No, the thoughts won't go together. That was altogether different.... What I have to do is simply to telephone Derek next week and say I'm tied up with my work and that I'm not sure I know when I'll be able to see him. It's not fair to lead him on, if that's what he thinks I've been doing. To be honest, I suppose there was some of that. I do like him and I am human. Maybe I'm closing things off too quickly. But, today, anyhow, I have other fish to fry—for one thing Adele's friend's show opens at five, and several errands need doing before that. There might even be a chance to get an hour in at the Library.

I'VE OFFERED to loop by the Connaught and take Adele to the opening but she said no, Fania wanted them to go together. When I step inside the Seabright Gallery two dozen people are already there, each equipped with a glass of wine and ignoring the photographs in favor of conversation with each other. There is Adele standing next to Fania, whom I have met only this past week but already like. Her pale blond curls glow with the luster of recent cosmetic assistance (one thing about having your hair go white is that being blond is made much easier). To see Adele and Fania together is to contrast two approaches to the problem of aging. Adele looks youthful for someone as old as she is, and Fania looks wan for someone as young as she apparently is. I go up to them, kiss Adele, and take Fania's hand. "This all looks marvelous," I say. "I'll want to come by later in the week and make a closer survey when there aren't so many people."

Fania nods and smiles and urges me toward the wine. When I return I see an older man talking to Adele, someone I don't know. I hesitate at a short distance, undecided whether to go up or not. When Adele notices me, she smiles and makes a beckoning gesture, with just a faint hint of nervousness.

"Avery, this is a friend of mine you haven't met. Max Wiesner, Avery Walsh. Max and I met on the plane coming over, I think I mentioned him. He has a daughter who lives in New York."

"Oh yes, you did mention him." Looking him indulgently in the eye, I say, "Adele told me you didn't find much to like about New York."

"If I were younger, no doubt it would be different. My daughter's very happy there." He smiled and turned to Adele. "Adele has almost convinced me to return and give it another try. I may not have met the right people."

When he speaks, I hear the slight gloss of an accent, so that it's possible to place him as a member of a group I have a soft spot for: older East European Jewish men with thoughtfully modulated manners, always slightly amused and invincibly charming. His thinning gray hair is brushed back on a sleek, narrow-gauge head, and deep smile wrinkles spread outward like a little gingko leaf from the corners of his eyes. He stands just at Adele's height, which is tall. So much do they seem absorbed in each other that I turn to Fania and begin talking to her under the cover of crowd noise. She explains that she knows Max Wiesner a little and had invited him to the opening. Yes, of course, he was from Vienna; had come to London in the thirties; owned a gallery specializing in African and Oceanic art. He'd been married twice but had outlived both wives. Fania expects him to marry again.

"Or maybe not, he never seems to be lonely," she says, gently aiming her gaze at him and Adele, who are laughing quietly together, looking as though they don't need any other company.

A group of people that I gradually identify as a family comes up to Fania and congratulates her. She introduces the Deanes to me one by one, Anthony, the father, Chantal, the mother (who is French), and Edward and Arthur, the two sons. Anthony reviews films and works for the BBC, Arthur does cultural journalism, and Edward wants to be an actor. Chantal takes care of them all. Something magnetizes me to her immediately if only because she actually seems interested to know who I am and why I'm here. Not conventionally pretty, nevertheless she has the sexual charm that French women seem always to keep right up into middle age and past it. Both boys are strikingly good looking and one can see an older, more battle-weary version of their features in the father, who is the most reserved of them, but who even so will break out in muffled laughter at the right provocation. Listening to them toss comments back and forth, to Fania and among themselves, I keep thinking that they seem, for lack of a better word, *American*. By which I mean what? That they are more like peers with each other than parents and children, and that for once the whole, boring process of "placing" everyone and everything (which always means subtly hinting at what's wrong with everyone and everything) is suspended. Instead, they seem available—to new people and new ideas; they don't refuse to be pleasantly surprised.

But now another group of admirers has crowded first them and then me away from Fania and from each other. Their heads turn around and around in the fray and I see Chantal cast a helpless mock-tragic glance back at me by way of farewell. I make up my mind to somehow get back to them again before I leave and see where things go from there.

Now, is there anybody else here I know? More people are streaming in all the time. It's going to be that kind of opening, the Victoria Falls roar of conversation already blanking out normal thought processes, enclosed air beginning to fog up with cigarettes. Then I see Corinne squeezing through the bodies, guiding someone over toward me, in fact, the same pretty woman she was with that night at Gold's.

"Hello, darling, this is—."

"*Susannah*," I chime in with her. "Corinne has told me all about you, and I was wondering when the unveiling would be."

Susannah smiles and says, "I warn you, she exaggerates enormously." She has dark hair and amused eyes, with long black lower lashes printed against her cheeks, skin of the pale satin finish most English girls seem to have, and perfect teeth. But as she banters lightly about nothing in particular, a part of me takes against her, probably not just because of jealousy alone. She seems a flawless example of the "Sloane Ranger," with just the right sort of white silk blouse and velvet bow tie, and already bored by everyone at the party. Us, too, I expect. On the other hand, these are not exactly ideal circumstances for getting to know someone since we have to shout into each other's faces if we want to be heard.

In the middle of a crowd packed together like spaghetti, I manage to separate the two of them and take Corinne over to Adele without Susannah coming along. Adele is still talking to Max; it takes a moment to get her attention. Exclamations of ecstasy from both women. I can see that Max thinks Corinne is attractive as he welcomes her into the civilized glow of his attention. Adele and Corinne exchange gossip about their friends in common. To watch them together is to recognize that they have a kind of rapport Adele and I don't have, the solidarity of New York sisterhood, a whole repertory of ironies, affirmations, and shared, untranslatable jokes. I slip in asides to Max from time to time, who always manages to find an oblique, unpredictable reply. Eventually he bypasses the rule against prying and says, "But this young lady and you are not a couple, are you."

"No. We're friends." He nods and I can see that he has "understood" Corinne and me, that he holds the information about our sexual preferences in his mind with no particular judgment for or against, just as part of the human pageant his seventy years have brought to his attention, the matter for further reflections and one more proof of his special gift for interpreting social relationships as they appear before him.

I overhear Adele mentioning my name and when I turn around she's congratulating Corinne for spending time with me. Corinne accepts this smilingly and says that Avery is a darling and she's really looking forward to going to museums and things with him. Then she turns my way and asks, "Do you see Susannah anywhere? I'm afraid she's been swallowed up in the crowd." I let her push off into the fray ahead of me, and, when she does finally meet up with Susannah, I let myself be jostled off course farther up toward the front of the gallery near the window. The idea of getting out of here begins to seem like bliss. But of course I'm meant to stay until it's over and go to dinner with Adele and Fania.

Meanwhile, the absorbing pleasures of people-watching, ideal for someone whose hobby is creative guesswork about the lives, occupations, and tastes of those around me. What for example to make of that thirty-five-year-old, with black leather jacket over a pleated-front white shirt and paisley bow tie, blue jeans and black boots down below, and a sort of stevedore's stretch wool navy-blue cap fixed on his head? He is handsome, with brush-like mustache and strong underslung lower jaw, the sort of face you expect to see in stiffly posed photographs from the 1890s, the subject's hand slipped into a pale jacket outlined in dark piping. I decide he is a brilliant young journalist, with an S-and-M tinge, presently unattached but not worried about it. His black-brown eyes meet mine for a moment and a small quantum of interest, superior challenge, and cool intelligence comes to me from them. But neither of us has the guff to go up and began talking just like that.

I turn to a young woman beside me, ultra-thin and swathed in the sort of Midsummer-Night's-Dream gossamer rags in subtly tinted pastels that Zandra Rhodes has made her signature. A halo of pre-Raphaelite hair surrounds the small face, made dramatic by blue eye shadow. She looks up at me as I look at her, neither smiling, saying anything, nor looking away. An empty glass dangles from her hand at the end of a crooked arm, but I don't volunteer to do anything about it. Instead, I add her and the black leather jacket to the by now enormous file of passed-up opportunities any fairly busy life racks up in the course of going out to parties and crowded public places.

One of Fania's photographs catches my eye, a picture of Cyril Ritchard making up in his room backstage before appearing in something Restoration, to judge from his peruke and the white lace at his throat. I let my thoughts wander for a few minutes, going over the "all the world's a stage" idea in the English context. Because, in fact, they seem the most theatrical of nationalities—not the most operatic, that's the Italians. First of all you've got to have a good script, and it's rare to find someone English—from Cockney on to frightfully Mayfair—who can't keep a steady stream of chat going. Like the French, they conceive of reality under a verbal sign, but whereas the French prefer to write, the English prefer to say it. In English, the best style is speechly. You might think that the novel was the central English form, but even there the dramatic perspective is the basis of construction. "Scene" predominates over analysis or revery (Virginia Woolf has never made as much headway here as in America), and, even when the story isn't done in the voice of a character, it still sounds like a monologue delivered center stage, with plenty of asides to the audience and naked judgments handed down about the unfolding action. The sense is always of a gathering of like-minded townspeople witnessing gross or heartwarming events of the story, laughing together or denouncing the folly or cruelty of the characters, occasionally applauding true and good actions. When not at the theater or reading, still each person carries everywhere in public and often in private a portable stage to perform on, coming up with the lines and gestures designed to insure acceptance and approval. To be left out, seen as bereft of a context, a supportive constituency, is the worst fate: life is life among other people, and that is that. No Daniel Boones or Thoreaus in English history and literature. Hence the entertainment value of English social life, where conversation requires participation, thought, anecdote, and wit, everything that promotes interest and lively reactions. Morose self-absorption and inarticulate sincerity, so much the rule in the great land across the water, close on Saturday here; nobody would risk it. Almost from birth the English are taught to provide verbal and gestural signs appropriate to the situation at hand; and to do a complicated obscuring dance around whatever won't go over in present company.

A fat, curly-headed person with a red tie starts talking to me as though he were my best friend. When I ask him if we know each other, he says, "Oh yeah, I met you at Bob Brown's birthday party last year, remember?" Cowardice strikes and I say I do, aware I'm condemning myself to hearing more about it all. When he finishes Bob Brown, the monologue moves to himself, how he answers phones for the gallery in New York that handles Fania's stuff, and, you know, Fania's really good people, she's made a lot of money for the gallery, a great artist, and when he told her he was coming to London, she made him swear he'd come to the party. He's glad he saw me here, maybe we could have a drink afterwards. This is a nice affair, but he's not that wild about the English, kind of snobby aren't they?

"I haven't had that problem with them," I say and then, "Oh, there's my best friend, catch you later." He starts another sentence but I squeeze through the wall of bodies and leave him to finish it. That conversation was my reward for being so analytical about our host country. And before I forget, if I'm going to get a chance to talk to the Deane family before they all leave, I better start looking for them. So now a slow search through the smoky crowds, eager to get back to the kinds of things we were saying. But—no luck. They may be scattered among all this noise, but more likely they've left, just as I would like to do but can't. Back to my post by the window, then, to gaze out at the people free to pass by outside. At an angle I can see the entrance to the Burlington Arcade. A figure steps out from under it and turns in this direction. Something about that particular silhouette and loose-jointed walk: it shouldn't be, but it is Derek. He comes toward the gallery. I find myself not turning around, not losing myself in the crowd, and when he passes in front of the window I give a quick wave. He breaks out in a smile, points to himself and then to the gallery with a questioning look. I shake my head and begin moving toward the door, slipping out past all the arms holding up glasses of white wine.

"Derek, what a surprise. Did I tell you about this party?"

"Em, you mentioned it, but you didn't say when it was exactly. Was I supposed to come?"

"If you wanted to." I gesture backwards with my head and say, "There's quite a mob in there. And nothing to drink but wine." He nods stoically. "Maeve telephoned this morning. I hadn't talked to her for a while."

"She told me. She said you have your, not your mother-in-law, but like that, visiting."

"Um-hm. My best friend, call it." He looks down at his feet, approximating the portrait of young dejection, in his denim jacket with the "Americanino" and "Fire Rescue Squad" badges. What probably can't be a real diamond glitters from his pierced ear, and his jeans have holes at the knees. "So, what have you been up to?"

"Absolutely sod all. Not even cleaning flats. Maeve's had political stuff to take care of, so we haven't been taking jobs or anyfing." Again he looks down and to the side. I focus on the short-shaved gold hair at the nape of his neck. Suddenly a group of people spill out the door of the gallery, the Deane family as it turns out. They stop to say "hallo" and seem quite happy to meet Derek, chasing away my own hesitation in their aura of uncritical good humor. They wave goodbye. But now another consignment of escapees from the party comes down the steps, two of whom are Corinne and Susannah. Corinne stops short.

"Oh there you are. I—we were looking for you. I thought you'd gone."

"No, I just saw a friend through the window and—and was going to bring him inside. Corinne, Susannah, this is Derek." They both nod to him and Corinne holds out a hand, which he awkwardly takes.

"Actually, I can't stay, I've got to meet someone," he says. Corinne looks at me and then at him and says, "If you're going in our direction, we've got a car."

Susannah trains an irritated look at her and says, "But we have to leave instantly, we're desperately late as it is."

"No, you go on. I want Derek to meet Adele," I say. "It'll only be a minute, Derek, then you can go."

He looks me in the eye, hesitates, and then says, "OK, but I really can't stay long."

We wave goodbye to Corinne and Susannah and step into the gallery. Others are squeezing past us, joining the stampede to get out, responding to some invisible but irresistible signal. The swillers are still jammed around the drinks table, though, and of course Fania and Adele are at their posts. The next step will be what's called a difficult moment, but you can't reach age forty without having gone through hundreds of those. I do a few quick mental calisthenics as I stride up to Adele (Max Wiesner still at her side), Derek ambling along in my wake.

"Adele, I'd like a friend of mine to meet you." She smiles benignly at me and then turns to Derek. "Derek Findlater." She and Max take him in, and then she smiles and extends her hand.

"You must be a photographer, too," she says.

"No, I'm out of work just at the moment," he says. "Music is more of my thing."

She exchanges a smile with Max, and then turns to me. "Fania wants to go to dinner soon, so perhaps she and Mr. Findlater could meet before the party breaks up." Then she bends toward me and said softly, "Fania has asked Max to dinner with us. Do you think your friend would like to come?"

I smile at her lovingly but shake my head. "He has an appointment." She nods gently, the relief she must be feeling showing not at all. I know that if I did get Derek included for dinner she would go through the evening with the appearance of perfect serenity. I've seen her in similar circumstances before.

She turns to Derek and says, "Avery tells me you have to go. I hope there will be a chance to talk another time."

Some of Derek's shyness begins to melt under the warmth of what I recognize as the Treatment. "I'm very glad to meet you," he says. I ask him if he'd like to meet Fania, but he says he has to get going, he really does. But he wants to talk to me and will ring me tomorrow. I follow after him to the door, give his hand a squeeze, and say goodbye. Something won't let me not stay there and watch him as he walks up Bond Street before turning a corner and moving out of sight.

The room has emptied out at last. When I turn back, I see Fania, the gallery owner and his wife, and Adele and Max moving toward me. Adele's arm is linked in Max's, and she smiles as she calls out to me, "Avery, I think we're all just about ready to go." For some reason, I glance back to the drinks table where the server, young and nice-looking in his white shirt and black vest, is clearing away the bottles. His eyes meet mine for a second and seem to know more about me than they plausibly can. Both of us hesitate; and then we smile.

Six

Since nine o'clock this morning I've been in constant motion, but now it suddenly feels brilliant, as Derek would say, to be restored to a few rooms, no one in them but myself. The days are getting darker earlier and earlier, and this morning began with one of those dense fogs that they say will be normal from now on until the New Year. I've got the BBC on the radio back in the bedroom, a program of plainchant broadcast from Winchester Cathedral. But meanwhile someone's car is parked out front with a tape deck blasting away at the public peace with heavy metal rock. Sitting here over a cup of tea laced with brandy (the heat doesn't seem to be on today), I listen to the collision of the two musics, visualizing them as a hopeless *pas de deux*, where a sexless thirteenth-century maiden is buffeted and wrenched about by a young punk in denim and leather, with head partly shaved and dyed several chemical colors. My loyalties don't go entirely to either one of these fantasy figures, however much they point to some of the contrasts composing the texture of everyday life in the postmodern U.K.—the half-timbered inn with sagging beams and leaded mullions next to a video store selling *The Rocky Horror Picture Show,* or the plastic-and-vinyl hamburger franchise where you can sit and listen to St. Paul's strike the hour not far up the road.

I saw Adele off today. She said she was ready to go home, though it had all been such a treat. We rode out to Heathrow in a taxi, she bundled in her black coat with the blue frogging and looking especially vulnerable in a way that lent youthful dreaminess to her face. As untendentiously as I could, I asked her about Max.

"Yes, I was going to say. He's a smooth proposition. And still—vigorous. He's been very attentive. I have to be honest, darling, I really like him. I never had any idea of coming over here and meeting someone, but he's being very urgent and all that. Says he's coming to New York in two weeks, ostensibly on business but mainly to see me. And his daughter again, of course." She sighed, "It's all such a surprise."

"He knows how to get in touch with you?"

"Sure, I gave him my address and telephone number, what do you expect? You did like him, didn't you?"

"Very much. You make an adorable couple. It speaks well for him that he likes you so much."

"Thanks." She looked at me to see whether I was being truthful, and seemed satisfied.

"It *is* a little surprising," I laughed, "since you told me you'd given up on romance et cetera."

"Yes, but it hadn't given up on me." She turned to the window, then back, reached up and touched the mole at the inner corner of her eye. "There are those split-in-half houses again. I don't know if I could live in one of those." We sat without talking, and I thought about last night, the opening, and the dinner afterwards. I'd wondered if she were going to ask about Derek, but she didn't, in keeping, no doubt, with her rule that each person's privacy is absolute. It's the kind of discretion that leads others to confide, but I don't think that's why she practices it.

"You know that boy I introduced to you? Derek Findlater?"

"Yes, who is he exactly?"

"Just someone I met at a political rally for South Africa. His sister invited me. I've sort of struck up an acquaintance with them."

"Oh, you do political work together."

"Well, no. We've been out to dinner a couple of times. And Derek took me to Madame Tussaud's." This sounded lame, if not downright implausible. Don't stop now, I thought; and then said, "We're not having an affair or anything."

Adele turned to look at me, with a faint hint of annoyance around the eyes. "Avery, that isn't any of my business." She fretted with her hands, touched the mole at her eye. "He seemed like a nice boy. Maybe you'll get more interested in him as time goes on."

This wasn't meant to be wounding, and yet something in it struck me as condescending. I started to speak and then stopped. Adele sensed waves of confusion coming from my way, hesitated, and then seemed to reach down to some bedrock foundation of Principle. She took my hand and said, "Dear. It's very tempting to fall into platitudes in situations like this, so I might as well go ahead and do it. You know and I know that we're always going to be close. I don't worry about that for a minute. The only thing I want for you is for you to be happy—for the short term and the long term." She nodded at me admonitorily. "You're not a fool, you're one of the canniest people I know. You can take care of yourself, you don't need advice or approval or anything but love from me, and you know you've got that, unconditionally." A willed smile gradually thawed into a real one as we looked at each other. She bent forward to kiss me, patted my hand, and let it go.

This was the real goodbye. When we got to Heathrow a few minutes later, checked her bags and got her V.A.T. forms stamped, the mechanics of the air terminals had taken over, and she was much more the brisk, professional traveler. Only as she was about to pass through the security check did she turn back for a final hug and "in case this is the last time" meeting of the eyes, in which affection blended with pain, and fear with reassurance, all of it conveyed silently, the gathering tears staved off until later. From just behind, a little boy stumbled into me and called out to his mother following along, a woman about thirty in a pink beret and green overcoat. I stepped out of his way, tousled his hair, which made his mother glare at me, and watched them follow Adele through the security check and down the passage to their flight. What I felt was one of those periodic pangs of deprivation that overtake the childless when they see an appealing infant or toddler in the arms of the parent they might have been.

JUST MAYBE another tea-and-brandy. After that, a shower and general overhaul. I've promised to meet Derek at some Indian restaurant down in Earl's Court at eight. He called this afternoon as he said he might and asked me to have a meal with him somewhere; his treat. Did that make sense, with his housecleaner's wages? Apparently. But Indian restaurants are usually budget-friendly, and Derek's "gesture" is touching.

The intruder car with its heavy metal rock has driven off and left the street in silence, and plainchant on the BBC has been replaced by one of those round tables where several fairly well-known critics discuss exhibitions of art, performances, and books, giving positive and negative verdicts so that it's always possible to find support for liking or disliking each artistic instance they discuss. A little paradigm for the current situation in criticism, where an argument can be made for or against anything, since there's no Academy handing down standards everyone accepts. Anyway, I can't agree or disagree with what they're saying because I haven't seen the exhibitions or read those particular newly published works. I also recognize that it doesn't matter: What's being purveyed is the emotional inflection of judgment, the syntax of appraisal, not actual information.

When I switch off the radio, my eye falls on Adele's collage, leaning in its frame against the botanical wallpaper. A cone of light shoots up from the lampshade on the bureau, as though the room were filled with smoke or mist. I empty my pockets, slip off trousers, shirt, and underwear. A brief inspection in the tall mirror shows everything intact. The six-footer's lank construction, always on the thin side ever since my teens, is the sort that holds up well enough as you go into middle age, pushups and sit-ups every day or so helping out. There's even a faint tan left over from last summer, to judge by the still-visible bathing suit line. Long, straight pencil strokes render the light pelt of chest hair, which continues down the center line of the stomach to the navel and then down to meet equipment that is, as they say of the Rolls engine, "adequate." Thighs that remember what it was like to jog, though we no longer do. If only the hair on the top of my head were less thin, if only my nose were a bit shorter—. But enough inventory for today.

Toweling dry after my shower, I switch the radio back on, this time getting a radio play that sounds peculiarly stiff until I realize it's set in the eighteenth century. But not one of the classics, a period piece by someone contemporary. I make half-conscious professional appraisals of it as I dress, preparing for my stint as critic on one of those chat shows, I guess. Faded jeans (he stole that line from Shaw), black shoes with big, rounded toes (she ought to have paused before saying that), a loose gray shirt printed with tiny pink squares in a nearly random pattern (the sound effects work well there). My hair, damp but drying, doesn't require much combing, unfortunately. (You can tell too easily that the play is coming to an end by the elegiac tone of the music). And let's see, the gray leather flight jacket, no doubt. There. Someone trendily unfamiliar checks out results in the mirror. Younger than I usually shoot for: a terrible beauty is born. The announcer comes on and credits the playwright, an unfamiliar name, but no doubt a rising star.

Outside a dark and misty evening greets me as I tap my way down Gloucester Crescent in the big black shoes. There usually aren't taxis at this hour, but no harm trying. A swarm of cars and pedestrians at the Parkway-Camden High Street intersection, headlights sweeping across the coats and boots of the trudging crowd. But no cabs, so the tube it is. Down the creaking wooden escalator, checking out youngsters riding up in the opposite direction to see what *they're* wearing. The contrasts are too extreme, though, and I put the whole issue on the shelf.

The Northern Line is the slowest and dirtiest of all. You know transport is on its way when tornado-like winds send a cloud of grit into the air from the direction of the train, which soon after shoots into the station out of its soot-black cylindrical tunnel. But that won't happen for nine more minutes, the lightboard suspended over the platform tells me. Meanwhile there are the inventive poster ads to scan while waiting. Toothpaste and telephone calls, some rave comments on "Queen" (the rock group, that is), a trip to Tahiti, Shakespeare at the Barbican, everything you could want is on offer. Plastered against the curving wall across the impassable tracks, there's one ad I've seen before that qualifies as a near-masterpiece of understated camp. What's being sold is "IMAGINE: the truly adult chocolate." A black-and white photograph of a young woman, French to judge from her dark, glossy hair with fringe across the forehead and generally *soignée*, high-heeled allure. She looks knowingly back at us over her shoulder, wearing a couturier silk gown, the shiny material stretched tight and highlighted over her hips, an organdy rose pinned strategically to the low neckline, her gloved hand resting on the marble balustrade of a stairway leading up to some undesignated room of the mansion where dazzling dramas of appetite are about to unfold. Several outsize bars of chocolate in pink wrappers (the one note of color in the picture) are scattered at the foot of the stairs. Underneath, in big letters, the caption: "Je Ne Regrette Rien." Well, precisely.

The train sweeps into the station along with its gale-force winds and hides everything on the opposite wall from view, impenitent Frenchwoman included. I step in and, surprise, find a seat. Directly ahead of me a punk-rocker in black jeans lounges near the door, his back pocket flattened against the glass partition between exit and seating. The label says "Guess," superfluous command for a confirmed people-watcher. I bump knees with the facing passenger, a West Indian youth with dreadlocks and silver chains around his neck. He vibrates back and forward gently and regularly to what can only be reggae music coming through his earphones, attached to some portable radio or tape-player concealed inside his black leather jacket. He doesn't seem to see the external world at all, and yet something makes it clear that he is aware of me and ready for any signals I might beam his way. And so on to the other passengers, one by one, including a long sober scrutiny of a man about forty, obviously gay and yet not "obvious," dressed approximately like me and very likely on his way to meet someone. "Je Ne Regrette Rien," the motto of the evening.

Leicester Square. Here I have to change to the Picadilly Line, which I've learned to do by taking a little-traveled shortcut at the end of the platform. It takes you downstairs and over to your next interminable wait among scraps of paper, advertisements, and people. I can never just stand, I have to stroll. Look as I will, I can't find another poster with my French lady of the night to fill the time and strengthen resolve. But it doesn't matter, the sheer, delirious mechanics of the thing are enough by now. Here's the train that will chute me on, station by porcelain-tiled station—*Picadilly, Green Park, Knightsbridge*—down to Earl's Court.

When I get to "Khyber Pass" restaurant, Derek is already there, sitting in the rear next to a mural of Krishna playing the flute. He half gets up and grasps my hand as I saunter over to the table, his eyes sparkling with suppressed excitement. Red cotton shirt with little green cartoon dinosaurs printed on it, denim jacket draped over the back of the chair: if he meant to charm me, it works. He has a little gold ring hooked into his earlobe and his hair looks newly washed with gold as well.

"You look great," he says.

"Oh, I'm just trying to compete with you. But I give up." He smiles, I smile.

We sit down and at the same moment fling open the accordion-pleated fan the napkins have been folded into. Asked how his day went, Derek describes the Chelsea flat he and Maeve cleaned, a new client from Dublin that they both like a lot. "He does newspaper work, you know, writes about sport. That's not exactly up my strasse, but he's a nice guy."

"Do you ever get to Dublin?"

"Sure. My Ma and Da live there. We go over every year."

"I thought it was Liverpool."

"They moved back. Got sick of England."

"You know, there's something I've noticed: you and Maeve don't talk the same way."

He blushes. "Yeh, I know. You should have heard me talk scouse when we lived in Liverpool."

"What's that?" He answers, as I should have guessed he would, that scouse was the way they talked in Liverpool; and gives me a quick demonstration. It sounds vaguely Irish to me, and he says it is, just with a twist and a new vocabulary. "But you don't talk it now?"

"No, that's what I was saying. I sort of talk what I hear. Maeve talks the way her teachers did. She was always better in school than me. Anyway, I've been hanging around King's Road trash so long I sort of talk like them. I mean, what do we ever have to do but stand around and slag each other off? If I start listening to you, I'll sound like a Yank, you'll see."

"Well, don't make a special effort. I like the way you talk, it's—gutsy." He seems willing to accept this. "And what did you do after you finished cleaning the flat?"

"Em. I had to leave a parcel off at the church."

"Church?"

"St. Anne's, Wardour Street. It's in Soho. I'd promised to deliver some NA literature to a friend of mine who chairs an NA meeting there."

"Oh, that's where you go to your meetings."

He looks levelly but tentatively at me. "Yeh, well, it's also where I go to church."

I absorbed this for a moment. "That's a Catholic church?"

"No. I was brought up Catholic but I don't go anymore. Especially with the Pope they've got now."

"So you go to the Church of England?"

"St. Anne's is different from most of them. The priest lives with another guy, for one thing. See, I started going to NA meetings in the church hall, and then some of the other recovering addicts said I should come to a service there. I did, and it was really OK. I saw a lot of people I used to see hanging around the Dilly. It's like this particular parish has got a different sort of idea, see, they want people like us to come. I guess the church was kind of dying and nobody was going there anymore. So they decided to make it more active and go out and bring people in. The priest used to do social work, he knows about the problems people have. Anyhow, you see recovering addicts and girls that used to prostitute and all. I got Maeve to come once but she says she doesn't need it and she doesn't like religion because she thinks it's against women. Even though they've got a woman who assists the priest with the mass and that."

"But you—believe in God?"

"I always did, deep down. But I didn't like the priests and the nuns. And you couldn't be gay and a Catholic, so—. Anyhow, in NA recovery, they talk about a Higher Power, which some people say is just the meetings but other people call God. It doesn't matter what you call it so long as you get connected with it." A slight strain has crept into his voice, and I can see I'm embarrassing him with my questions.

"It's good that you found that," I say and drop the subject. The waiter takes our order and avenues of lightweight talk open up again. And yet a low-level unease runs through it all. The "politics" of the evening have shifted for me. Before, I could see myself as the older, more reasonable party, letting himself be drawn along the path by hot-blooded, amoral youth. Now it looks as though I'm sort of a thousand-year-old, glittering-eyed bird of prey, offering nothing more than the blandishments of lust to someone with his sights set on higher things.

Throughout the rest of the dinner—negotiated over vegetable fritters, heaps of pungent curries, soft flatbread, and fragrant rice—I have recurring moments of vertigo, wondering how I got myself into this particular situation, talking to this person with his own definite history and character traits. A bruised sense of probability balances off against the memory of specific incidents that brought me here, chance encounters, reflexive actions, and conscious decisions. Memories of childhood tree-climbing come back to me: getting to the lowest branch was the biggest challenge but seemed paltry since it was first and closest to the ground. Each following upward leg of the climb would seem risky but still manageable until suddenly you were aloft among unfamiliar, down-bending top branches, throat catching with the vista out onto fields and houses, a red car winding along a curving road until it vanished behind a jagged leaf in the near foreground—which left you with the task of looking straight down and wondering how you were to find your way back to solid ground....

But here I am, and it's not very nice, is it, to drift off during a one-to-one dinner when someone is talking to you. What seems to have a calming effect is to look Derek square in the eyes, overshadowed by straw-colored brows, tufts of which almost meet across the bridge of the nose, especially when he frowns. He has a clear and guileless gaze, punctuated now and then by a quick blink before the green beam flashes out again. It's one of the most magnetic faces the casting director in me has ever seen, the porcelain-white smile that breaks out from time to time, usually with a noticeable leftward bend, the strong jaw line, and that way he has of tucking his chin under and looking directly at you. No one needs to be told that one of the punishments attached to the loss of a spouse is physical deprivation, which seems unnatural and unbearable after the comfort of daily physical contact. I drain the last of the lager in my glass. Of course I feel what has to be described as a bone-deep ache to touch and hold all the boyish freshness opposite; but it is specifically him and not just a generic warm body that attracts me, and that wave of electricity overrides all the reasonable objections that crop up. Joshua would understand this instantly, I feel certain.

The Indian woman at the till looks at both of us interrogatively as Derek counts out pound notes to her. I know, I tell her silently, I should be paying, but he insisted. We go out into the night, and I can't prevent myself from asking, as innocently as a lamb, "Where now?"

"My place. I want to show it to you."

"Where is that?"

"Just off Redcliffe Square. Five minutes from here." We walk on in silence, eventually passing through the square with its small stone church and on to a small street nearby. Up the stoop, lit by one lantern, its twin on the other side not burning. Crumbling yellow stucco and a heavy glass-paned door, which Derek unlocks and holds for me. As we go into the entryway a door opens a few inches and an oldish woman peers out. She says, "Eh, it's just you." She looks glaringly at me and then back at Derek. "You 'aven't seen Ahmed, 'ave you? He owes me three weeks' rent now, and 'e keeps sneaking in when I'm not looking for 'im."

"Ahmed? No, I haven't seen him," Derek shakes his head.

"Well if you do, tell 'im he better settle or I'll have the police on 'im." She gives me a final glare and then slams the door. We make our way upstairs to Derek's room off the first landing.

"Tenant problems?" I ask, just to say something.

"The guy next door to me. He's a Paki. They never got on, and now he's out of a job." Derek switches on a bright overhead light as we step into his bed-sit. Just what I imagined: a high-ceilinged room with a few indiscriminate pieces of furniture, in particular, the name-conferring bed (metal, its white paint flaking) and chair to sit in (an odd, once rather modern armchair with brown cushions). One small table with a box of cornflakes sitting on it next to a few plates and bowls, and a little sink in the corner. Derek's personal touches include posters of Boy George and Stevie Winwood thumbtacked to the wall (painted a nondescript beige), a small but healthy looking rubber plant, a dog-eared copy of *Playgirl* lying on the bureau (a black athlete featured on the cover), and a stack of music tape cassettes on a shelf near the door. Something peculiar casts a little shadow on the wall above the bed, and when I bend closer to look at it I see a small crucifix nailed to the plaster and painted over the same beige as the walls, the small contorted body as well as the cross.

"That's strange," I say.

"Yeh, when they painted the room, they just painted over it without taking it down. That was before I moved in, but I left it, I don't know." He looks at me and grins. "Does it bother you?"

"No, I was just curious." Derek turns on a bedside lamp and then switches off the glaring overhead light. A circle of golden illumination falls on the threadbare green carpeting that covers the floor. He slips off his jacket and tosses it on the armchair.

I take mine off, and Derek reaches for it, pausing before he drapes it over the chair to say, "Nice. I bet that cost a packet." He takes a step toward me and then stands stock still, his arms hanging at his sides, staring at me. Traffic noises outside register insistently loud. It's been too long, I've forgotten how to do this, I think, not meaning sex so much as the gestures of "romantic passion." But then I quietly say his name, nothing more, and he steps toward me and puts his arms through mine. Drawn-out curry-scented kisses as I hold onto him, feeling the resistant ribs underneath his thin shirt and the lightweight, springy musculature of his back. A deep sigh escapes me, and I simply crumble against the trembling quickness of his body and a new series of kisses worth writing home about. Both of us giving rough mutual assistance, clothes get flung off in several directions. But there is time to take each other in, the banquet for me, Derek's broad-shouldered, loose-jointed frame with the flat turtle belly twenty-year-olds have. And he is, well, baited as beautifully as anything in *Playgirl*. None of this would mean much but for the way it is animated by Derek himself, whose gestures and expression waver between a sort of movie-idol suavity and an indelible, awkward innocence. I will never have enough of him. Coverlet stripped off, the bed decides to add a realistic note by creaking energetically as we fall into it and turn over and then back again. One last resistance makes me pause and ask in a half-whisper, "Um, you know, I guess, that I'm at risk?" Derek says nothing but smiles and reaches over to give me a kiss and a rough squeeze.

Suddenly from downstairs a door slams. Footsteps thumping upstairs, followed by a high-pitched, "You come back 'ere, you bloody thief!" We hear a lock outside rattle and then a door slam.

"It's Ahmed," Derek says, pausing. Then we hear another slower series of steps coming up the stair. Then a pounding on the next door.

"Open the door," the landlady screams.

Muffled and faint, an entreating voice calls out, "I pay you tomorrow, I promise to pay tomorrow."

"You'll pay me now or I'll call the police on you, you devil!" More pounding on the door.

"He's bolted her out," Derek says. "This will go on a while." Then he begins to kiss me, our noses getting sexily in the way as we breathe hot breaths in and out. Next door the pounding and verbal lashes keep going, but we ignore it in favor of the rising mist inside consciousness, a cloud of bright steam that takes its color from the lamp and finds counterparts in the glowing aura hovering around a flank momentarily hunched up or the fevered sleepiness glimpsed in partly closed eyes, or the scent of fresh sweat that builds even in the cool air of the room. Derek stops for a second to take the little gold hoop from his ear, which is being pulled painfully around by our wrestling.

"Let me in there, or I'll break the door down!" *Pound-*

pound-pound against heavy wood. Which matters not at all as we stretch and turn and bend, Derek's hand strongly clasping my wrist, the light wisps of his armpit matted into curls, his knee against my shoulder, and then the funny delicate deference I always feel when someone isn't circumcised, as though they were more vulnerable or supersensitive, anyway, requiring the most thoughtful attention possible. But now some more modern dance, inspired by Hindu temple friezes, Krishna or whoever, our improvisations bringing every part of us against every other part in silken abrasion, all to the accompaniment of an inner sounding of the depths, just the grateful, hardly bearable rightness of it all. Not wanting to be obvious about advancing the plot, nevertheless, at what he judges to be a decisive moment, Derek produces from nowhere the extendable, expandable latex sheath and deferentially slips it on me in a way that manages to be not just practical but part of the rapture, a kind of protective homage due to what in life is both sweet and grandly serious at once.

Freed now to go forward with every held-back impulse tugging inside me, I join the ranks of the happy somnambulists, dazed with sheer opportunity. Begin with a fresh appreciation of the strong perfection of the human back, the jutting twin shoulder blades, the downcurving spine supported by flexible muscle on either side, Derek's skin taut, smooth, and white with a pink flush. We don't forget after all, do we, but still it's unfamiliar, to the point where just how much has been pushed down under the surface of permission comes rushing back with the sense of a reprieve: this—remember, and now this, turn here, go there, and then that feeling…. Maybe there is just the faintest envelope of anxiety, if I notice it, but look how boyish his face is, turned slightly to the side, mouth partly open in an ecstatic scowl, only now and then looking at me when his will tells him he must put aside modesty in favor of something more important. I start choking up long before the final slide, and the sight of bare emotion, a risk much older than immunodeficiency after all, stuns us onto a new plateau of empathy that sends him hurtling helplessly on ahead of me but, since we are joined, carries me along with him spinning out over the edge, rocked with the certainty that we've "gotten away with it" as we scramble against each other—arms, legs, hips—in thrilled selflessness, the bed ringing like a tambourine, while—ah, for you, THERE! and then for me, HERE!...

In the drenched, silent aftermath, as we lie tightly clasped together, breath still coming in jags, hearts pounding, we can tell by the still angry but appeased tones outside the door that Ahmed has given in and paid at least one installment on the rent.

I turn drowsily to Derek and ask, "When you came to the opening yesterday, you knew I was going to be there, didn't you? I mean, it wasn't an accident, right?"

He gives a smile that mixes embarrassment and mischief and says, "Right, love."

Seven

Derek said he had promised to meet Maeve this morning to clean one of their clients' flats, so there was nothing for it but to disengage ourselves from his bed (which now looked permanently unmade) and go out for early breakfast. We were stopped by his landlady, guilty and full of apologies for the noise. The tricky way I have with women elders came into play, and within minutes she was asking me if I needed a room or a job as a handyman. She told me to call her Dora, but I said, "Oh, no, Mrs. Finchley, I couldn't do that yet," which made her blush with pleasure.

Derek and I made our plans over eggs and bacon. It was quickly settled that he will be coming here for dinner tonight; so I didn't mind too much just kissing him goodbye and going off on my own. I went back to the flat first, pottered around for an hour, humming under my breath, tidying, and throwing out old magazines and newspapers. Then I set out for the British Library, glad to have something to occupy me the rest of the day. I counted on the proven soothing qualities of that blue and gold dome.

Not that concentrating on what I was doing was especially easy. A sort of infantile elation kept washing over me (the famous sex cure, I guess), so that I'd have to stop reading and just look up for a while at a square of empty space above my head until I could get a grip. I'm gathering material on the period of Cibber's years of triumph, when he was made director of the Theatre Royal (on Drury Lane in his day) and after that poet laureate. It's the model success story. That a moony, stagestruck boy with little education and no funds should begin as a bit player in the 1690s and by 1730 be famous as a character actor, a playwright, and theater director, retiring within a few years to enjoy his laureateship and warm approval from cultivated and fashionable society under the second George puts a strain on credibility; but, on the other hand, it shouldn't, there are so many parallel examples. Shakespeare, to begin with, who was one of Cibber's idols— which didn't mean he avoided making a hash of *Richard III* when he patched together his own stage version of it. No one seems to have minded, though, and apparently his remake was used until the early 1900s all over the English-speaking world. Some of it is even in the 1955 Olivier film of the play.

One of the most interesting chapters to develop will be the, so to speak, cockfight with Pope. Like so many antagonisms, it began with friendship and professional respect (always more sincere from Cibber's side, certainly). The first hint of trouble seems to have come with the staging of a play written by Pope, Gay, and Arbuthnot, in which Cibber played an unflattering role, one where he was given lines that directly satirized himself. To get back a few points, he put some slighting references to the play in his next stage adaptation. Warned to omit them, he refused and then found himself after a performance confronted in his dressing room by an enraged John Gay. The resulting dustup doesn't seem to have left anyone a clear winner, but what's more important is that the

Cibber-Pope feud was now engraved in steel and became one of the lasting themes in the lives of both.

The next attack came in Cibber's *The Non-juror* of 1717. He translated *Tartuffe*, rewrote it, actually, transforming it into a tract against Jacobites, Roman Catholics, and nonjurors in general (those who would not swear allegiance to the king and Anglican church doctrine). This is the only really shabby thing Cibber ever did, but naturally it won George I's approval and is probably the main reason Cibber was named laureate when the post became vacant. Cibber never fancied himself much of a poet.

After *The Non-juror*, venom-dipped barbs from Pope began to appear in print with some regularity but generally went unchallenged by Cibber, who tried to laugh at them along with everyone else, correctly foreseeing trouble if he persisted in goading the greatest satirist of the period. In the very first chapter of the *Apology* of 1740 appears a passage about Pope's attacks; one of the central motives for these memoirs must have been to set the record straight and disarm Pope. He says, "Not our great imitator of Horace himself can have more pleasure in writing his verses than I have in reading them, tho' I sometimes find myself there (as Shakespeare terms it) dispraisingly spoken of. If he is a little free with me, I am generally in good company, he is as blunt with my betters; so that even here I might laugh in my turn. My superiors, perhaps, may be mended by him; but, for my part, I own myself incorrigible: I look upon my follies as the best part of my fortune, and am more concern'd to be a good husband of them, than of that; nor do I believe I shall ever be rhim'd out of them."

This mixture of praise and abdicating balm may have had a faint chance of satisfying and neutralizing Pope, but Cibber's review of the traditional charges against his competitor, pretending to dismiss them in an equivocating way, still allowed readers to make up their own minds. Pope responded almost immediately by giving Cibber a more glaring place in the *New Dunciad*, published the following year. Then came a printed letter of Cibber's designed to sling mud in the grand old tradition, ridiculing Pope's physical deformity and his sexual unsuccess, a letter that, according to Dr. Johnson, "made Pope writhe."

Cibber must have known that literary vengeance wouldn't be long in coming, but that doesn't mean he was prepared for the final *Dunciad*, where he is moved to center stage as the ringleader of the Dunces (the whole herd of Grub Street hacks) and proclaimed the favored consort of Queen Dulness herself. Not that Pope's mock-epic, with its runaway footnotes and scholarly apparatus, entirely escapes the empire of that Hanoverian Goddess. But its faults finally leave the impression that at some level the work is sincerer, was closer to Pope's real concerns than, say, his *Essay on Man*. *The Dunciad* is Pope at his most Swiftean, with moments of almost surrealistic comedy. Something about that dim, dreamlike, smoky atmosphere stays in the mind, a purely literary Inferno, filled with sharp (and useful) comment on the art of poetry even when you haven't a clue who the characters were in their own day or what writings of theirs are being lambasted. Cibber must have realized that his immortality had been guaranteed by being made the hero—not in the way he would have preferred, but as an eternal figure of fun. He gave up trying to outflank Pope; in a few years both died.

This last decade of his will be the hardest to write, partly because it involves the life of a better-known author, and partly because Cibber begins more and more to retire from active duty. Making an accurate assessment of Cibber has always been difficult because Pope's attacks have tended to guarantee condescension as the only possible stance to take toward him. Of course it's not the book's last chapter: the story takes up afterwards with the next generation of Cibbers.

As I was copying out a paragraph, suddenly a pair of hands closed over my eyes. A familiar perfume; but I would have known in any case that it was Corinne, who giggled quietly when I turned around. She sat down in the empty reading post next to mine and asked me to go out for coffee with her. "Come on, you've worked enough for one day, look at all those notes." Absolutely true. I packed up my paraphernalia and followed her out the glass doors and into the lobby. We stopped for our coats and were slipping them on when she said, "Oh, before we go, let me show you the most beautiful thing. Or maybe you've seen it—the head of Hypnos? No? It's right upstairs." None too eager, I followed her up to the next floor of the British Museum as she told how she'd stumbled on it yesterday while strolling through the collection not looking for anything in particular.

Near the entrance to a large room devoted to Hellenistic Roman artifacts was a plexiglass case with a hollow bronze head in it, blue-gray with ancient patina and identified as having come from second-century Iberia. The straight Greek nose, the partly open lips, the downward gaze of the empty eye sockets, all of this was familiar and standard. But then I saw the feature that makes the work what it is: a wing, and one wing only, emerges from the left temple. Hypnos, the God of Dreams seemed himself to be caught in the grip of a sample dream, his own, verdigris in color and two millennia old, sponsoring billions of shorter sequels that have overtaken all sleepers in the world since the head was cast.

"Isn't it fantastic? They don't have a card of it, but I've already ordered a dozen photographs. I'll give you one."

"Lucky find. How many hours have I spent in this Museum, and never once came across it."

"You see? Stick with me, I'm a tremendous guide. So, shall we go for coffee?" She edged away from the case as a tall man in glasses and pin-striped suit zeroed in on it. We walked back downstairs and out into the courtyard, thronged with people going in and out of the Museum, but an image of the bronze head kept coming back like a refrain, associated illogically in my mind with the last line of *The Dunciad*: "And universal darkness covers all." Besides that, I saw or thought I saw a certain resemblance between that verdigris face and Derek's, something about the jaw and the set of the brows. But then, I was seeing him in everything and everybody.

Corinne took me to a little coffee shop she knew about on Drury Lane, down from the Shaftesbury Theatre. We found a table and sat down as she slipped off her coat and gloves. Then she went directly to the topic on her mind. "Who was that good-looking guy you were with at the gallery?" I let a few beats pass in silence, and she shot a mischievous, worldly smile at me and said, "Come on, I won't tell anybody."

"His name is Derek Findlater. I met him at a rally against apartheid in South Africa. We've started going out."

"Oh, that's nice. He looked adorable—and so young!"

"He's twenty-seven," I said, taking my medicine.

"Really? What's he do?"

"Not much. On the dole. Cleans houses sometimes."

"Ah-hah. How interesting. And—do you like him?"

"Yes," I said in a low voice.

"Oh, Avery, that's so nice." She twinkled her eyes at me and nodded, giving another turn of the screw to the awkwardness. "Susannah liked him, too," she added, less spontaneously.

"She did not, they didn't exchange two words."

"Mm-hm, but she told me she thought he had very striking looks."

"Well, he does."

Seeing that I wasn't going to go an inch further she laughed gently and shook her head. "I hope you'll let me meet him again some time." And then, more seriously, "I'm glad you're feeling better. I was worried about you."

"You shouldn't. When people worry about me, I start thinking there must be something the matter; and that undermines confidence. I'm indestructible, OK, so let's leave it at that." She made a face and then smiled. We started out again on other subjects: Her book was going well, she could begin to see the end of the tunnel. Susannah was to get a promotion in a few weeks, something that would put her in a position of real responsibility. The BBC was in a period of transition, all sorts of changes could be expected.

She gave a sort of dry laugh, "The question is, whether she'll still have room for me, once her new duties begin. She's so busy already."

"Are you being serious?"

"Maybe. I don't know. I suppose there was a built-in time limit from the beginning. And Susannah never misled me or anything. She's older than I am, you know, and a lot more sophisticated. She spent most of her teens in Paris at some ritzy school. I think she likes me because I'm so American and normal-minded, et cetera. But that probably wears thin after a while." Corinne's voice was low and a little hollow. "Well, anyway, I never planned to move here permanently, right? What about you?"

"No, no plans. But, I suppose you could both visit back and forth."

"Yes, if it turns out that's what she wants." She was being breezier about it than she actually felt, I could tell.

"Just, I wish things looked better for you and her."

"I'll be all right. I'm indestructible, to coin a cliché." She smiled in a way that showed experience, a light case of the blues, and a dependable resilience. "Listen, darling, I better go. But I'm so glad we talked. Can you pay today?—I didn't get to the bank. I've got bus fare and that's it. Thanks a million. I'm so glad about your friend. Call you." She kissed me and then swept out, leaving me to wonder if I should have been more supportive. How much of that self-reliance was a pose?

When I got back to the flat, I took a shower, checked my watch, and then telephoned Adele. She was pleased I called, deep in jet lag, but happy to be home. "I miss you, but we had some good talks, and I think it cleared the air. Come home when you can." Then she insisted I not run up my telephone bill. We said goodbye, and I held the dead black phone in my hand before putting it back in its cradle.

So that's done. Now a few preliminaries for dinner. Silver, plates, and glasses on the table. Yes, I have soda for him—or juice, if he wants it. As I fill the boiler with water for pasta and began to chop vegetables for the sauce, a small worry crystallizes. It's the point that Corinne raised about Susannah, the built-in time limit to any transatlantic romance. Silly to worry about that already, since there are other obstacles just as grave and even more immediate. Besides, I really don't plan to take any big plunges just at present. And yet, the fact is that at the start of any liaison, even those that don't have any prospects for permanence, you always do allow imagination to run directly out to the far horizon of possibility—the vanishing point, I guess—to estimate just how far things can go. It's not wildly different from doing your plays. No sooner are they drafted than you begin to wonder how long they'll run.

Once again I fail to live in the present. There's a lot to be said, in favor, though, of weighing chances, trying to take the measure of a new love. What's implied is that you are, underneath everything else, idealistic—or do I mean positive, in some sense. That you go into the new relationship, head bowed, as it were, with a fundamental wish for this to be *the one*, the one that will not end, that goes on being reciprocal and completely satisfying. A prime difficulty in starting a new love is the enforced recognition that you are now sealing off the earlier one. Face it, it's over. Well, maybe not altogether, unless amnesia can be willed. It can be, for a while.

My watch says eight o'clock. Where is he? But why am I worrying, people his age are easygoing when it comes to punctuality. Let's see, open a can of nuts and put them in a dish; maybe a few celery sticks, since I have the time.

Coming back from the kitchen, I glance around the living room: maroon sofa, blue armchairs, nothing either glaringly modern or quaintsy antique. The dining alcove, glassed in like a greenhouse, has a view of the garden, still producing flowers even this late in the year. Low lamps at strategic places around the room give a comfortable light not quite intense enough to read by but fine for quiet conversation. The little pot of daisies on the coffee table looks cheerful rather than forbiddingly formal, as roses might have. Magazines and newspapers carefully scattered about—*The New Yorker*, *TLS*, *Time Out*—also add to the impression of careless spontaneity. Two minutes till curtain, Mr. Walsh.

But no Derek. Better go turn off the burner under the pasta pot, which is roiling and clattering impatiently. Easy to reheat when the time comes. There. A cloud of steam veils the inside of the window, which faces out toward the street. Wait, is that—yes, it's Derek. After a second's hesitation, I go throw open the door of the flat, then the door of the house. But there's something wrong: He's holding the side of his head.

"Derek, what's the matter?" He drops his hand and I see a cut, oozing blood, just below the hairline at his left temple. His hand and a handkerchief are covered with blood also, some of it dried, some not. I hurry him past all the props and preparations of the living room into the bedroom and then the bath. He lets me wash the cut and find a bandage for it. I notice a little vein in the middle of his forehead with a visible, rapid pulse.

"Tell me what happened."

"Skinheads throwing rocks. They thought I was a faggot," Derek laughed.

"That's disgusting." A flash of anger shoots through me. "Where did this happen?"

"I was walking down from Tufnell Park. I'd been to see Maeve. They just came up from across the road and started throwing. Three or four of them, just kids, really. I can run fast, though. And I started yelling like a right lunatic. Then a couple of blokes dashed up from somewhere and they got scared and ran away."

"Did you call the police?"

"No. I never really saw who did it. I wouldn't be able to identify them or anyfing. And if I'd got cops involved I'd still be down at the station now. I wanted to see you."

"OK, but they should know so they can put policemen up there and stop it from happening again."

"Yeh, well, I didn't call them. I don't get on with cops." He bends forward to kiss me. Right and proper action begins to blur in my mind. And goes on blurring. Good thing I turned off the burner in the kitchen.

Of course I have to be careful not to dislodge the bandage and, in general, to handle Derek with care. He's had a shock. But it doesn't seem to show, in fact, if anything he's more masterful, like a war hero. But events go pretty quickly this run-through, and when we fall back on the sheets, I have time to wonder if it wouldn't have made more sense to put everything on hold for a night. Just a bit late for that scruple. Derek leans up on an elbow and looks at me, the lamplight behind him adding a bright outline to his silhouette, bandage and all.

"Guess what," he says. "I'm going off the dole."

"Oh really?"

"I got some work around the office of the Terence Higgins Trust."

"That's the AIDS organization, no—yes?" He nodded. "Well, terrific. That's good news. What about housecleaning?"

"Maeve can do most of it herself. And then when she needs help we can work together on weekends."

"Sounds like a good plan. I'm glad you found something you like."

He smiles at me with a significant gleam. "I've found something I like, all right."

"It certainly looks that way. You can be pretty convincing." I pause and then begin again. "There is one thing. I think we've got to keep our wits about us a little more. I mean, we got a little carried away last night. I do believe 'safe sex' is safe, but—within limits."

"I'm not worried. We didn't take any risks."

"Yes and no. We seem to have gotten away with it, but people don't always. Even balloons have been known to pop, you know."

He shrugs. "You're never really safe anyway. Somebody could throw a rock at you on the street and you'd be dead. People die every day that didn't do anything risky. It's just, like, you guess the odds. But if you're worried—. You know, I took the test four times. You could take it, too."

"That's a difficult subject with me." I explain, haltingly, about Joshua and me and the test results.

"Right, but it's got more accurate now." He looks at me. "But you don't have to take it, it doesn't worry me. We're brilliant just as we are."

Yes we are, he's right. I'm content just to sit and stare at him. The rest of the evening flows by as though we have always been together and are familiar with every one of our personal quirks and habits. We have our dinner in the glassed-in alcove listening to the rain that begins to patter on it, warm, candlelit atmosphere around the table contrasting comfortably with the general cold and damp outside. Safe in our shipshape glass envelope. Conversation is about nothing in particular, though at one point Derek hints that we might think of taking Maeve to a movie or something, so she won't feel left out of the new arrangements. I say that we will, absolutely.

When we finish, Derek helps me clear, in fact, goes ahead of me into the kitchen. When he comes back I'm still brushing away crumbs. Raindrops patter and tap on the glass alcove. I see him pause to look at the yellow-and-white daisies, bend down to smell them, and, disappointed, regretfully say, "I should have brought you some roses." I would probably laugh at this except that, at just that moment, attention focuses on his bandaged cut, and I feel sorry for him again.

Eight

London has begun to gear up for the holidays. All along Oxford Street the shops have interspersed coveted merchandise with stars, glass balls, holly wreaths, tinsel, and snow. The crowds on Regent Street are jammed to a standstill, and yet somehow new thousands manage to push into Liberty's every hour. Harrod's lets in a milder-mannered, better-dressed pandemonium and manages to supply nearly everybody's friends and family with cashmere. The striking clock over Fortnum's door sends out two mechanical guardsmen every hour to stand at attention as a bell strikes, dismayed at the number of shoppers forcing entry. But enter they do, fighting their way toward counters weighted down with Christmas pudding, pâté, pickles, teas, and mustards. Nothing will be allowed to interfere; for many of the customers are non-British, and these short days of shopping will be their one chance—for this year and possibly for this life.

The past two weeks have trundled on like a baby earthquake, low on the Richter scale, but continuous and unsettling. Derek spends most of his nights on Gloucester Crescent, then goes off to his job at the Terence Higgins Trust. We've had Maeve over for a meal and all gone out to a production of *The Marriage of Figaro* at Covent Garden, Derek putting on a black bow tie and something resembling a dinner jacket that he picked up secondhand at Camden Market. Corinne and Susannah got tickets for the same night, with the plan of meeting for a drink during the interval. Susannah took a liking to Maeve but still had nothing much to say to Derek. Corinne seemed to like both and has begun calling them "the twins." Neither "twin" warmed to Susannah, but they found Corinne "brilliant, a darling." I don't see signs that Susannah is slipping away from Corinne, but she and I haven't been in close touch. So much of my time is taken up by Derek.

I never subscribed to the Lawrence-style canonization of sex. For one thing, love somehow gets left out of the picture in favor of "dark gods" who steal up out of the murky deeps of the psyche. But there's no denying that love at its most physical changes everything—the kind of sleep you sleep, the way morning light looks as it filters through the curtains, your feelings about the children running up the streets chasing each other and calling out names, or about the shopkeeper who for no reason looks you in the eye as she hands you your parcel and pleasantly holds your gaze for a moment. Just to rest your hand on a tablecloth and feel, almost with a tingle, the faintly rough weave of the ironed linen can seem resonant; or the smell of the wet, fermenting leaves gathered under the trees in Regent's Park; or the sudden scuffle of a bird flying out of the shrubbery up into the upper atmosphere and seeming to vanish into a thin, gray-golden afternoon cloud.

"What are you thinking about, love," is a question I've heard Derek repeat a number of times lately, which means that I've come down with visible symptoms of public daydreaming. But I don't remember daydreams any better than I do night dreams. So of course I always make up something, like, "I was thinking about apartheid." (We attended another rally with Maeve.) Or "I was thinking about that gang that threw the stone at you." (The wound healed very well, with just the faintest papercut of a scar.)

Different from daydreaming are the times of conscious thought devoted to Joshua. These take the form of a not quite verbal meeting, a strong exchange of fact and emotion, accompanied by a soft-lit image of a face, or maybe everything that is expressive in a face. Doubt or recrimination seems active on my side solely. What I "hear" from him is affirmation, solidarity—which doesn't entirely calm every worry; but then, I'm still in the land of the living. You are entirely aware of that, Joshua, hence the unqualified beam of reassurance from your quarter, as the best thing that can be sent to me from where you are, freed from the claims of life that tend to erode support so selfless—yet not entirely free because still concerned for those remaining behind. And of course the memory of what it means to be "pure in heart," once summoned, is the strongest admonition.

I haven't talked much to Derek about the past. Only enough to make it clear that no taboo is in effect. I certainly don't want him to feel like an interloper or latecomer, and I've avoided comparing him to Joshua out loud. True, he sometimes seems almost too confident of the present situation, which I can attribute either to my not saying how much Joshua still means to me, or the twenty-year-old's sexual pride (adding to the attraction, naturally). But more than that, it seems to be a working-class thing, a tough, fundamental conviction that "we are the good guys," and that, given the opportunity, anyone accessible to common sense and evidence will see that.

I've had to revise my shorthand sketch of him as "disaffected youth on the dole." He puts in long hours at the Trust, is always volunteering to do errands for me, and has insisted

I terminate the cleaning service I've been using, and let him take care of the flat. A rabid worker, he gets very restless when he has nothing scheduled, and he doesn't count reading as anything more than a sort of filler slipped in between other more compelling activities. But when I tell him I want to just stay in for the evening and catch up on a few books, he will dutifully imitate me, go through all the magazines, and now and then poke into one of the novels on the shelves. The only one he seems to have finished is *Lucky Jim*, his comment, "This is terrific, but, you know, the hero needs AA, he's really on the edge."

He also goes to his NA meetings, one of which I was invited to. It was held in the social hall of a church on Portobello Road, a high-ceilinged but small room with Gothic windows, used on Sundays for the children's school, as evidenced by the crayon drawings of houses and trees and clouds on the wall. Derek likes this particular meeting because it is attended mostly by gay men, so there's no need to censor anything he might want to say. The format was simple enough. The twenty recovering members sat in a semicircle facing a little table where the group leader presided. A book describing the general problem of drug addiction was passed from hand to hand, each person reading a paragraph. Then one of the members "chaired," that is, told the story of his life—how he became a drug user, and then how he got off drugs with the help of NA. Some of the incidents were screamingly funny, others appalling. The time when he woke up on a flight to Rio with no idea how he'd got on it. The time when he saw his best friend die of an overdose. He would pause at moments, letting the import register, an intelligent, bardic light in his dark eyes. After this the other members spoke voluntarily from the floor, commenting on the story and its similarities to their own. They sometimes went on to talk about problems they were faced with and how they were trying to solve them within the guidelines of the NA program, a series of "steps" that involved self-examination, spiritual assistance, and changing destructive habits of thought and behavior. It was, well, civilized, and many of the speakers as eloquent as truth is, talking about their lives and what they hoped to do one day. Afterwards Derek introduced several of the other members to me, always careful to explain that I was "not an addict," but a friend. Even those who obviously assumed this was a subterfuge adopted for my sake were friendly and welcoming, urging me to visit again whenever I wanted to. Possibly I will, from time to time, because it's such a large part of Derek's orientation to experience and it will help me understand him.

We left the meeting and walked down Portobello Road, lighted by old and somehow soothing lamps, which cast a pale illumination on the two-story, pastel stucco houses along the way. Shrub-like trees bent into our path so that we had to duck from time to time. "What did you think of it?" Derek asked.

"It was nice. I enjoyed it. Especially the boy telling his story. Hard to believe he survived all that. And you'd never guess from looking at him."

"Probably not from looking at me either. I haven't told you all of it." I let this pass. "But I will if you want me to."

"Right here on the street?" We had turned onto Pembridge Road, brightly lit and lined with shops, because it would take us down to the Notting Hill Gate tube stop, where we could get a taxi.

"No, I didn't mean now," he scowled, then smiled. "But sometime."

Sometime turned out to be when we got home. I saw that for whatever reason Derek wanted to tell "everything," and that I should listen. Actually, the general outlines I already knew. And the rest I probably could have figured out on my own had I tried.

"So, after a while," he said, "when I couldn't pay for the

drugs, I found this older guy. He told me he would keep me supplied with stuff if I would go with him—you know, be available. So that's what happened."

"Did you live with him?"

"No, he was married. He paid the rent for a studio flat I had in Soho."

"How long did that go on?"

"Em, about six months. Then he got put in prison for embezzling. He worked in a bank, vice-president, actually." Derek leaned back against the pillow he had propped up against the bedroom wall, maybe just the tiniest bit proud of having snagged someone that important.

"What did you do then?"

"I found another john. A priest. A Catholic priest. Really weird. He never actually wanted to go all the way. What I had to do was let him chase me around his flat, wearing just my briefs. He had this long feather. He would try to catch me and tickle me with it. And when he caught me—I would always let him catch me after a while—he'd start tickling me. And I would scream and laugh like a lunatic. And then he'd go off by himself. That's all he wanted. A good thing, too, because by that time, with the drugs, I was able for sod all. When he found me shooting up one day, he didn't want to have anything more to do with me. Like I was a piece of shit or something. It wasn't long after that I heard about NA. You know, it doesn't come to you till you're ready for it." He looked at me, eyes blinking, trying to fathom my reaction.

"I'm glad you told me," I said. "You were lucky that the story turned out to have a happy ending." I might have left it at that, but the imp of the perverse made me ask, "Did you ever have a relationship with anyone your own age?"

"No. I'm not attracted to guys my age. I don't know why. They just don't seem serious."

"Do I seem serious?"

"You do. And you remind me of Stevie Winwood, who is probably the best-looking face in pop music." He reached over to kiss me.

"You're good at flattery," I said, hoping I was wrong. "And *you* look like *this* character." I held up the British Museum photograph of Hypnos, which Corinne had sent me that morning. Derek regarded it and asked what it was exactly. "It's from the British Museum, the head of a Greek god, a sort of movie star cast in bronze."

"I always wanted to be one of those. I used to have fantasies about the statues—have you ever seen a picture of the one whose arms are broken off?"

"There are a lot like that."

"Well, there was one that I had a picture of. I used to keep it under my mattress. And then one day my mother found it and said it was pagan and I oughtn't to be looking at stuff like that."

Vistas of an ammonia-scrubbed household and a cheerless childhood came into focus. "You still talk to your mother, right?"

"Sure, my Ma's OK. We'll go—Maeve and me—to Dublin next month to see her and Da. She said come Christmas but I didn't want to." He nestled up next to me, putting his head against my shoulder. "We should have a little time together first." He looked up at me and smiled, and then, "I'm glad my story didn't make you think I was hideous. I just didn't know then, I was confused by the drugs."

"Doesn't matter at all. And, you know, NA—the whole thing—is very interesting. I'm glad you found your way to it." We lay there quietly, listening to faint creaks from the heating system and the sound of wind outside. When I looked down again I could see that Derek was sleeping as calmly as only children are supposed to; soon after that I began to follow after him, a sensation of weightless ease overtaking me and wafting me toward—.

MAEVE AND I have agreed to attend a service at Derek's church. It's the Sunday before Christmas. His St. Ann's is having the nighttime "Ceremony of Lessons and Carols," which I've seen at home on TV, broadcast from some suitable cathedral or Westminster Abbey, can't remember. Derek is going to do one of the readings, and he wants us here with him. We sit in semidarkness. He fidgets nervously next to us as the choir begins to assemble at the rear of the church. It's a Wren-style structure, built of brick, with arched windows and clear panes of glass, a white interior with gold trim and dark wood paneling around the altar, which is decorated with red and white flowers. Everyone stands as the organ strikes the opening chords. Congregation and choir begin singing the words, "Once in royal David's city stood a lowly cattleshed...." By the time the hymn concludes, the choir is installed in its loft and the priests in their seats beside the altar.

The priest (Derek's friend) pronounces words of welcome and then sits down for the first lesson. As the reader walks up to the lectern, Derek whispers, "She used to prostitute." But you would never know it. She reads the Creation story from Genesis, in a clear, unaccented alto voice. The red silk blouse she wears and the white sweater match the altar flowers, and she looks unassailably ordinary except for her hair, which is frizzed out in a large mane around her face. The lesson finished, we hear a carol from the choir, the one with the refrain "Jesus Christ, the apple tree." Some of the voices are obviously trained, others not. But the tune is irresistible.

Of course I haven't, except as a tourist, been to church in twenty-five years. Presbyterianism slips away easily by the time you leave home. Like all my friends, I'm an agnostic—no, wait, I know some very devout atheists. To be at a church service reminds me again how unnatural religion seems to us all. Robes, candles, incense—you might as well be at—at the theater. But of course it's natural to all these people here, or most of them; and to Derek. OK, a willing suspension of disbelief then, for the duration.

As each of the participants goes up to read (some of the texts familiar to me from Handel's *Messiah*), Derek whispers a word or two about their background. They all seem to have been part of the Picadilly Circle scene; but those days are over. Now it's Derek's turn. Maeve gives him a pat as he steps out of the pew and walks to the lectern. I can see by numbers of smiles in the audience that he is known and liked. One boy with spiked hair leans toward his neighbor and whispers something I'd give a lot to be able to hear. "And there went out a decree from Caesar Augustus," Derek begins, a nervous quaver in his voice. He quickly warms up, though, and the rest goes smoothly. We did a little rehearsal this afternoon, and I gave him some hints on voice production. When he returns and takes his seat again, we all stand and sing "Away in a Manger." Even I can bawl out that without much trouble. Maeve reaches over to squeeze Derek's arm and flash a congratulatory smile at him.

Finally we get the Incarnation text from the Gospel of John, read ringingly by the priest while we all stand. When it is over, we hear a short sermon from him, this friend of Derek's, who is middle-aged, vigorous, and, judging by his words, not a hypocrite. I keep thinking he certainly doesn't look gay, but then I should know better than to traffic in stereotypes. The service concludes with a procession to the hymn "O Come All Ye Faithful," which I know also and like, but can't sing all the way through, it goes too high.

"So that's that," Maeve says as we go out into the cold air, after shaking hands with Father Hartley, the priest. "Derek, I thought you read extremely well."

"Avery and me were practicing all afternoon," he says. "Wait, there's someone I have to see." He runs over to the boy with spiked hair, almost knocking over an older man in a pinstriped suit and horn-rimmed glasses. Then he comes back to us, explaining, "That's my mate from one of the meetings. I was supposed to remind him that he has to speak tomorrow night."

"Well," I said. "Where shall we go?"

"Would you like to go to The Harp?" Maeve asked. "We won't stay long," she said, realizing that Derek and I would need a little persuading. We walk down to Picadilly, looking for a taxi. The air is misty, smoky, lit up orange from the street lights. Crowds of people sweep by, laughing and yelling. Cars thunder by, by the hundreds, but no taxis. We stand opposite the bronze monument at the center of the circle, the steps at its base crowded with young people who may very well be reading lessons at St. Ann's next year. At the top the winged statue balances on one toe and holds aloft his wand.

Derek, seeing me look at it, says, "That's Eros, you know." (He pronounces it EE-ross.)

"Actually, it isn't," I said. "When the monument was put up, the Victorians would hardly have stood for anything as risqué as that. Its actual name is the Angel of Christian Charity."

"Really? Like, everybody said it was Eros." He looks up at it with fresh interest. "Where did you hear that?"

"In a guidebook to London. I pride myself on keeping a lot of trivial information at my fingertips."

"That's amazing. So all the time I was coming to the right place." He grinned and then Maeve came out of the crowd.

"Forget finding a taxi. There's a bus down there. It'll take us directly to Parkway."

When we get to The Harp, it is crowded and several people greet Maeve as we make our way to the bar. Smoke hangs thickly in the air and the smell of spilled Guinness and crowded bodies mixes in with it to compose a familiar, staunchly human atmosphere. No question of sitting down. I get pints for Maeve and myself and a Coke for Derek. We stand and let the crowd buffet us as we try to talk, constantly interrupted by friends of Maeve who come up to kiss her and hand her pints one after another as she finishes them. A man in the rear starts playing tunes on a penny whistle, and the rhythm gets taken up infectiously by the crowd. A raspy tenor voice adds words to the tune and many begin clapping. By now Maeve is more with the crowd than with us. A kind of wild light comes into her eyes, and I begin thinking that there is much more to her than I have guessed, something out near the edge of the irrational that leaves the rest of us a little behind. I wouldn't be surprised if she became one of those "charismatic" figures one day, at the vanguard of a band of volunteers, urging them on like Joan of Arc. Raising her glass now, she suddenly loses her balance and stumbles backward, but the press of the crowd holds her up and her friends join in when she laughs. Derek and I exchange a look, and I know exactly what he is thinking. The times we've gone out together, I've noticed that Maeve errs on the side of indulgence when it comes to drinking. I also know neither Derek nor I will ever say anything to her about it. Nothing wrong with getting tipsy occasionally. And how else negotiate The Harp?

When we ask her if she's ready to go, she says she's not, but never mind, don't wait for her, a friend is going to take her home. She gestures toward a curly-headed man in his thirties with a red complexion and pretty eyes, who introduces himself as Danny O'Shea. We say goodnight and begin forcing our way out.

As we walk up Inverness Street to Gloucester Crescent, Derek sniffles a little and I ask him if he has a cold. He shakes his head. "Maeve's terrific, isn't she? I mean, she's got a lot more going for her than I do. She goes out and talks to, like, construction workers, trying to get them interested in politics. I wouldn't have the bottle to do that, really." Then he looks at me in the lamplight, a strangely tragic expression on his face. "Whatever she wants to do, I have to support her in it, don't I?"

"Sure, I guess so."

"I mean, she really wants the world to be a better place and that."

"She does. And she actually puts some legwork into it. But I still think there's room for the rest of us who don't have her talents. Or who are trying to do other things."

This seems to soothe and even thrill him. There's no one on the street, so he suddenly stops, grabs my shoulders, and kisses me. He says, "It was great that you came tonight, I was really glad you were there. I really loved that." We stand and stare at each other with starry eyes misting over, not like grown men at all. And I can just glimpse real stars through the tree branches above. Then, hearing the sound of steps and voices coming up the street, we push on toward our door.

Part III

One

You cut your hair!" Derek gives a sidewise nod and won't look at me. He is standing in the middle of the living room, hands in his pockets. A short fuzz muffles the outline of his head, which looks bony and sculptural in the gray light.

"I got tired of bleaching it," he says. He slips off his leather jacket (a Christmas present from me) and tosses it on the sofa.

"Well, let's have a look." His hair is light brown, at least will be when it grows out. "Don't want to be a blond god anymore?"

"People are always staring. I used to like getting noticed, but I'm fucking tired of it. Like, yesterday, I was standing in Tottenham Court Station and a couple of old dears started talking about my hair, I heard what they said." He slumps down in an armchair, hands in his pockets again. "I just want to fade into the background and be normal."

"I doubt you'll manage that. A haircut's not going to make all that much difference." He turns aside from me and faces over toward the glassed-in dining alcove. I've said the wrong thing, suggesting he's not going to achieve normality, what-ever that is, so he changes the subject.

"Looks like we might get a little snow."

"I wouldn't mind especially. It's that time of year." The holidays are over now, which is fine with me. From Christmas Eve until New Year's, London goes into a contented general strike, with shops closed, public transportation at best off-and-on, with an overall somnolence that can seem peaceful or provincial, depending on mood. People call on each other, drink port around the hearth, and indulge in the British passion for inactivity, but it all happens behind closed doors.

What Derek, Maeve, and I did was go to spend New Year's afternoon with Corinne over in St. John's Wood. She has a garden flat, with chairs covered in old floral prints and dozens of nineteenth-century French fashion chromolithographs on the walls. Susannah was there, talking about some friend of theirs who had shown up at last night's party in a Christian Lacroix dress, looking, as she said, "like a boiled sweet." Without ever seeming overbearing, Susannah always manages to keep conversation revolving around her topics, which meant that two hours passed at an amused, gliding speed never dragged down by anything too informative or depressing. A gilded clock under the bell jar on Corinne's mantel adjusted its hands quietly and, presto, we were all standing up to say goodbye and Happy New Year. Derek and I aren't exactly at the center of the party circuit, so that was our only invitation. Just maybe Derek has been a little bored the last few days? Myself, I can always read, but that doesn't necessarily solve life's problems for him. One night we went down to a big dance hall in Brixton, a sort of converted hangar, elbowing our way into the middle of hundreds of hip-hopping West Indians, which was fun to do once. Now that January's safely settled in, the comfort of routine comes back, Derek at work, me shuffling my filecards.

This afternoon, notebook in hand, I went to the house and museum of John Soane, in Lincoln's Inn Fields. It had been on my mind to go for months, and then research is much less a strain when fact gathering sends you outdoors. The square, which stopped trying to make an impression ages ago, was once the site of the theater that set itself up in rivalry to Cibber's Drury Lane. His actor children Theophilus and Charlotte, at different moments, both performed there even though the troupe was one of Cibber's competitors. It would have been pulled down long since by the time Soane built his first house there, which he later bequeathed to London, as one of its earliest museums.

A longish wait after the bell and the door was opened by a gray-haired curator, who politely took my trench coat and hung it by the door. From the little entrance hall, he led me to the right of the stairs into the dining room, briefing me on the founder. "... born in 1753 ... built the house next over in 1792 ... then completed this part in 1813. It houses his extensive collections of art and architectural ornament." Mild comments about the dining room and adjoining library began to dwindle and trail off. The curator stood quietly a moment, then went away, leaving me free to wander around on my own.

An eccentric arrangement of arches, something like Gothic groining, connects the ceiling of the library to the bookshelves, over which Soane installed mirrors to multiply details and throw spatial relations into doubt. Colors are dark red and dark green, with wood moldings interspersed. At unexpected spots (pendentive formations among the arches, and on column capitals), little round mirrors also crop up to provide extra ornament in the form of tiny convex reflections: over and over the reflected room, in a sort of Mercator projection, looms behind the large, bulging face of the visitor gazing innocently from a framed circle of silvery glass. The general effect is like being caught inside a Neoclassical funhouse or surrealist's jewel box, whatever tingling aura of disorientation you experience, all of a piece with the museum-quality stillness and marble melancholy of the statues posted about at strategic intervals.

This was absorbing, but not why I'd come. I had to tug myself away to find the Picture Room, where Soane's outstanding collection of Hogarths are hung. He actually owned all of the *Rake's Progress* series of oils, not to mention the less well-known "Election" paintings. My day's agenda was to study the fable of Tom Rakewell's decline and fall, hoping to get started on the job of conveying the atmosphere of Georgian England. Hogarth's the best one to look at for that. Besides, Theophilus Cibber, Colley's only son, willingly or helplessly, did everything imaginable to qualify as a model rake himself. The play he wrote, called *The Harlot's Progress* (and based on that series of Hogarth prints), was either a half-conscious acknowledgment of his failings or an attempt to divert attention away from them.

My eye went first to the scene in the tavern, based, commentators say, on one called The Rose, which stood in Drury Lane, not far from the Theatre Royal. There is Hogarth's Tom in self-satisfied dissipation, leg in the lap of whoever she was that week, his curly peruke askew, and a look of drowsy, wine-embalmed complacency on his face. Tumult around the table takes the form of overturned crockery, a discarded gown and stays on the floor, a cracked mirror on the wall, stageworthy glares projected across the table (along with a few crude insults, silent but easy to imagine), deep décolletages acting as magnets to fevered hands, partly devoured fruit on the table, dedicated swilling all around. You can smell snuff, sweat, melted tallow. Trying to visualize Theophilus Cibber, you could do worse than cast him in this particular scene.

It's probably better to look at the series in order, so I went back to the first picture, where Rakewell calmly loiters in the drawing room while the household of his miser father, only a few hours dead, is being dismantled. Equipped with inheritance and a malleable, featherweight brain, he whisks himself off to the second tableau, a smart residence in London. He has come downstairs to receive those who will cut this particular piece of country cardboard into a man of fashion—fencing partner, dancing master, gardener, music teacher. Rakewell has found his true vocation in cash outlay, and you think of the root meaning of "prodigal," the son's extravagance a predictable wine-and-roses reflex to his father's stinginess. But there's no paternal embrace for him to return to when funds run low. The third scene is the three a.m. bacchanal at The Rose, then comes the first crunch: out of pocket, the Rake tries to attend the Queen's levee at St. James in hopes of drumming up royal sponsorship. Unfortunately, he is arrested for debt by Welsh constables, just outside of White's, which has no doubt unburdened him of a hefty percentage of his capital. Odd to see that familiar vista—in a painting, that is—down to the gate of St. James, which I know in a context altogether different (White's now a gentleman's club, as respectable as it is dowdy). And, farther on, Locke's hatters, largely unchanged since, say, 1890, its floorboards rough and unswept, sample headgear displayed as is, without the flattery of window dressing; and then Berry's wine shop, a century and a half's layers of green-black paint accumulated on its façade, bubbled and blistered in spots; and then St. James Palace itself, where no monarch has lived since the Regency, guards outside in tall beaver hats reminding one nevertheless whose palace it is.

Unlike Auden and Kallman, Hogarth didn't introduce any special surprise or plot complexity into his Rake's "progress." Marriage to a rich, one-eyed widow ("this deformed and withered sybil, ordinary even to a proverb," as one Georgian commentator puts it); squandering of a second fortune at the gaming tables; imprisonment; and finally madness, most likely brought on by advanced syphilis as much as by adversity. In the Age of Reason, madness is a form of exotica, so the Rake and his fellow patients are actually on display for sundry noble visitors to Bedlam. Did they recognize in his pose the resemblance to Caius Gabriel Cibber's *Melancholy Madness* at the entrance to the hospital? That was Hogarth's model, apparently, the resemblance not hard at all to see once pointed out.

Standing there in the velvet stillness of the museum, I had a little thrill of circular coincidence, going from Caius Gabriel's incarceration for gambling debt, to *Melancholy Madness*, to Pope's couplet about Colley and the statues at Bedlam ("Where o'er the Gates, by his fam'd Father's Hand,/Great Cibber's brazen, brainless Brothers stand"), to Theophilus and Charlotte Cibber and then Theophilus's *Harlot's Progress*; then to Hogarth's Rake and finally back again to Caius Gabriel. Dizzying. But then, coincidence spreads through experience like electromagnetic waves; it broadcasts to us the news of who and where we are.

In the interest of completeness, I went downstairs to see Soane's "Monk's Chamber," a half-serious spoof on the new Gothic fashions of his time. Harmless enough; but a bit more disturbing was a little cell nearby with actual chains and handcuffs attached to the wall—suggesting what, exactly? The taste for Gothic didn't begin with Madame Tussaud—or with *Melancholy Madness*, for that matter. Always the dark underside of consciousness, springing up like uncouth fungi even in the Age of Reason.... The next display was the alabaster sarcophagus of Seti I, one of Soane's special treasures. Nothing makes my mind go blank quicker than a stretch of hieroglyphics, if only because of the settled conviction that they're never going to be anything except routine praises of a godlike ruler. Well, good timing: as I turned aside, the museum guard came up and with a regretful gesture implied that the day's viewing was now at an end. Throughout the museum there was the sound of shutters being closed. I walked upstairs again, took my trench coat from its hook, and went down the steps to the street. It was nearly dark out already, but the silhouettes of the trees in Lincoln's Inn Fields stood out against the dim light of the sky. Then on into the rock concert of light, horns, and traffic in Holborn, where I found a taxi.

DEREK IS helping me clear the table when we hear the bell. I glance at my watch, walk to the door of the flat and then to the outside door. It's Maeve, who furls her umbrella and shakes off a powder of snow before entering. She lets herself be led inside, where I take her coat. Derek lopes over and gives her a hug. A partly suppressed giggle. She runs both hands back through her hair and sinks into the sofa. Over a black turtle-neck she is wearing a grape-purple jersey whose folds take on a soft glow in the lamplight.

"I thought of ringing first but couldn't remember your number, Avery. I hope I'm not breaking in."

"No, we've just finished dinner. Want some rice pudding?"

"Lovely. Got any coffee? Oh, don't bother, a tea bag will do just as well."

"No, no, it only takes a second." Derek goes off to the kitchen.

"It's so cozy, really lovely, the way you two have become so domestic, getting up rice pud and things."

"Well, we bought it at Marks and Sparks."

"Oh, I didn't realize they did that, I never shop there myself, too expensive."

"The lines, um, you know, the queues are shorter. It's worth it."

"I agree, but you've got to be able to afford it. I love the way Americans always seem to have lots of lolly. Makes everything easier."

It's not clear whether she means this to have the edge it does for me, but while I'm looking for a response, Derek comes back, bringing a dish of pudding. He says, "There's coffee coming in a minute."

She smiles up at him. "You spoil me rotten. On that topic, I have a favor to ask, since tomorrow's Saturday. Could you possibly help me with Liam's flat? I've got things to do, I don't want to spend the whole day."

Derek pauses, and then nods. I feel a quick sear of annoyance since we had the plan of making a day trip down to Brighton. Derek partly saves the situation by turning to me and asking, "Do you mind? We could go to Brighton on Sunday."

"But you'll miss St. Ann's."

"I could go at eight."

"Whatever you want to do. I suppose there are errands I could run tomorrow. Besides, the weather may turn out bad, and we couldn't go anyway."

"Sunday also, come to that."

"By the way, who's Liam?"

"You know, the one from Dublin. We're best of friends now. But the flat still needs doing, he can't get anyone else. He's lots of fun. I keep saying I'm going to have you and him to my place for a meal, I've been so busy," she says. Then she turns to Derek. "So, we'll meet there at nine-thirty, that all right, Del?" (I've noticed she uses his nickname whenever she wants him to do something.) He nods and goes off to fetch her coffee.

"What happened to that one you were seeing, you know the one we met at The Harp?"

"Oh, Danny. Well, nothing much. I'll run across him again, I expect. Eventually." She rearranges the folds of her jersey and regards me gravely. "It's adorable, the way you and Derek have settled down. I might like to do the same myself some day. But not just yet. Oh, lovely, Del," she says, taking the cup from his hands.

"What not just yet?" he asks. She gropes for a cigarette in her bag, lights it, and inhales rhetorically.

"I was just saying to Avery I wasn't quite ready to settle down with anyone in particular."

"He'd have to fit himself around your political work."

"Not bloody many who'd be willing. Maybe in Ireland...." Trailing off, she looks up toward the ceiling, her face deeply shadowed in the lamplight and wearing an expression that in its resoluteness and dreamlike absorption makes me think of photographs I've seen of the early women suffragists.

Derek asks her for a cigarette—unusual, because he almost never smokes. He bends over as she lights it for him; and then stands there taking drags at intervals a little too rapid to seem natural. No one says anything, and I play over my feelings for Maeve, tonight a mixture of admiration, jealousy, annoyance, protectiveness, and, what, a sort of family feeling based on eight weeks' association with a pair that Corinne is somehow right to call "the twins." They begin talking between themselves about the trip to Dublin they're planning, a visit to their parents. That's about ten days off. Derek has told me he'd like me to come over as well—not straight off, but after they've been there a few days. He's been telling his Mum and Dad about me. I haven't made up my mind yet. It sounds a little Victorian: would I be expected to declare intentions or something?

Derek calls Maeve over to look at an ad for a special discount flight he's found in the Camden Town newspaper. I watch them as they read it together, Derek's newly shaved head looking somehow vulnerable and Maeve's intelligent features focused intently on the ad. Derek's arm is around her shoulder. I am not a blood relative, no, just an outsider, an older generation, excluded. It's all been a mistake, it will never last....

First Derek glances up at me, staring directly into my eyes, and then Maeve does. They look question marks at me, not so much puzzled as embarrassed. At last I stand up, still without saying anything, and go off toward the bedroom. I get undressed, climb into bed, and switch off the light, listening to their detective-novel whispers from behind the door.

Later on, when Maeve goes, Derek tiptoes into the bedroom and without turning on a light undresses. He slips in with me and snuggles up, touch becoming sight in the darkness. His skin smells of the cigarettes they've been smoking, which in a way is sexy and in another way annoying. We lie still, breathing softly. He has forgotten to take off his watch; the radium dial glows greenly against the sheets, and I can hear it tick faintly.

Stroking the fuzz on his hard, round head, I grumpily whisper, "Little Tom Rakewell," knowing he won't understand; and not really sure myself why I call him that. Unless there is a secret retaliation or consolation, sometimes, in saying things no one can possibly follow, not even the speaker.

Two

In my free-floating, sometimes disorienting schedule, the working materials and papers of the biography have become a sort of anchor. On the work table (in what I still don't quite call the study) are stacks of notecards and notebooks, some with trial drafts of chapters in them. A bronze lamp with library-green shade stands guard over all this, on the right side of the desk. And the concept "work" covers so many activities, from the most menial to the exalted. Suggestibility; hints taken up or discarded; the gold vein of the mine found among so many false leads. There does turn out to be a such a thing as passionate research—a word that has better connotations in French, where it also means "search" or "quest."

The biographer's search is less metaphysical but can be at moments just as hectic, odd facts pounced on to the accompaniment of an inwardly sounded "ah-hah" of discovery whenever they interlock with details gathered earlier to establish a pattern of behavior or support a presiding theme. The circle of lamplight comes to resemble a small arena where the principals—ruled page, felt-tip pen, blue pencil, supportive cup of coffee—all interact in a scenario of hesitation and discovery, retreat and advance that may seem either like combat or sexual courtship. The drama and the naïveté of this, partly material and partly immaterial, accounts for writers' willingness to put up with long hours alone, the hardness of almost any chair sat in for the length of time required to produce a good paragraph, and the cold sweat of self-doubt, absolutely indispensable if you don't want the process to disintegrate into mere private entertainment.

My last generation of Cibbers promises to be the most colorful. I don't mean the older daughters, Catherine, Anne, and Elizabeth, who were conventional enough and married off to decently dull husbands (some of whom uncooperatively died). No, the spotlight will mostly be aimed at Charlotte and Theophilus, the two theatrical children, in whom you can see a further development of that family essence I've been tracing through the two previous generations.

Charlotte, the youngest and clearly her father's darling, turned out to be a rousing disappointment. A little spoiled and headstrong as a child, she was probably thought of as charmingly high-spirited. And certainly she began by trying to please her parents, though not to the extent of learning cooking, sewing, and housekeeping. She liked to dress in men's clothes and later on to hunt, which she did day after day when the Cibbers were in the country. A pivotal incident: in the summer she turned fifteen, she and her mother were at Hillesden while Colley Cibber was off on a jaunt to France. Knowing that he planned to buy a horse when he returned, Charlotte decided to give one of the candidates a preliminary test on her own. She took it for a gallop through the countryside, unfortunately running down a child in the process. This was somehow blamed on a groom, who after being fired for drunkenness threatened to get even. An inflamed Charlotte managed to find herself a gun and sat up for several nights firing at shadows. Nobody was killed, but the shock gave her mother an asthma attack and drove in a bit deeper the suspicion that, as a daughter, Charlotte was going to be too exciting.

Cibber must have thought some of this behavior would resolve itself once she accepted the disciplines of the stage and marriage to Richard Charke, who seemed reasonably credible as a son-in-law. The wedding at St. Martin in the Fields and her debut in *The Provok'd Wife* took place within a few months of each other. As an actress she was talented but uncontrolled and erratic, and the same description could be applied to her in the role of wife and mother. In any case Richard Charke turned out to be the standard Hogarthian rake. Within a few years she gave up on him entirely and transferred all her distracted family feeling to her child Kitty. A life of outlandishness and worse awaited her, compiled of feuds with anyone in range, especially theater managers, the results predictable as wet weather in London. Outrage unrelenting as Charlotte's could qualify as comedy for anyone who didn't have to live it or live near it.

After she performed in a farce that satirized her father, she was summoned to a family council and told it was reform or take the consequences. I can probably make something of the fact that the last straw was a *theatrical* offense. Charlotte's staunch impenitence failed to impress her sisters, who disowned her, hustled her out the door, and acknowledged the victor's gleam in each other's eye. Colley Cibber himself had conveniently stormed from the house before this disciplinary maneuver was staged, but in any case he ever after turned a deaf ear to Charlotte's wheedling for subsidies. She quickly became unemployable, her scheme of throwing together a renegade troupe of actors and staging (in a sort of warehouse) a satirical piece she'd written not, needless to say, really workable as a permanent solution. The farce just happened to pillory those theater managers she felt had wronged her, which may have served as a blissful release of pent-up hostilities but also settled forever the question of whether she might be forgiven and rehired by any of them.

The remainder of her life is a mixture of black humor and pathos. She began dressing as a man "for substantial reasons" never explained but obviously having to do with the greater mobility available to the male gender at the lower end of society. She was a tavern keeper on Drury Lane, a waiter in Marylebone; she took both men's and women's parts in strolling companies, went off to Wales and worked as a pastry cook; then as a puppet-show manager; then as a performer at Bartholomew Fair; then as a magician's assistant in Petticoat Lane. One of the last glimpses of her is as the resident of a thatched hovel "in the purlieus of Clerkenwell," where she wrote and had published installments of her *Narrative of the Life of Mrs. Charlotte Charke*. Here private disasters were made public and a father's forgiveness begged for, but on that score she was wasting her breath. When he died he left her "five pounds and no more." She soldiered on through gross poverty and neglect and even managed, just before she died, to marry off her daughter Kitty to a strolling actor. Charlotte's last public appearance was a pre-season performance at the Haymarket in 1760. Daughter and new husband went off to America, where Kitty became a noted comic actress, and where she died shortly before the Revolution.

As I sit here and think about it all, oscillating between pity and the opposite, something makes me wonder how my own life would read in synopsis. The simplifications required to turn experience into text operate on a different plane from the actual process of undergoing events and emotions—fear, anger, lust, love, and confusion over happenstance as it tumbles down around you; though of course well-done narratives give us the illusion that *we* go through those events and feel those emotions. It's easy, when making the summary of a life, to drift into a mood of something like arraignment.

In order to be "gripping," biographers often take the short cut of playing on the register of judgment and satire, throwing conflicts, backstabbing, and pratfalls into high relief—the sort of biography that for notables "adds to death a new terror," as Wilde once said. If I object to biographies that turn into court cases, then I have to make sure I understand the difference between narration and exploitation. In Charlotte Cibber's case, tempestuousness might inevitably follow from the collision of an independent mind with the restrictions placed on women, restrictions symbolized in the cumbersome dresses and hoop skirts she seems to have sniffed at except when a theatrical role required them. It all depends on how things are accounted for. Well, one tack to take is to give lengthy quotes from her *Narrative,* even though she wrote it as fast as she could, hoping to sell it and be able to pay for dinner. She could plead her own case. Obvious faults I could present as evidence of circumstances that deserve pity more than ridicule, maybe? I'm certainly not capable of writing a biographical "Last Judgment." The pile of notecards and notebooks suddenly looks enormous. I lean back in my chair, let out a sort of "hmpff," and then notice that it's dark out. The day gone, and shopping for dinner still isn't done.

WALKING BACK from Marks and Spencer with my little bag of groceries, I realize I forgot onions. Too far to turn back; the solution is go over to Inverness Street to see whether the vegetable stands are still selling. They are, and, while I'm waiting for my ten pence in change, breathing out gusts of white steam in the middle of the jostling crowd, I see Derek farther on, stepping into the doorway of The Harp. By himself. He's probably meeting Maeve there; but he hasn't mentioned that he was going to.

When I go through the door at first I don't see him in the dim light and haze of cigarette smoke. All the clients are men, dressed in gray or brown; but no Derek. Wait, there he is, off in a corner, sitting by himself. He looks up surprised when I walk over and not all that pleased, apparently.

"Well, hello. Thought that was you I saw come in here just now. Been out shopping." I sit down and put my bag into an empty chair next to me.

"I was, em, just stopping for a minute before going back to the flat."

"Meeting Maeve?"

"No, I don't think so. I mean, I'm not expecting to. I'm just sitting here, just like all the rest of these berks." I glance at the other customers and then notice the glass in front of him: brown ale with a cap of foam on it.

"Wai-i-it a minute. What's going on?"

"I'm trying to decide if I want this or not."

He couldn't have surprised me more if he'd said he'd been diagnosed with a fatal disease. "But NA doesn't let you drink. What is this? What's going on?"

A hangdog, green-eyed gaze: he looks at me the way homeless people do when you ask them how long they've been on the street. "I felt like I wanted to. I didn't have any yet."

"Come on, let's go. Just leave it right there." Powered by a flush of relieved anxiety, I stand, lifting my bag with one hand and holding the other out to him. He looks at me, and then gets up without touching the glass, dropping coins on the tabletop. We walk out of the pub and into the street. In the lamplight, the vendors are beginning to pack their goods and close for the night. We lope along in silence to Gloucester Crescent and climb the steps to my building. A light mizzle is falling and there are dead leaves on the mat.

Inside, I set the groceries down in the kitchen, then turn around and go back to the living room where Derek is standing by the TV, running through the channels. "Why don't we talk for a minute without that, all right?" I say. He shrugs, switches it off, and then turns to look at me. "Want to sit down?"

We go to the sofa and I put my arm around him. "So, what's going on?"

Derek sits there silently. He shifts around, pulls away, and finally says, "I've had things on my mind. I probably wouldn't have taken that drink. I had just about figured that it wouldn't be worth it when you came in."

"Did you have a bad day at work, or what?"

"No." He sits with his eyes focused on the floor.

"Well, what is it?" I can see his eyes begin to glisten. He closes them and a tear squeezes out. Then, almost sheepishly, he releases a low, unconvincing laugh.

"I don't know. I'm a fucking alcoholic-addict, I don't need an excuse."

"Does this happen a lot?" He shakes his head. "Maybe you're not exactly looking forward to going home. Maybe you should cancel."

"I've got to support Maeve," he says. "You agreed that was so."

"But—what's that got to do with anything?"

"She feels better if I go with her. We were always a team."

"If you're on the verge of drinking over this, it must not be a good idea, right?" He brushes a hand across his face, sniffs, and then looks at me.

"It's really not a problem. Maeve would hate it if I didn't go. But I will miss you."

"Is that a problem?"

"No. Just be sure you don't find anybody else while I'm gone."

This sinks in for a moment and then I say, "I won't be looking." I tighten the hold of my arm around him. "Well, if that's all you're worried about—."

"I'm not worried, really I'm not. *Really.*" He looks up at me, his eyes moving from left to right and back again.

"What are your plans for while you're there, by the way? I mean, do you just sit at home with your parents or do you go out, or what?"

"Emm. We'll go out. Actually Maeve wants me to go up to Belfast with her for a day or so. To see friends of hers."

"Activist friends?"

"Probably. Almost everybody she knows is."

"That might be risky up there, no?"

He shakes his head. "I don't think so. It's just friends of hers." He looks at me with a mild, innocent expression, blinking his eyes.

"But if they're her friends, why should *you* go?"

"I sort of like it up there. I've met them once or twice, they're OK." I realize I've come up against a wall of unshakable intention. Derek has made up his mind to go along with Maeve, to take the trip, and any danger signals like his flirtation with drinking, or cautionary comments from me, he's just going to ignore. This is one of those moments, not too frequent, actually, when I feel the age difference between us. There's a sort of quasi-fatalism of youth that simply goes along with everyone's plans, doesn't want to make a fuss, is content to waste good time because the group wants to waste it. But if it's my choice to be with Derek, then I have to let him make his own choices in turn, however pointless they seem to me. Times like these always send me through a quick review of the reasons we're together. By now I know how to find the reasons by feel in the darkroom of the mind.

"Now, you go to Dublin on Thursday." Derek nods. "And when do you come back?"

"Wednesday after that."

"When was it you wanted me to come over?" I realize I

haven't before now had any intention of going.

"You could come on Monday. Is that OK?"

"Should be all right. But now, when do you go to Belfast?"

"Saturday morning. Back to Dublin on Sunday. It's just for a day. I told Ma and Da you might come." He looks at me hopefully.

"Well, I probably could. But you should check out the terrain first. Will you telephone me?"

"Sure. Will you be in Sunday, say, around four?"

"Yes. By the way, I would want to put up in a hotel. That way you could come and stay." He smiles and nods. "I guess it's settled then. And look, you didn't drink over it," I say quietly. "That's good." We stand up at the same moment and hold each other tight. I feel his heart beating through his shirt, his chest expanding and contracting, the loose boyish way his limbs are attached to his body. There are creaking noises coming from the room heating and the low thunder of traffic from outside. With my own kind of fatalism, I tell him that I love him and that we have nothing to worry about.

Three

I've noticed before that moments of tense transition, like an emotional razor strop, sharpen perception. This morning I find myself observing how gray light coming through the windows gives everything a hard, glassy aura, the bowl of oranges on the coffee table, polished brown wood of the chairs, leather jacket tossed on the sofa. Derek and I are sitting in the living room waiting for Maeve to arrive in the taxi that will take them to the Gatwick bus. He has told me not to go with them to the airport. We'll say goodbye here. He keeps wandering around the room, coming over to my chair from time to time to take the hand held out to him, grab hold, and then let it drop as he turns away and goes over to the window.

No matter what I have said, Derek hasn't been able to feel calm about the trip, and his agitation has rubbed off on me. I've given up trying to make everything right and been simply drummed into a state of blank acceptance of the psychological weather. I wish I knew exactly what it was that is bothering him, but since he doesn't know, I can't. One possibility is that the symbiotic relationship between him and Maeve has been disturbed; there's a tug of war between loyalties. Clearly he wouldn't be making this trip except at Maeve's instigation; he'd rather spend the time with me. He's not very close to his parents, the trip to Belfast was planned entirely by and for Maeve. No matter what he says, it's a dubious project for them to go up there and mix with people involved with—is it the IRA? He doesn't seem to know and pretends not to care, either because he wants to reassure me or because he doesn't want to make his own disquiet conscious to himself. It's not that I'm opposed to Maeve's activism. Her views about the British in Northern Ireland are humanly sound, granted, and there's no point in holding convictions you're unwilling to back up. Just that, now and then, I'm bothered by her nonchalance, her lack of what I would call realistic thinking. And I'm angry with her for involving Derek in her plans when they have nothing at all to do with him. Could it also be true that she feels a tug of war from her side and is testing to see whether she still has power over Derek? I don't like the drift of that suspicion and am certain she has never consciously considered it. But how big a role does the conscious mind play here?

I've been so wrapped up in ruminations about all this the past few days there was hardly any convincing sympathy to spare for Corinne when she telephoned two days ago to say she'd been called home: her brother had been hospitalized for pneumocystis again. She left yesterday with no definite idea when she'd be back. I think she was a little hurt at how little response she got from me, but it was as much as I could do just to avoid going into my own perplexities. I think also that any reminder of Joshua's death—and this was a truly threatening one—is still impossible for me to deal with normally. Everything I said was unfocused, formulaic, lame. When she comes back, I'll try to do better and make things up somehow. Her voice sounded unfamiliarly low, with a sort of enforced calm, when she said goodbye.

Any odd event that occurs seems to attract others. Why otherwise would I have had a visit this week from Max Wiesner, who'd just returned from seeing Adele in New York. He wanted to drop off a present she had sent me, a sweater, cable stitched in dark purple wool. Apparently the two of them had had a festive week together. Max told me all about this over a cup of tea, in a tone so affable I temporarily forgot to be anxious. He sat there in his nicely cut tweed jacket, paisley cravat tie, and pale blue shirt, his fine-boned hands gesturing as he reported on Adele; a perfect sample of the older man, dry, still physically active, quick-witted, and cheerful, who makes seventy look enviable. Plans are settled now: he'll be opening his gallery in New York some time in the spring. An assistant will run the one he has in London until he makes up his mind whether to close it or not.

He asked to be brought up to date about my doings, nodding at what he may or may not have recognized as a selective summary, one gray eyebrow arched over the bright eye that regarded me as I dutifully reported on the part of my activities that I thought would make sense to him. After a few minutes, he seemed to catch on that I wasn't in a good mood. He smiled at me shrewdly, and said, "A cab's coming in a few minutes. I was going to look at a few galleries, but it needn't be done today. Would you like to come with me for a drive? Just for the pleasure of it?"

The first reflex was to say no, but then the prospect of getting outside for a while, with no special errand or goal, suddenly sounded good. "You've persuaded me, Max." When the taxi arrived, we bundled in and the driver was told there was a change of plans, we'd be going down to Hyde Park. Then Max settled back to talk. The sky was silver-gray, trying to clear, above the bare branches of the trees. When we got down to Marylebone he pointed to a medium-sized building in weathered limestone, saying he had lived there for several years when he first came to London. During the war he hadn't seen combat but instead was in what he called "special services." But he wouldn't talk about this because he still con-sidered it confidential. He'd been through the blitz and the Finest Hour and all that, you got used to it, soot in your tea and so forth—though a number of friends had been killed, which was terrible. He gave me a special look when he said this and then took up his story again. What London was like after the war, emerging from the rubble. And how you couldn't get things, everyone just bumping along through the shortages and restricted liquidity. The really big changes hadn't come until the sixties, when suddenly the old haunts became unrecognizable.

"You have no idea how different things used to be. And it's still going on. The last time I went over to the City, I couldn't get my bearings. All the tobacconists I used to know are gone." He said he thought skyscrapers suited New York better than London. "I remember when I was younger, how boring people seemed to me who objected to new art and architecture, as though they wanted everything to stay frozen forever in the eighteenth century. But we didn't know just how far development would go. No way to stop it, really. You've got irresistible pressure from people wanting things they didn't used to. Well, observers have always thought the world was going to the dogs. And it was—for them. I'm sure you're perfectly content with the way things are."

"Well, maybe not," I said. "I see your point. London's changed even since the first time I was here, back in the six-ties. You notice it more than you do in New York." We turned onto Ring Road and down into Hyde Park. The sense of open expanses and a lowering of the noise level made us both quiet and thoughtful. We drove past the Serpentine, glass smooth and reflecting the featureless sky above. A solitary jogger made his way along one of the paths, an older woman pushing a pram trudging along from the opposite direction. Because the jogger was tall and blond, I thought of Derek. To break the silence, I asked Max where he lived exactly.

"Ennismore Gardens. Knightsbridge. Small place, but it's quite comfortable," he said unapologetically. "Like to stop in?"

"No, I should get back. But thank you. That's not far from here, is it? Why don't I drop you off, and then go back to my place by myself?" He agreed to this only on the condition that he pay return fare as well: it was his party. A few turns and we were on his street. He stepped onto the pavement from the taxi, a tall mansion block in red stone looming behind him, then turned and gave a slight bow and salute to me as we drove off.

When I telephoned Adele that night, she had just been talking to him and had already heard everything secondhand. She was thrilled that we'd had such a nice afternoon together. News was all from her side. Yes, she really, really liked Max and was glad he'd be moving to New York. "This feels like it may be the real thing," she said in a musing voice. "He is an extraordinary person." They had sat up late one night while she showed him old scrapbooks and photo albums with mementoes and pictures of Joshua, and she said she felt a wonderful sympathy from him. It had been nice to meet his daughter, who was very bright, worked at Christie's, and was going to marry an American boy next summer. And Max had told her how much he admired and liked me, she said. "Otherwise, I would have had my doubts about him." She implied that this last hurdle had settled the question for her. I asked whether marriage had been mentioned and she said, of course not, that was the farthest thing from her mind. I wondered, though, whether it might not move a little closer after Max relocated in New York? Adele said she was afraid she'd now gone past the age of consent. This made us both laugh, but then an odd silence fell. Neither of us wanted to look into it, so we ended the phone call.

Derek and I were conscious of last night as being important in some anxious sense. When I got back around six, he
was in the kitchen peeling potatoes. "I'm cooking tonight," he
said. The dining table was already set, and there were florist's
red roses in a vase at the center of it. We sat in the alcove and
ate our sole and potatoes and sprouts, with BBC Haydn on in
the background, both of us being as sharp and funny as we
could manage. Derek is a good satirist when he wants to be.
I've suffered a few slingshot wounds at his hand over the past
couple of months, but last night he had nothing but gooey
compliments for me. I could see a very self-conscious will to
please in that but still enjoyed the sensation. He had on the
same red shirt with printed dinosaurs he wore the night we
went to his room in Earl's Court for our grand audition. Was
he wearing it on purpose? Probably not; I'm the only one ever
to remember things like that.

To finish up with, Derek had some Black Forest cake he'd
found somewhere, a confection I never buy but always reflexively eat when it's given to me. We sat back in our chairs, the
plates before us a smear of brown crumbs and whipped
cream. I was about to clear everything away when he told me
to wait, there was something he had just thought of that he
wanted to say. It sounded a bit more premeditated than that,
but I sat down again and looked at him expectantly.

"I'll be back in a week," Derek said.

"I know."

"And if you come over to Dublin, we'll fly back together."

"Right."

"You said you were getting to the end of your research."

"Nearly."

"So you'll be thinking of going home before too long."

"I haven't made any plans."

"OK. Well, I just wanted to say that, when I come back—
or we come back—if you decide, you know, that it's time to
leave, and that we have to split up—"

"Derek, who said I was planning to go away?"

"Nobody. I mean if you decide to. I just wanted you to know that this has been over-the-top, the happiest I ever was, and that I really love you and feel like I was really lucky to know you. You are a great guy." He looked at me levelly with a mixture of defiance and vulnerability in his eyes.

"You don't need to say things like that. We've gone beyond that level, haven't we? I don't have any doubt that something really wonderful has happened, all I have to do is stop and think." I coughed at a crumb stuck in my throat. "As for the future, I have no idea why you think I'm about to say goodbye. You—." But suddenly I realized that he didn't really think so either. Derek was the one about to say goodbye, just for a short time, but then you never know, the plane could crash, or whatever.... And the speech about me going away was just a pretext for making a formal statement about his feelings—what he wanted to leave me with before he went to Ireland. Hence the slightly inflated "last words" tone.

"Derek, when we come back next week we will sit down together and look into the question of where we go from here. I'm not planning to leave you. Let's have our little trip and we'll figure out the rest later."

He knocked over his glass as he reached for me, paused to right it, and then reached again. We got up from the table and dragged each other across the room in something like a dance or a boxer's clinch. Pretty soon we were going at it on the sofa, inconvenient, and yet, because of its oddity, a fiery nest for love—shoes, socks, jeans, dinosaur shirt flying off, to leave us for a while tantalized on purpose with briefs, a single scrap of stretched cloth between us and entire free play. Always the same conflict: wanting to plunge over the cataract into oblivion and also to slow things down, to treasure each irreplaceable time frame for what it is, to congratulate circumstance for having come up with a Derek sprawled against the sofa cushions, arms spread out, milk-blue skin perfectly smooth except where a thin dusting of golden hair was just visible at the center of his chest, the delicate carving of the rib cage, the faint biscuity fragrance of his skin as I kissed it. I couldn't altogether put aside the pain of the approaching separation, and therefore "complete abandon" wasn't going to be possible even though much of what I did and said *resembled* it. All I knew was that I wouldn't trade the feeling of that sculptured cranium with its soft brown fuzz in my hands, the bulge of just his and no other person's Adam's apple, the articulation of bone and muscle in his back, or the sleepy, trusting look he gave me over his shoulder during the obligatory pause for safety measures, or the duo sighs we both breathed out as we got past the point where you think in distinct thoughts, as body English replaces coherent seeing or saying.

MAEVE HAS just come in to say that she has a cab waiting outside. She gives no explanation for why she has brought a small leather suitcase in with her. She comes up to me, gives me a hug and with a convincing lightness of tone says, "So we're off to Ireland, Avery. Do your best to come over. Actually Dublin can be fun, there are places we can take you, and the parents aren't so bad, really."

I don't say anything at first. Then, "I wish you luck," with just a little too much emphasis.

Maeve looks at me and then at Derek. "I promise to take good care of him, Avery."

"He's promised to do the same for you."

"Has he? Del, you are the sweetest brother." She goes over and gives him a hug.

They both look back at me, Maeve biting her lip and frowning sympathetically. It's been too easy to forget that she really likes me, is concerned that Derek and I should be happy together, and wants to be useful to both of us. I go up to her and put my arms very gently around her shoulders, then let them drop.

Derek gives me a last kiss and pulls away. I walk with them out to the front of the house and down to their taxi, which they board with irksome efficiency, Maeve first. What must be Maeve's everyday suitcase is sitting on the seat. Derek leans out the window and tries to smile. I see Maeve in the twilight of the back of the taxi give a jaunty wave. "I'll be here expecting your call on Sunday," I say. "Hope the trip goes well. My fingers are crossed. I know you've thought of everything." I bend over and whisper in Derek's ear, "I love you." He looks on the point of tears, so I back away. "All right, driver," I say. They both wave, and, when the taxi starts off, I watch until it disappears. When I turn around one of the neighbor cats (a long-haired calico) is sitting on top of a brick fence-column, regarding me with mild but alert apprehension. The split-pupilled eyes blink as I pass by, but then the cat runs off along the fence to some secret lair. How do I know that there's something Derek isn't telling me?

Four

After Maeve and Derek left I had a call from Susannah. She wondered if I had any evening plans. "Corinne and I had been planning to go to a drinks party in the East End, in Spitalfields." I wasn't clear about where that was. Susannah explained that it was near Liverpool Station, an old part of town that had begun to be renovated by artists and other adventurous sorts over the last few years. "I solemnly promised the host—his name's Toby Arnold—that I'd come. He's even got a theme. It's supposed to be the 'Anarchists' Party,' whatever he means by that. Anyhow, Corinne said your friend was leaving town, and I thought that you might—."

"Do you have to wear costume," I asked, "or will regular work clothes do?"

"Whatever's comfortable. I'm wearing a black jumpsuit. I suppose I'll add an attention-getting scarf or a belt or something. Want to come?"

"Sure. Though I'm not feeling especially anarchic right now."

"Look, we'll take my car. Corinne says you're on Gloucester Crescent, but I don't know where exactly." I mentioned the number and was told to expect her at nine. My earlier plan had been to go to a movie, but, in fact, there was nothing I particularly wanted to see. The party sounded silly enough to take my mind off other things for a few hours.

Derek telephoned just after six to tell me they'd arrived safely. His parents were expecting to meet me. He'd call tomorrow again. Everything was OK, his parents were OK, he wasn't bored. I could hear voices in the background, voices with lots of intonation, over the clatter of dishes. It was a little gleam of Ireland, a new frame to imagine around someone up to now pure London.

With Derek gone, I had time as I pottered around the flat to look at our situation with more perspective than usual. We had in effect been living together for more than a month now, though he kept paying the rent on the room down in Earl's Court; he went there from time to time to water his rubber plant and check in with Mrs. Finchley. (She had finally managed to evict Ahmed, I gathered.)

It had been a simple luxury to spend night after night with Derek, and even to function as a couple. Maybe there was something lopsided about the tandem, but that seemed to be the rule with most gay relationships, one partner noticeably older than the other, or ritzier, or more domestic—anyway, something to reestablish the difference that gender made in the male-female counterpart. It's very hard to love someone "exactly like you," though, as I stop to think, I've seen that also. On the subject of love, at some point in the past few weeks the word had begun cropping up a lot between Derek and me, as it helplessly does in an atmosphere of physical warmth, pleasure, and mutual admiration. Putting aside the question of what he meant by it, what did I? The coolest, though not necessarily the truest, appraisal I could make of the situation was that I was having a very good time with someone to whom I'd become attached largely as a reaction to the loss of Joshua. I'd been lonely; Derek was eager. Actually, that probably would have summed everything up pretty well until recently, and the practical side of me still wished, in a way, that there was nothing more to it and that the relationship would fade and flicker out as soon as I left London. But in fact I felt like staying in London with him; or taking him back with me.

Just what would that involve? Even putting aside questions like foreign residency and naturalization (English friends in New York had given me some idea of the obstacles), there would be problems. What sort of work could he do? And what friends would he have, apart from me? (Just now I recall him asking me whether I knew anyone in America who was a member of NA.) As for my friends, I knew that they would at first be surprised by Derek's sketchy education, his slang, his peroxided hair—no, that was gone now. But they would adjust, people always do. There's a good chance that they might get past objections based on background and like him for his pep and natural charm. (Otherwise they aren't friends.) You only have to go over a private list of acquaintances to realize that knowing about books and performing arts and so forth is no special guarantee of lovableness. Sometimes when we're together I compare all my "sophistication" to his lack of it and feel that he comes out miles ahead. He has a way, just in a glance, of showing up pretension for what it is. And I welcome that. From his side he seems eager to learn whatever it suits him to learn from me. As he ages, he will change, certainly. We'll be more alike, and partly that's because I will move in his direction also.

But what if he changes in an incompatible direction? What if, for example, he became more and more confrontational like Maeve? Since taking the job at the Higgins Trust he had begun to talk about politics more than he used to. But that's all right. At least gay political groups don't, at least so far, seem to be attracted to terrorism. The great end-of-century topic. I had tried to get a fix on it in *Listen to the Waves*, which was done in the early seventies, but never made any headway, partly because it didn't come out in favor of bomb-throwing. The characters, who were in a group like the Weather Underground, were based on some people I knew slightly. What I tried to show was that middle-class revolutionaries' reasons for participating are purely personal. They don't really know much about the underclass; they're angry at their parents (usually for good reasons). But their actions tend only to win sympathy for the conservative side—often as not among the underclass as well, who don't identify with them for a minute. The play had some good rants in it, too many to work as a well-tooled evening of theater, probably, and saying that that's the way people actually talked in 1970 doesn't get around the aesthetic issue. I have no plans to rewrite it.

On the other hand, Maeve's activism hasn't struck me up to now as being in any way blind or dangerous. She is vehement and unrelenting, but I don't disagree with her. Women and gay people shouldn't be treated like second-class citizens. Racism is dead wrong and the means used to reinforce it evil. The British ought to get out of Northern Ireland. And meanwhile no real progress seems to be being made on any of these fronts. What's the answer? Up to now, as far as I know, Maeve seems to have steered away from illegality and violence. But suppose she—and Derek, for that matter—lose patience and begin a new sort of involvement. I shouldn't jump to conclusions in advance, but there's no getting around the problem that, if they did become something more ... in deadly earnest, it would inevitably drive a wedge between us. Adding that to the series of circumstances—nationality, age, experience—dividing us would probably be final. But where are these speculations coming from, given that Derek hasn't suggested he would ever turn into a stone-throwing activist? It must have to do with him being with Maeve now and in some sense under her control.

SUSANNAH AND I are driving in her Peugeot over to the East End. Her quick glance at my jeans, boots, black cashmere shirt and leather jacket seemed to say that I would do. She is in fact wearing her jumpsuit, with two pins on the collar: a black-and-white miniature cartoon doll and a gold preying mantis with garnet eyes. When I ask her about them she says, "They're from a collection a friend of mine has been flogging all over town in order to raise some money so she and a friend can escape to Capri and open a shop there. To help her, everyone bought things, but I don't expect to wear them much. Tonight's OK, I suppose." Susannah seems to have put on extra eye makeup and her mane of textured hair is bunched and secured at strategic points to make an arresting asymmetrical effect.

"I've spoken to Corinne," she says. "Her brother's condition seems to be stabilizing."

"That's great news. I so want to talk to her. Do you have her number?"

"Yes, I'll give it to you. She'd like it if you rang. Of course she's bored sitting around all day with nothing to do. All the family are there, but that's a mixed blessing, I imagine." After a moment she asks, "Did she tell you she's thinking of going back?" I said she had mentioned it briefly. "I think she will pretty soon. Which is too bad, but I've been expecting it. I've known other New Yorkers. Eventually they miss Fifth Avenue or Tribeca or both and they go back. It's quite hopeless to compete. Knowing that, I always tried to keep things in perspective with us. And it's been lovely, she is adorable." Not knowing what to say, I just nod.

We are making our way down City Road, dim embodiments of minor commerce in the form of old brick buildings partly visible in regular flashes of intermittent lamplight as we drive past. At Old Street we turn left and then soon after onto Great Eastern Street. I've never been in this part of town before; there doesn't seem to be anything remarkable in it. I ask why the trendy people are moving there.

"We're not in Spitalfields quite yet. I don't know, really. It's cheap, or used to be. There are lots of old houses crying out to be redone. And then it's just seedy and sinister enough to attract artists. Did you know that Spitalfields was where Jack the Ripper's murders happened? No, I suppose not. I didn't know, either, but they're all very proud of it over here." As if to confirm what she is saying, a pub with the murderer's name on it glides past. Also, a Wren-style church that looks closed up and nonfunctioning.

"We must be there now."

"Yes, we are. That was the Spitalfields Market we passed just now." It isn't hard to see that Spitalfields is a rough equivalent for New York's SoHo (or Tribeca), where gritty wholesale, old buildings, and new renovations mix in together to compose just the right "anarchic" tone for artists. Susannah makes a few turns in a practiced manner. "White's Row. Here we are." She pulls over and parks, releasing a sigh. "Better lock up," she says.

The houses on the street are dark brick, about four stories, with little pediments over the doors, some grimy and dilapidated, others looking spruce with fresh white paint. We walk to one of these and ring the bell. The door is opened by a young man in waistcoat and ruffled shirt front, hair dark and short as teddy-bear fur, and a small diamond in his earlobe. Susannah smiles her way past, wafting a falsetto "Hallo, Jamie" toward him as I follow. The house is flagrantly bare of furniture, and the renovation, if it's still going on, far from complete. Someone has gotten as far as scraping down all the paneling to the original oak, but it's been left in its variously discolored and unvarnished condition. The windows are covered with plastic sheets and everything looks a little dusty. We go up a flight of stairs, my hand sliding along a smoothly worn banister that must be the original one. At the top we can hear the party-tone of a dozen competing voices coming from the front room.

This floor is a little more finished than the one below. Guests in little four- or five-headed knots stand around a long table with bottles of wine on it and some difficult-to-identify party foods. There is a grand piano covered in Handiwrap. When she sees me looking at it, Susannah whispers, "I suppose the cling film's to keep out dust." Then, louder, "Toby! There you are." She lets herself be kissed by a not quite young and not quite fat man with a long fringe of ash-blond hair around a bald pate. Over a jumpsuit in some soft gray material, he is wearing a black silk cape with a scarlet lining. A necklace of little ivory skulls completes the effect. We are introduced but it's apparent Americans don't interest him unless, possibly, they are younger and better looking. I leave them to talk, and sidle over to the drinks table.

There doesn't seem to be a barman so I pick up a glass and am about to reach for a bottle when a hand darts out and takes it. I look up at the owner of the hand as icily as I can, then realize he is trying to pour me a glass. I let him go ahead and then thank him.

"I'm just doing it to be polite," he says. An asymmetrical smile, half good humor, half irony is directed at me. He doesn't look as though he has come to an anarchist party, unless what an anarchist really wears is a tweed jacket and bow tie. We begin chatting and, in no special rush, conveying relevant information: what I'm doing here, where I'm staying, who I came with. He doesn't know Susannah but he's heard of her. He is the curator of a museum whose name I don't recognize. In London there must be a hundred or more, not all of which anyone is expected to know about.

Other guests have come in, some taking the evening's theme a little more seriously, that is, frivolously. A man in his thirties, wearing a tutu over black tights, with several dildoes strung around his waist. A woman with a Salvador Dali mustache, with what I hope is a stage prop machine gun slung over her shoulder. These and others in irreversibly chic but not necessarily anarchistic clothes mill around under big paintings of male and female nudes at play, bodies as much fat as muscular, not quite in the Botero category, but close. The curator tells me that these were painted by the host's lover, an Argentine coming into vogue just now, but for some reason not at the party tonight.

He is also responsible for some of the trompe-l'oeil that appears on the walls at unpredictable intervals, including a Tiepolo blue sky with theatrical clouds on the ceiling over the stairs. This is surrounded by a trellised balcony dripping painted ivy, two startled baroque heads peeping over to see who might be staring back at them. But the main attraction is the painting of a nude male figure suspended at the center in a crouched posture, like a deity parachuting down from Olympus, his neat genitalia plummeting head-on at the viewer. I see all this on my way up to the bathroom, which is on the top floor. When I pull open the door, the hinge squeaks too loudly for the effect not to be on purpose. Next to the door, at floor level, a clever trompe-l'oeil dog is scratching a flea behind his ear. Too bad. I step inside.

Later I stop at the top of the stairs and look down at the milling crowd, which is like so many others to be seen in New York, Berlin, Paris. Tonight's "anarchy" is a just a way to have fun, of course, but jokes point up realities. Makes you wonder what forces at work in today's artistic milieus make exotic attitudes, strange clothes, and ironic stance the rule. Clearly this rarefied populace is prospering under the "system" being mocked, receiving from it an admiration that often takes the form of solid payment. Of course that admiration is mixed with fear, bruised self-esteem, and not a little contempt as well, something like the feelings of a king for the mocking little court fool he can't do without. Because law and social rules are impersonal and inflexible, even those who are their chief beneficiaries now and then like to see them flouted. But court fools knew just what rung of the ladder they were on, and that their necks belonged to the king— nothing like the bland assurance of the Now People. Given that in some sense I see my own attitude as contestatory, why don't I identify? Partly accident: I didn't become attached to any of them at a crucial formative moment. Living a life marginal to the "system" that they have so much fun sending up, but marginal as well to them, I feel (as everybody does) that I have wider information; or have one less set of illusions. If only I could state in so many words exactly what it was I did own in place of those illusions, the pilgrim's progress would be a lot easier for me; not that I'm any good at taking things easy. I don't imagine tonight's guests would have much interest (except as visual images) in real politicos or actual terrorists, either, since the kind of change they instigate begins in fashion magazines and therefore has prescribed limits not aimed at anything so large as governmental or economic order. Really, it is astonishing to think of all the seething vehemence coming from so many different quarters, devoted to undermining the status quo in favor of no one really knows what. Certainly the trendies have no idea; or haven't broken silence yet. Whether anarchists or "bourgeois," we're all monumentally discontent with things as they now are, we say so constantly, in almost everything we do.

And what is it that we most despise about the present? Constraint? Violence? The make-it-or-break-it spirit of competition? Consumerism, or rather the consumption of so much that is ugly, tasteless, banal? The stupidity of the majority? Social inequality? Racism and oppression? The bankruptcy of family and community? Capitalist engulfment of the globe?

The snuffing out of the spiritual dimension? All of the above? Whatever the problems are, a battering-ram of negative criticism was long ago put in operation against the Fortress State and has never stopped hammering since. Impossible to tell whether the established order is about to topple or is quietly gathering strength—even from the attacks themselves. Our activists are certain that it is about to topple; if I doubt them, that may derive as much from a fear of what the collapse would then usher in (some form of Stalinism) as not being convinced by evidence offered that the day of reckoning is really that close at hand.

When I go down to the party again, it is very crowded, but I can see Susannah off in a corner absorbed in conversation with a young blonde who looks like a New Wave Marlene Dietrich, all in black sequins and rhinestones. I also see a couple I recognize but can't at first place. Hard scrutiny at last releases their names: it's Gillian Fournier and David Hunt. But where is her husband? It occurs to me that I may have got it all wrong that night at her house. Maybe David Hunt isn't gay after all, and they are having an affair. Do I go up to them? Well, in the spirit of anarchic risk—. Thinking she might not remember me, I reintroduce myself to Gillian. "Oh, Avery, you're here as well. It's been ages. Corinne tells me you've been having lots of fun." She smiles in a teasing way, and I realize that I'm glad to be talking to her. "I want to have you over for a meal again, and will get 'round to it soon, I've been busy," she says, reminding me that I haven't reciprocated but in a tone that lets me know single men aren't really blamed for that. "And you remember David," she says, gesturing toward him.

David and I smile amiably. I've forgotten why I didn't like him; it comes to me that being a Sanskritist was never his fault in the first place. Last October seems a long time ago. We stand and talk and I ask about Henrietta and the De Comptons.

Henrietta has gone to teach at Nottingham for a term, she does that sometimes. Julian De Compton was ill but is now better. He and his wife are collaborating on a new book, a sort of overview of the Pre-Raphaelite Brotherhood, which should be fascinating.

"How long have you known Toby?" she asks.

"About an hour. Susannah Kynaston brought me—do you know her?"

"Yes, I know her," Gillian answers, something unyielding in her voice making it clear that they don't get along. Which might explain why Corinne and she haven't been seeing much of each other—though obviously there were at least a few telephone calls. I explain that Corinne is away and that we are keeping each other company for an evening.

"Are you enjoying this? The anarchy and all?" (She herself is wearing a black leather jacket over a flowered blouse and a long skirt over boots.)

"Well, actually, no. But it's part of soaking up the London scene, I guess. This is the first time I've been to Spitalfields."

"It's getting to be the thing. Actually, this is where my family lived when we first came to England in the seventeenth century. We were Huguenot silk weavers. Spitalfields was the capital of the silk trade, right up through the nineteenth century."

"You wrote a book about that, didn't you? I haven't read it, but I know about it."

She smiles and says, "I had a look at it recently, and it holds up pretty well. Now that you've seen Spitalfields you might like some of it—but maybe not, it's very scholarly work."

David Hunt says, "No, it's first-rate. I recommend it."

Somewhat guiltily I promise to read it and then say I better get back to my companion. As people always do, I make the suggestion of lunch, this time with a real intention of following through, and then begin threading my way over to Susannah.

She turns aside from her Dietrich look-alike and says she was wondering where I was. "I was thinking maybe of going," I say.

"Oh," she says with a slight frown.

"I didn't mean you had to leave. I just wanted to let you know."

"Well, actually, I thought I might stay a few minutes more. Do you know your way back?"

"The cab driver will."

"Yes, that's true. So then, I'll ring if I hear from Corinne. Thanks for coming along with me, I hope you weren't too bored."

"No, it's been brilliant," I say, trying out Derek's all-purpose term of praise. Then I wish her goodnight, nodding as well in the direction of the blonde whose name I still don't know. I decide this particular occasion doesn't demand a goodbye-thank-you to the host and slip out unnoticed.

The street is quiet, partly lit by lamps, with no one in sight, no one to stop me from going off in what looks like the direction of Liverpool Station to find a taxi. Footsteps: a quick turnaround, but—Jack the Ripper isn't there. Obviously just an echo of my own steps against the brick façades. And this is London of the late eighties, when Madame Tussaud's heirs devote their skills only to the careers of football players, pop stars, fashion plates, renegade royals, and other anarchists. Black, shining pavement, old brick houses with new people and fashionable things glimpsed through the windows. Let me go home where I can miss Derek in peace.

Five

Reshuffling my notes and drafts, usually a homely pleasure, this morning counts for more than that. Work, because of its routine normality, makes other anxieties and terrors shrink a little. I'm feeling Derek's absence, and I guess, after all, that I want to tell him about my test results. I mean, I don't want to tell him but I have to and need to. I suppose he'll make his telephone call later on—or will he? They were going to Belfast today. He may not get to it, which adds another twinge of loneliness. So I'm kept hard at my task, as an antidote, the only one I have, to useless fidgeting.

Theophilus Cibber's section is fairly well outlined now. The keystone events are those surrounding his second marriage to Susannah Arne (sister of the composer). She began as a singer but under Colley Cibber's tutelage became an excellent actress—more popular than her husband, as even he must have recognized. Meanwhile he impoverished them both with his drinking and gambling, so that, when a moneyed admirer of his wife appeared, Theophilus chose to encourage the intimacy. William Sloper was a country gentleman, with even a certain refinement. The pinnacle of

the story comes when Theophilus compels his wife at gun-point to spend a night with her new gallant. And the rest is …
farce, at least for the rake. It took Susannah perhaps ten min-utes to see that Sloper was a better bargain than her husband;
she fell in fond love and the real thing shortly after. Ready cash was enough to appease Theophilus for a while, but when
he saw that he had lost his wife (along with her stage earn-ings) and that public knowledge of the liaison was affecting
audience reactions to him, he reversed his plan and began to rage and thunder against his rival.

He also sent a band of men to bring Susannah home. Sloper conspired with her family and staged a counter-abduction. By now she was pregnant with Sloper's child and wanted nothing more to do with Theophilus—who brought suit, asking for five thousand pounds in damages. The deci-sion went nominally in his favor, but the judge of the case thought ten pounds ought to do. Long-term creditors began baying at his heels louder than ever. He was made a laugh-ingstock at the theater. A litigious laughingstock, though, who brought suit again, on the grounds that her pregnancy had prevented Susannah from working and deprived him of income. The judge awarded him five hundred pounds, from which stiff legal fees had to be deducted. After this, he gave up on Susannah as a wife and as a source of income from the-atrical or any other performances.

The rest of his story will be hard to convey with anything like sober logic. We get, what, creditor-dodging; sporadic public appearances; disaffection of his father, and death of the same, after which he stages at the Haymarket a play of his own concoction called *The Insolvent, Or, Filial Piety*. Across intervening bodies of water, scandal is easily confused with renown, so Theophilus more than once consented to come over and draw crowds of the curious to Dublin's Smock Alley Theatre. Furthermore, he had begun to venture into enterprise, publishing a ghostwritten *Lives of the Poets* and laying plans for merchandising "cephalic snuff." An outline of a company had been set up, as a prelude to securing capital, when another bid for him to appear in Ireland came through. He took passage on an old trading ship, the *Dublin*; but then a storm blew up in the Irish Sea, the ship was wrecked and Theophilus drowned, in October of 1758. This "act of God" probably spared him other slower deaths, alcohol or syphilis; or a pistol shot in a tavern. He died while it was still possible for some observers to pity him. He certainly can't be described as one of fortune's favorites, but, after two absolving centuries, notoriety and a theatrical innovation or two have at least earned him a place in the *Dictionary of National Biography*. Since we didn't have to live with him, we can smile at the comic scenes in his life. One more theatrical casualty. One more casualty....

Yesterday I decided to follow through on an incidental project I'd set in motion more than two weeks ago. It had to do with the HIV test. I still have a lot of anger about Joshua's false negative results, but, after some thumping interior quarrels, I went and gave a blood sample. This was at the communicable disease clinic of St. Stephen's Hospital, down in Earl's Court. The London gay switchboard had told me it was one of the best places to go, if you felt that you must be tested. There have been several articles lately about the advisability of doing that; it's certainly more accurate than it used to be, and some of the new treatments look promising.

If I changed my mind, that had to do, first, with Derek. He had a clean bill of health to offer, and there was a chance I did also, but I couldn't be sure. He never once suggested I take the test after I explained about Joshua. And I don't think either of us considered the lovemaking we were having too tame. What were the motives then? Almost metaphysical, I guess: wanting to offer him a lover who had a clean slate, with no holdovers from the past, no liens on complete freedom. Or, if that wasn't the situation (if I was HIV-positive), then not to try to go ahead with the assumption that we had "forever." How else to make plans based on realistic estimates?

St. Stephen's Hospital is on Fulham Road. You go through several corridors and up a flight of stairs to get to the clinic, whose large well-lighted waiting room is, these days, filled with clients. The first visit, after a half-hour wait, they sent me to a consulting room where I was interviewed by a woman doctor, soft-spoken and solicitous. She wanted to know my reasons for taking the test; explained that testing positive didn't mean I had AIDS or would necessarily get it. I said I knew all this. "Should the results turn out to be positive," she said, "please remember that counseling here is available for you. It's not as though we'd simply give you the results and leave you to cope on your own. We're here to help." I thanked her, told her I hoped I wouldn't need it, and then went up to a room on the next floor to give my sample. A Scot with red hair, young and mechanically efficient, took three little vials of claret-colored venous blood from my arm and said to come back in two weeks, which I meant to do. But then Derek's trip interfered, and I didn't think about the test or getting results for it—in fact, I simply forgot. They telephoned yesterday and said results were in, if I wanted to pick them up. It was against clinic procedure to report on the results except in person.

I went back down to Fulham Road, walked upstairs, gave my name to the receptionist, and then sat down in the waiting room. Soft-core classical music was being piped in over our heads, but played apparently on a broken tape machine: the sound sagged in and out of pitch and rhythm in a way that enforced an irritated, helpless attention. Nearly all of those in the room were men, most of them young. One, looking very much out of place, was a middle-aged man in a pinstriped suit and horn-rimmed glasses. He sat upright and motionless in his chair, with feet placed together, and stared forward at nothing in particular. Two seats over from him was a twenty-year-old in denim jacket, hair a sort of dark brown mare's nest, his body slumped forward, his head resting on his hands. As I watched him, his name was called, and he left to go upstairs where the consulting rooms are. Since the exit was through the stairs, I knew I wouldn't see him again when he left with his positive or negative diagnosis.

By now I found myself, typically, staring at everyone who was there, people who might be living in the shadow of frightening possibilities. There was a bodybuilder wearing a tight T-shirt, his brown hair streaked blond. Despite the eyes of a number of the men patients trained intently on him, he looked neither right nor left, gazing fixedly at a magazine, without, so far as I could tell, ever turning a page. A young Indian woman in a long dress sat next to the window with her eyes closed. Someone who looked as though he might be a dancer, with a black leotard under his jacket, one leg bent, one stretched out, let his head loll around in a complete circle and ticked his foot back and forth, presumably to keep tendons limber. His name was called. He walked to the exit stairs past a framed tomb rubbing, gold impressions on a black background, the funeral portrait of some medieval seigneur with a Norman name. Taped orchestral music swooped and wobbled. The dancer disappeared to the sound of steps as he climbed up to the consulting room. A young couple came in, both dressed in King's Road boutique clothes. They gave their names to the receptionist and sat down. The man in the pin-striped suit was called, and responded with a brisk, leather-shod step. A feeling of dizziness or disorientation began to steal over me. I noticed that my heart was pounding, really thumping, and I wondered if the others heard it—no, of course they couldn't. But something must have looked odd; I caught the questioning eye of a mustached man about my age wearing a striped shirt and black jeans. Or was he just cruising? Even here? A Strauss waltz came on, swooping and diving with its own and the tape's crazed rubato. The gold tomb rubbing shone where a ray of sunlight hit it. The Indian woman was called and padded out noiselessly. I looked at my nails and began picking a bit of dirt from under one of them. And if the results were positive? Was there still time to join one of the undergrounds and use my single trump card, my life, in some meaningful "action," an immolation that might serve a purpose instead of amounting to little more than a random accident? But that was just an empty attitude, a bit of ironizing meant to avoid face-to-face confrontation with finalities. I felt a light wave of nausea thrum up through my throat, then told myself to be calm. The music staggered on; a cloud temporarily overpowered the sun. I heard my name pronounced, but as from a long distance, miniaturized, crackling with faint static. I stood up, swaying a little, and made my way to the exit.

Afterwards—after the consultation (seated) in the doctor's office and the session with their counselor (they insisted), and after yet another blood sample for a second test, I walked back downstairs and out the glass doors into the traffic of Fulham Road. And felt nothing, a sort of void. I believed and didn't believe what they said. I had known all along; but of course it couldn't be real. If it was real, the cars and pedestrians would all have stopped in their tracks and stared at today's marked man. It wouldn't all continue as it always has; the sky would crack open or something. You can swallow only so much absurdity and then no more; I had to stop myself from laughing. And of course I'd secretly known all along. Which would account for the absence of shock or outrage. Just a numbness—a boredom, really, in the way that death was boring.

The question is whether to tell Derek now or when he comes back. I should wait, and yet I don't want to. There's no one else to tell. I certainly don't plan to mention anything to Adele. Or not yet. It seems melodramatic, I don't think I could convey it to her the right way. Telling Derek would be a sort of practice, making it begin to seem real. Anyway, he has to know, unfair for him not to. True, he never asked me to take it in the first place, and I suppose that, as long as he was willing to live with the chance that I might be "positive," it might not make any difference now that I am. But that's easy to say. Because everything between us has gone so well, I was lulled into thinking that I'd somehow become invincible, free from any sort of threat. So much good luck crowds out the possibility of bad, right? The results were simply going to confirm the happy premonition I had already felt deep down.

Techniques of self-deception (rationalization, wishful thinking, superstition) always stir feelings of solicitous protectiveness in me, whether I see them from the outside or inside. Self-deception has to go by the board now, but I don't hate myself for having the will to illusion before. Or maybe— just maybe—the test was a false positive, and I will be all right. Here I have to laugh, tears or no tears. And I think of Joshua, see him in my mind, with the most gentle expression of concern possible on his face.

The soft sunlight coming into the living room puts a strange cast on everything this afternoon. It's still bothering me somewhat that this is the day Derek was going to Belfast, as though he has slipped a bit further out of range. I wish he'd never gone at all. Well, you have to visit your parents now and then. Walking over to the dining table, I notice that nearly all of the petals of the roses he brought a couple of nights ago have fallen from the stem, and the water in the vase is greenish. I'm just going to leave it there for the time being.

As a change of subject, I think back to my telephone conversation with Corinne two days ago. Her brother is on the mend and she thinks she'll be back next week. Glad of that. I told her about going to the party in Spitalfields with

Susannah. Not everything about it, but just to give her an idea. She seemed only mildly interested—understandable since she'd been spending most of her days in hospital waiting rooms. I thought how far away and trivial all these doings in London must seem to her from the perspective of the intensive care unit.

Funny how it's possible to sit in an armchair with the newspaper, reading, or mulling things over, or just staring at an end table, and have a quarter of an hour pass without being able to remember a single thought you've had. Then, looking up at the tree branches through the window, I suddenly am reminded of the time the street gang threw a stone at Derek. And the cut on his forehead. What made me think of it? Well, there's an article here in the paper about a racial incident in Brixton—probably that.

Might as well make a pot of coffee. No point just sitting there like a paralytic waiting for the nurse. Actually, there's some mocha-java left over from this morning, which I can reheat. (But stop it before it boils.) When it's reheated, I pour myself a cup and find myself looking out the window. For no special reason, memories of my first weeks on this street come flooding up. The loneliness, the disorientation, before I had met Corinne or Maeve or Derek. Oh, and that afternoon I wandered into St. Martin in the Fields and heard someone deliver a eulogy for his lover.... Today I miss you, Joshua, as I haven't for a while. Of course I can see you plain as day, you're smiling a painful smile and nodding, but I wish you were here to talk some of this over with, right now, and not feel teary. Outside, a taxi rumbles past along the curve of Gloucester Crescent, a single passenger in the rear seat.

When the telephone rings, loud and shrill in the quietness of the living room, I jump in my chair, then get up and answer it. A crackling noise and then: "Avery! I can only talk a second. We've had some trouble. Some of the Oranges came into the pub where we were with Maeve's friends, and there was a fight, I mean, one of them got shot. He's alive but we're going to lie low for a while, or we may try to get back to Dublin, I'm not sure yet what they want us to do but—. Look, Avery, I can't talk now, I've called my parents, they're expecting you to come. I'll telephone you later, tomorrow maybe."

"ARE YOU ALL RIGHT?"

"I'm OK, but Maeve has a sprained arm. Listen, I have to hang up. When I can, I'll ring my parents—g'bye." Click. I knew it, I knew it. And now? Have to find him. I'll go there and find Derek and Maeve.

Six

A piece of luck for me is that, when emergencies arise, I react by becoming suddenly very calm, seeing what steps need to be taken and in what order. Derek's grenade of information had gone off. I sat for a minute in the living room, letting the impact subside, and then made two telephone calls: one for a seat on the next Aer Lingus flight and another to Derek's parents. The international operator seemed to take an outrageously long time to make the connection. When a man's hoarse, low-pitched voice answered (Derek's father), it was clear from the strained mixture of anger and interrogation in his tone that he had been told. I identified myself, described the frightening telephone call, and asked if he knew anything more than I did. "I know nothing," he said, "I'm only waiting. Do *you* know anything?"

I repeated to him what Derek had said and then proposed coming to Dublin. "This is a terrible thing that has happened," I said. He excused himself and whispered something away from the phone. Then he came back on and said, "Mrs. Findlater and I would be pleased if you could stay with us."

"Thank you, but I'm not sure that's the best plan, since your house may be being watched. I'll stay in a hotel. I hope I can see you, though, while I'm there."

"Any time. We'll be here waiting." We said goodbye.

I took one change of clothes in an overnight bag that could be put under the seat, so there wouldn't be any delay for baggage. When I climbed into the taxi and told the driver to take me to Gatwick, his face lit up; disaster always benefits somebody. Once at the airport, travel preliminaries went ahead at a dreamlike pace, though I felt an odd panic as I passed through security check. I knew the flight lasted something like three quarters of an hour and so was a little surprised when the stewardess brought her passengers a sandwich. I wasn't hungry, but she looked too authoritarian—a bit older than most stewardesses and with a large head of hair—to be told no. My seatmate, a man in his fifties, opened the wrapper of his, sniffed it, and put it aside. Noticing that mine was still wrapped, he said, "Yes, I wouldn't trouble. A bit off, mine was." I gave a half-smile for complicity's sake and was about to go back to the travel magazine when he said, "You're Irish?"

"American. Of Irish extraction, partly. You must be, yourself," I said because of his voice and easy manner, and perhaps his pale green shirt under a tweed jacket in forest colors.

"Dublin born and bred. Business takes me to London four times a year. Now that's done till the next one."

"Actually, I wonder: do you know of a good hotel in Dublin? I didn't have time to book."

He gave me a once-over and said, "You could try Buswell's. A bit pricey, but not as bad as some. They don't usually have vacancies, but this time of year—." A gesture completed the thought. His red cheeks bunched up around his eyes as he smiled. "It's just behind the Shelbourne. Do you know Dublin?"

"A little. Over by Stephen's Green, you mean. Sounds ideal."

"You could do worse. And if you require worse I can make suggestions for that as well. I know the town all through." But he could see that was as far as I wanted to take it, so he nodded and went back to his paper. Later he got up and went to talk to the stewardess. When we landed and were beginning to move to the exit, I heard her say, "So will I be seeing you again, Harry?"

"Please God," he answered and made his way to the door.

Once in the terminal, I asked the travelers' desk to get me a room at Buswell's. A room was available for two nights only, but that should be enough time. Outside, a cold, cloudy day. The taxi sped into town, wound among the streets of the old city, and dropped me off at the awning of the hotel, where a hatted doorman stood, indulgently sizing me up as I got out and paid the driver. The hotel was a bundle composed of several adjacent Georgian houses, not over five floors high. Inside there was a fire at the hearth in the small lounge, tables and wood chairs of no particular period, a bar and restaurant off to the side, the bar beginning to fill up and emit noise and smoke. I was checked in by a clerk with enough personality to avoid coldness, yet not toppling over into familiarity. It felt odd to be a traveler again—and with the mission I had.

All right, and what exactly was I here to do? Time to get that clear, I thought, as I looked around my small room, which was comfortable because not at all posh or fussy. After I had telephoned the Findlaters and invited them to the hotel, I put things away, then stretched on the bed for a few minutes. Possibilities: that Derek and Maeve might have come back from wherever they were and would reappear tonight or tomorrow. But that didn't sound very likely. What else? That things would take longer, after who knew what sort of machinations. It had sounded as though some concrete planning

was being done, but that the timetable hadn't been set up yet.
Derek had said he would telephone as soon as he knew. If
only he could have given a clearer idea of what was going
on—but then his friends probably didn't want him to. A final
possibility was that neither Maeve nor Derek would ever
resurface again, but that was the black hole among eventuali-
ties, one I had to avoid thinking of.

I put on a tie and a crew-necked sweater and went downstairs. A wing chair next to the fire was empty so I sat in that.
A few minutes later I saw a middle-aged couple come in the
door and look timidly around. I went up to them and said to
the man, "Mr. Findlater?" He looked relieved and brought his
wife forward, who nodded and tried to smile, dark green eyes
crinkling up and almost closing under the pressure of emotion. She had short gray-brown hair and wore a little gray felt
hat on the back of her head. Her gray suit wasn't new; the
pleats of her white blouse were neatly pressed and a black rib-
bon fastened with a gold pin at the neck completed the effect.
Her husband, large-boned and gray haired, wore a sweater
under a brown jacket, but no tie. We went back into the lounge
and sat down. I noticed that he walked with a slight limp.

"Would you like some tea—or a drink?" looking first at
her and then at him. They both convinced me they wanted
nothing at all. We sat for a moment absorbing each other. "You
haven't heard anything more from Derek," I said.

"Nothing—nor nothing from Maeve," Mr. Findlater said,
shaking his head.

Choking back a sob, his wife said, "We're so worried about
our children. This is the most terrible thing." Something in her
voice suggested refinement, and I caught on that she was a sort
of D.H. Lawrence's mother, a little above her husband, somewhat his captive. Maeve's and Derek's personalities suddenly
made sense as a response to that parental difference. Maeve,
with her feminism and political involvements, had given a

new turn to her mother's stance of offended superiority. Derek played up belonging to the working class like his father; but with the difference that this particular son was gay. I realized that I'd never asked Derek whether he'd told his parents. Meeting them and listening to them, my guess was that he hadn't. In order to undertake such a project, you have to have some assurance that the words used will convey shared meanings. These people, who came of age around 1950, might have some idea what "poof" or "queer" meant, but those words didn't describe Derek. If he told them he was "gay," would they understand what was being communicated? That he was a normal bloke who was attracted to others like himself and, more to the point, did something about it. And who otherwise made no claims to being cursed or blessed, to being court jester or renegade, pariah or redeemer, however much the present day might need one of those figures to shed light on its confusions.

Derek's parents seemed glad that he had an ally in me— someone older, more settled, and financially secure (not that I really am). Their son's friend was American, which effectively clouded over what might otherwise need explaining. It somehow made sense that an American would take an interest in Derek, who, Lord knows, had run a bit wild but then straightened out after all and was a good boy, no better son anywhere—and now he and his sister were in this terrible trouble. Maeve was as clever as they come, they loved her for it, but she'd gotten ideas, they'd known there'd be trouble some day. Now what could they do?

"Did you inform the police?"

"Del said we mustn't," Mr. Findlater said. "But if we don't hear soon, I'll do it all right. You can't sit by forever."

"How long do you think you'll wait?"

He paused. "Well, surely, if I don't hear in three days."

"Do you think we should tell them now?" Mrs. Findlater asked.

"I would. But I can see the arguments against it. And, obviously, the decision has to be yours."

"I don't want them to get in trouble with the authorities. But if I don't hear in three days' time—." Findlater seemed to be underlining his position as paterfamilias and commander-in-chief. "If there's one thing I've learned in thirty-five years of driving the bus, it's that a little patience pays off in the long run. Those that won't wait five minutes, they're the ones who miss the opportunity." He folded his hands in a way that showed me we were going to have to deal with the emergency according to his lights. I sat without saying anything.

"We should be going, dear." Mrs. Findlater stood up, and so did we. She held out her hand and said, "We do appreciate your interest and concern. And how long will you be staying in Dublin?"

"Until I hear something. They may end up returning directly to London, in which case I would go back. You wouldn't necessarily have to. You have my telephone number here at the hotel."

She nodded. "The instant we hear anything we'll ring." I thanked them for coming as we walked to the door. When Findlater turned to nod goodbye, something in the way the light struck his face emphasized a resemblance to Derek, and my throat tightened. I must have stared a little; the blue eyes in his rugged face blinked and then he went out the door. I watched them walk past a waiting taxi and farther down the street—I suppose to catch a bus. After they left it occurred to me that the traditional presentation of prospective bride-groom to parents had taken place, though without the betrothed being present. Under the pressure of anxiety and incongruity, I felt terrible. Magazines scattered around the lounge looked monumentally pointless. For form's sake and to fill time, I had dinner in the hotel restaurant, putting food that I didn't want in my mouth and mechanically swallowing it. All around me was cigar smoke as an accompaniment to political discussions from men dining with other overweight men, who glanced at me, took in my solitude and returned to their roast beef, cauliflower, potatoes, and comments on the balance of trade. The soft yellow light from the little lamp at my table fell on the white linen and did what it could to soothe. With an intensity like seasickness, I missed Derek.

AFTER BREAKFAST I went out for a walk, first through Stephen's Green and then over to Merrion Square. Cold air but clear skies. Times like these you inevitably drift into magic thinking. I looked at every passing car, every fellow stroller, hoping to see who it couldn't possibly be. But then you never know. The houses on the square were solidly Georgian, except for a corner one that had added a sort of elaborate loggia with ornamental detail painted blue and white. At the end of a vista, a neoclassical church rang its bells and summoned Sunday morning worshippers inside. I went back to the hotel, checked for messages and found none. After sitting in the lounge for a while and attempting to read *Town and Country*, I gave up and went out again, this time down Grafton Street and over toward Trinity. But there was no reason to go inside. I pushed on down to the quays, getting to O'Connell Bridge but not crossing it, on down to Wood Quay and the Capel Street Bridge. Across the Liffey sunlight emphasized neoclassical shadows in the architecture of the Four Courts, crowned with its domed columns, a small Pantheon or graceful Temple of Love atop the halls where sentences are handed down. Trembling waves on the river rose and fell, dousing and darkening a green smear of algae just above the water line on the gray stone blocks of the quay. Staring at the churning waters I felt a faint nausea as the whirlpool of feelings—disorientation, fear, mourning—began turning and accelerating inside. I was still nursing an irrational hope that I would catch sight of

Derek somewhere—if not on the street, then through the window of a pub, or down by the water. And that it would all be over and he would come back with me. Even though I knew this was nonsense, I let myself think those thoughts just to break the monotony of pain. After a while, I decided to go back to the hotel.

No messages. I spent the afternoon in my room, sleeping, waking up, reading, sleeping. At five I telephoned the Findlaters. No word from Derek. Would I like to come there for dinner? I told them I still didn't think it was a good idea, since there might be some sort of surveillance. I would wait at the hotel. Derek's mother got on, thanked me for my kind support, and said I should return to London whenever I wanted to, she was sure they could manage on their own. And that we should hope for the best, it was in God's hands. I thanked her, agreed that it was, and asked her to let me know the instant she had news. We said goodbye.

As I was getting dressed for dinner the room telephone rang. Shirt still unbuttoned, I answered and recognized Derek's father's voice.

"Hello? Mr. em—Mr. Walsh, yes. Findlater here. Yes, my son just rang. There'll be a delay of a day or two. He says he thinks it best if you go back to London. He'll get in touch with you there."

"Did he say he was going back there directly?"

"He didn't inform us, but he thinks it's best if you go back. Should you need any assistance, why—."

"Oh, no, not at all. Well, if that's what Derek wants, I'll go back. There's a flight early tomorrow. But—if he telephones again, you might tell him where I am in case he wants to reach me here."

"I did inform him of that," Mr. Findlater said. We both thanked each other and said we hoped it would be settled soon.

The sleepless night that followed I got through by a combination of silent incantation, deep breathing, and a couple of aspirin. Next morning I telephoned the Findlaters to see whether there had been any new message. No, but they wondered whether someone might not be trying to reach me in London, so perhaps I would be well advised to return. No argument against that. Off I rushed without a backward glance at the hotel, the city, or the green land our plane was plucking us away from. The morning flight was full with what were obviously businessmen. I talked to no one, read my newspaper, tried not to feel sick as the jet wobbled down through the clouds.

THE FLAT seems stale and empty now, the more so in that as the door pushes open I seem to hear a noise and feel a rush of hope that Derek might be there waiting for me. Pure imagination, but not impossible, given that I was told to return. The bag sits on the sofa, and I can't bring myself to take it into the empty bedroom and unpack. Instead I wander around the living room, going over the past two days, not so much searching for clues as for a sense that I have done all I could. Yes, no doubt I have, but what now? Pronounce the usual mantras about patience, grind your teeth if you have to, and remind yourself that the world is real.

Soft white cloudlight filters through the glass enclosure around the dining table where the vase with Derek's dead roses still sits, the water all evaporated now, the petals fallen to the table and dried to a brutal dark purple. But I don't sweep them up and throw them out. No, I slide into one of the chairs and put my head down on my folded arms. I can see that the chances aren't necessarily in favor of this all turning out well. In the small dark cave where my head rests, dry sobs, by their own volition, rise up from the gut, small, steady convulsions shaking me into a kind of forgetfulness that blots out where I am, the image of the missing person, and the prospect of the hours and possibly the days ahead of me.

Seven

Since it was a Monday morning no different on the surface from any other, I made up my mind to go through the motions of life. As I pulled on a pair of corduroys, a shiver went through me at the memory of several scenes from last night's dream proscenium. I also had a flashback to one of final afternoons at New York Hospital last spring. Adele and I were sitting together in the glazed stupor that overtakes anyone who has been sitting in waiting rooms too long. I have a mental picture of Adele in a pale lilac blouse with an orange scarf pinned around her neck; and her sad expression, something more resigned than despair. We'd just been told that Joshua had lost his sight and were debating whether to bring it up with him. He hadn't been in possession of all his mental powers for a while, but still he did talk to us and in some sense depend on us for an understanding of what was happening. This one defeated us, though, and we ended up never devising any special formula to sum up his situation for him. Mostly we just sat and held his hand and made reassuring noises, while stroking his hot, dry forehead.

Instead of replaying all that again, a slouching, unshaven stand-in for me boiled water for coffee, put bread slices in the toaster, and turned on the BBC. I looked beneath the slot, and sure enough there was mail, in particular, a letter from Robert saying that plans were in the final negotiation stage for a Hampstead production of *You Had to Be There*. News that might under other circumstances have sparked a complacent surge of self-satisfaction today left me hollow.

When I got to the desk, a third cup of coffee at my side, I whispered "So far so good" to the stacks of papers there and began pulling some of them out for inspection. Within a few minutes, though, it became clear that nothing much was going to make sense today. Notes on their little cards, drafts in the big red notebooks, might as well have been written in Sanskrit. It was all so much gibberish, the names, the place-names, the pointed citations with odd Augustan spellings and expressive capital letters. Southampton Square, Marshalsea prison, *The Non-juror*, "... impatient to doe me that sort of Favour," Henry Brett, the Lord Chamberlain, Anne Oldfield, *The Relapse*, Bedlam, *Raging Madness*.... Slow down. As an exercise in keeping calm, I set myself the task of just sitting there and putting the desk in order; that way, when all of this was over, I could get back to work. Put this set of notes in that envelope, this handwritten draft, folded, in that notebook. Arrange the notebooks in chronological or thematic order....

And then I did something I knew was irrational, and so of course useless in the present dilemma. But still somehow helpful. It was the part about Theophilus's death in Dublin. I wrote up some "notes" from an imaginary book, one that explained how in fact he hadn't drowned in the Irish Sea. How he had been found clinging to a ship's spar, brought to shore, and nursed to health. That was my answer to what-ever or whoever assigns destinies to creatures with few defenses. I felt pleasure and defiance in typing my own anti-factual sentence: "Theophilus survived and even acquired a more realistic estimate of his own life, along with an idea or two how to improve it." This wasn't the first time I'd practiced home-brew magic, so I wasn't all that scandalized by this particular spell. It occurs to me that I may never finish the biography, if only because I prefer fiction to fact, which seems almost the same thing as fate.... And so, with irrational pastimes, coffee, and tightrope-walking on the lines of my own nervous system, the morning passed.

To leave the flat was to risk missing a possible telephone call, but there was no food in the fridge. Around twelve-thirty I scuttled out to the street market on Inverness and snatched up eggs, cheese, some bread, and a few vegetables, swearing under my breath during the long waits at each stall. Three of the vendors got to keep their change when they rummaged too long in their coin boxes. On the brisk walk back a quick glance at the sign of the Irish harp at The Harp unleashed a wild shearing sensation around the thought that if I looked inside Derek and Maeve might be there. Not likely. I also wondered (bizarre concern at this point) whether he had managed, in hiding or wherever he was, to avoid drinking. I was glad not to be under any such obligation, in fact, decided to have wine with lunch, to see if it helped.

When I opened the door of the flat, some half-perceived nudge or suspicion made me look down at the floor. A folded piece of paper lay just beyond the sill—it had obviously been slipped under the door. I put the bag of groceries on a chair and picked up the note. It said: EXPECT TELEPHONE CALL 11 A.M. TOMORROW TUESDAY. Hand-printed, but not Derek's writing. A jolt went through me and my heart was pounding as I sat down to reread it. Ordinary paper, ordinary pencil, no distinguishing characteristics. But it meant Derek and Maeve were all right—at least it probably did. What would the note have said if they weren't? Assuming they were, why not telephone *today* and say so? Hopeless to try to second-guess any of this. I sat there as much in a rage at not being told more as relieved to get news, any news, even this cryptic fragment.

Wait, the Findlaters might have heard something. I went to the telephone and set up a call. When Derek's father answered, breathless and hoarse again, I told him about the note. "Yes, yes," he said, "we've had one as well. Eleven tomorrow morning. That means they're safe, surely. I wish I knew more," he added, his voice darkening in tone.

"And obviously it means they have friends in London as well as Dublin," I said. "I guess we don't know for certain where they'll reappear, here or there."

"We'll know tomorrow, certainly," he said. "We were just about to ring you. Mrs. Findlater sends her regards and asks me to thank you for your concern."

"Thank you. Goodbye."

I could see that he was more reassured by the messages than I had been. There are much-discussed drawbacks to having an active imagination, and mine is more in tune with drama than anything else, with plenty of energy for speculation about the possibilities—multiplied, in this case, by the separate Irish and English venues involved.

Lunch was going to be perfunctory, so I followed through on the idea of throwing in some non-perfunctory burgundy to go with it. Three glasses swallowed down along with a little wrinkled yellow omelette went without any persuasive result, so I finished the bottle. Around three o'clock or so, I fell asleep on the sofa, to the sounds of bare branches scraping against the glass of the alcove. Sit here until....

Waking came at the foregone conclusion of darkness; because of unroutine circumstances I hardly knew where in Zambia or who I was. But then lucidity came back and told me all of it again. My throat burned, my head throbbed, so I went into the kitchen and poured a glass of soda; then added some whisky to it, sloshing it around the glass as I went back into the living room to switch on lamps. Half past five. Clockwatching goes better with a drink in hand, but even so—*tick-tick-tick*—-eventually palls. The glass finished, I decided to relocate to the bedroom. Bit of a mess. The master forced the servant in me to put away some clothes that were lying on a chair and, without exactly making the bed, at least pull bedclothes up to the top and stack the pillows. Fluffing them, I felt something under the bottom pillow and pulled out a little condom packet, which looked innocent in a sinister way. I threw it on the floor.

Do something, keep busy. Shuffling some papers and books strewn over the top of the bureau, I came across the photograph of Hypnos that Corinne had given me. Too late to point out that I ought to have gone over the flat and made it less of a minefield. Once again the set of the cheek and the mouth reminded me of Derek's face. The bronze mask, eye-sockets empty, was still caught up in its own internal fable, lips seeming to be on the point of forming a word. From the left temple, an unfurling wing of dream sprouted and became, like a disease, communicable. I stared at it for a while. I've got to get out of here, I thought.

Heat didn't seem to be doing much in the radiators, and the chill air more or less vetoed the idea of a shower, but I forced myself to take one anyway. When I came back into the bedroom, wrapped in my bathrobe and toweling my hair, there, sitting underneath the lamp, was Hypnos again, magnetizing me toward him. It suddenly came to me that I didn't have a photograph of Derek. And what if—. Push that thought aside. The first thing to do when he came back would be to get a camera and commandeer someone to take snapshots. But this lack of an available image underlined his absence. Sharp pains in the chest told me just how much I missed him, just how tightly wound among my ideas and

hopes he had become. Which I might not have known if he
had never gone away in the first place. Until he returned,
Hypnos would have to serve as his likeness. I brought it very
close to my eyes until the details—eyes, cheeks, lips—began
to swim and blur ... then put it aside.

Going over possible projects for the next few hours, I
decided on dinner out; being in public reflexively calms you
down. Dressing went fast, but there was a wait while my hair
dried. Then I slipped out the door and walked to Parkway to
find a cab. I told the driver to take me to St. Martin's Lane,
which he seemed already to expect at this pre-theater hour. I
could settle back and let the phantasmagoria of early evening
traffic stream past without having to think about anything.

The Cafe Pelican, the place I had in mind, was only a cafe,
but then solitary diners would be less noticeable there. In fact,
you can get small tables up near the window that make it look
as though you're waiting to meet someone before going to
your play. One of these window tables was vacant, so I took
it. A whisky and soda was the first order of business; trying to
find something on the menu that seemed possible to eat when
you have no appetite could come after. During the wait, the
active little video of daydreams projects easily onto a white
tablecloth, which you can depend on having here.

The windows directly onto the street are framed in green
with brass trim, part of the bistro chic of the place. The waiters (some of them women) wear black ties and trousers with
a large white apron draped over them, which makes me wonder why they don't call it the Cafe Penguin. Plenty of time to
note all this since I have no distractions and nothing at all I
want to think about. A steady stream of cars—headlights and
red taillights—glides past, stop, start up again. Dark silhouettes of pedestrians tramp by, breathing steam. The noise of
traffic, the fracas of ticket distribution hour in the West End.
Just opposite in fact is a theater, a Corinthian portico blazing

with light, a line of beaded white bulbs turning on and off to give the illusion of a series of bright jewels sliding 'round and 'round the marquee. Theatergoers go up the steps into the lobby. Traffic slides by with unbroken confidence, part of the irreality.... Why does the first drink always go so quickly?

A couple at the next table get up and leave their tea behind. It occurs to me that the several objects on their table are a little family. A small metal teapot, smoothly armored in silver-gray, is Father. The porcelain creamer is Mother. Blue-rimmed teacups in their saucers are Tim and Jane in their sailor outfits. An aunt and uncle stand modestly apart from things, one salt, one pepper. The sugar bowl is the car they have all just stepped out of, waiting for Father to give them directions. What he's about to tell them is—I'm not sure. Oh yes, they're all going to Brighton, a seashore town, something like that. And then a mugger comes up to them—.

"Do you want to order?" the waiter with short hair asks me. I fumble with my menu and tell him to bring me a glass of wine and a roast beef sandwich—annoyed at being interrupted, just as he is annoyed that I'm not ordering a complete dinner. He repossesses the menu and, when I look back at the Tea family, they are gone; one of the other waiters has taken them away.

But I have wine instead of tea. It comes before the sandwich and goes down without any fuss. So that when the sandwich does come, I order another glass, which also arrives quickly. Overheard fragments of other people's talk do for dinner conversation while I swallow bread and cold roast beef. "... no, he put up in some flash hotel in Kensington, he doesn't usually stay with me nowadays." "She thinks I'm ready for that part, but I want to wait until I've got it well and truly down." "I thought I was going bananas, but then he told me he had brought it himself." "I like Michael a lot, really, but I don't fancy him and he knows that." "No, we were going to dine at Caprice. As it was desperately crowded we decided to come here. But it's not much better, is it?" "Actually, Faber nowadays are very different to what they used to be." "If she hadn't insisted on cold cash, we'd be home and dry already, but...." I put down the rest of the sandwich, wipe my hands on the napkin, and glance up at the window. Some effect of reflection superimposes the transparent image of one of the waiters over the dark street outside. Toplit and in high contrast his face registers as a series of shadowed hollows; it looks like—what? A trendy bunching of the hair to one side gives his head an odd asymmetry, like a wing.... Oh yes: Hypnos. He looks like Hypnos. My wineglass is empty. But I'm tired of wine and this time I order whisky. That goes pretty quickly; and so I decide I should go, too. Exactly where doesn't matter.

The street outside to begin with. Into chilly dampness, but I don't mind that much. The rest of them have all slipped into the safety of a nice overheated theater. Should I find a movie? Wait, here's one: *The Sacrifice.* No. But do I really want to be outside, trudging along like this? There's that bar, the one I've never been in. I step down to the entrance and push through the door.

Darkness and dimness, boys in the latest Armani or Yamamoto idea posted all around. I can't face it—but I don't have to, I'll drink at the bar with my back to everything. Unfortunately there is a mirror, but then of course there *would* be (to use the conditional tense of sardonic probability). Then I'll look down at the counter, which in practice means my drink. Disco music, thump, thump, thump, but no one's dancing. A lunge to the gut, the piano and steel chords breaking into bright shards over our heads. And then her voice, Miss Disco Universe, drawing the note along behind her like a stretched-tight leather cord, whipping it from side to side and throwing in quick kinks of vocal ornament, up to the top of the lucite-and-steel sonic staircase and then a greased swoop down into some resonant basement where the captive groans and sobs. *I'll never let you go-o-o-o....* This is not soothing. I don't like it here. May I finish the drink, pay, and go-o-o-o. The word that follows me out the swinging door is *Lo-o-ove....*

Fighting the crowds in Leicester Square is always good for a comedy turn. Punks with heads selectively balded push their ebon leathers past me, one saying, "Dead right, dead on...." Anonymous aggression of the crowds. And who is this human casualty? His face misshapen, the result it's fair to guess of fetal alcohol syndrome. He looks at me, grimaces with his teeth, a dirt-caked hand held out to beg. "I don't want to stay in the Shelter. There's this Killer, 'e got claws like hammers, I'm afraid of him. 'e gets at me if I go there, 'elp me please, can't you give me anyfing." I ward him off with some change and get past. That man there, fallen in vomit, is he awake? But not moving. Moving now, covered with vomit. Dead on. Straight on. If I can get Derek back. French tourists, eating from cups. "M'enfin c'est vrai que Paul il a le Sida ou non?" "Qu'est-ce que j'en sais, moi, c'est pas mon affaire." *THE SWISS CENTRE,* in blazing lights. Maybe they were Swiss from Geneva. Movies, movies, but I don't want any of them now. Just wash along with the foot traffic.

And while you're at it, Piccadilly. What if he were here. But that's the last place. Silhouetted against the light, in a frozen arabesque, the Angel, hypnotizing all of them gathered around the base of the monument. The faces, most of them young, in three-quarter profile, gazing absently upward or to one side, never looking back at you, waiting to be approached. Derek isn't one of them, thank God, but where is he? A stampede of cars and buses, lights wheeling and crossing. Joshua, please help me find him. The swirl of faces, West Indian, Pakistani, Mediterranean, and, what, Irish? Clamor of voices gusting up toward the black sky. If I close my eyes, I can see him so clearly, the blond hair—no, not any more, brown, and the ears, and the green eyes blinking at me and then admitting me. Nothing could be so sad.... Have to get out of here. If I cross to that corner, then across again, I'll get to Shaftesbury Avenue. Taxis up that way.

No, nothing along here, go farther on. Wardour Street. That's where his church is, maybe he's there. Or am I confusing it? Was farther down, maybe. No, there it is. Dark, for Monday night in the night city. Nobody around. They don't keep them open, do they? I could try. Of course not, just as I knew, not open. "Come back tomorrow." Why do I just stand here. To kick it, that's why. This is for you! *I-i-i-i*, that hurt! Lunatic to kick the door so hard. All right but you had no business getting him into trouble, he hasn't done anything, he's been good, and I want him back. GIVE HIM BACK! Choking, just leaning against the fence and choking. I want him back. Remember that time we took a walk in Regent's Park and he tripped and fell and scraped his knee but said it didn't hurt, only later it began to bleed....

"Um, excuse me. Aren't you Del's friend?"

Wait, I know this boy. Spiked hair. I have to, first, clear my throat. "Yes, but—. I don't remember you. Have you seen him?"

"I met you when he read here at the carols ceremony. I haven't seen Del for a couple of weeks. Is he all right then?"

"He went to Ireland. He may come back tomorrow. You haven't seen him?"

"Like I said, not for a couple of weeks. He'll be back tomorrow, you said? Tell him I said hello." He looks at me. "You sure you're all right?"

I nod. "I've got to find a cab."

"If you go down there, there are masses of them. I'll walk with you." He gestures in the direction of Shaftesbury.

"All right." We walk together. But in fact there are no taxis the whole length of the street. Charing Cross. Well, I could take a bus. He tells me where the stop is, and even waits until the bus arrives. His name is John, as I just barely remember. Says good night and to tell Derek hello tomorrow. I swing aboard the big red ark.

But no seats, so I grab onto a chrome pole, along with everyone else. Him, for example, who must be all of twenty, black, a little gold loop in his earlobe, his jaw taut and trembling as though with tetanus. Or that one, blond, bearded, a slightly bulbous nose, red eyes—like a figure from a Dutch painting, and in fact he may well be Dutch. Bodies and heads in the bluish half-light as we speed up toward Camden. Her small-featured face, leather cap, black curls framing a milk-white complexion, one mole near the mouth. All of us jolting along, stopping, letting off some, taking on others, station by station, an underlying, unspoken complicity between us based on crowded conditions and shared inconvenience. At this hour most everybody's young or at least we're all in sympathy with being young. Them against us. The huddled brick fronts whiz past as we clear the traffic.

And here's my stop, Camden Town Station. Down two steps and the bus roars off in a puff of diesel fumes. Deserted. No, a derelict, ensconced against the wall. He has fallen asleep, his hand still holding a half-eaten scone. He sits on top of two stacked crates, a little improvised throne his counterpart to Her Majesty's, in this dirty, wind-swept, Camden Westminster. Ribbon-cuttings and other royal duties done for the day. Sensing someone there, he raises his head unsteadily and stares at me with bleary, half-open eyes—not really surprised at all when I bow to him slightly, turn, and then walk away through the litter toward Inverness Street. Light comes from the windows of The Harp, and just a faint thump and whistle of music as I pass. The air is very cold, and when I look up a few stars sparkle down at me against the blue-black night.

Eight

Just after ten o'clock the telephone rang. A surprise, since yesterday's message had said eleven: but when I answered with a trembling hello, I heard a familiar voice, a woman's, and it was Corinne.

"Hello, Avery, it's me. I telephoned last night, but you were out."

"I was down in the West End. Wish I'd known. I'm so glad you're back. It's wonderful to hear you. And—how is your brother?"

"He's better. It was difficult but he pulled through." She cleared her throat and, in a sort of public broadcast tone, said, "The only thing is, I've decided it's time for me to go home. I'd just feel less anxious if I were a little closer to him from now on."

"That's probably for the best. When were you thinking of going?"

"Right away. As soon as I can."

"Have you told Susannah?"

"Yes. She understands. We've talked about this before."

Neither of us said anything, and the jointly composed silence suggested resignation for her and support from me.

"But she can come to New York some time."

"I suppose so, if she wants to. I'm sure she will if she wants to."

This was as long as I could keep to a normal conversational frame. I said, "Corinne, something's happened while you were away. I wonder, if it isn't too much trouble, could you come here this morning?"

"Sure. Is it Derek?"

"Yes. And Maeve. Can you come now? I'll explain when you get here."

"I'll be there in—about twenty-five minutes."

I thanked her and said goodbye. Either because I knew I would soon have company or because something had snapped the night before, the wait didn't seem oppressive now. By the time Corinne arrived, all the breakfast dishes were washed and put away and there was a pot of coffee for her. I decided not to have any more because my head ached and my stomach was feeling a little sensitive. It isn't really news that I can't drink the way I used to be able to do.

Corinne was wearing an orange sweater and purple trousers, the two colors jarring in an interesting way that may have been purely accidental. She looked thinner, and her hair was longer; in fact she said she was going to let it grow down to her shoulders so that she could try a Lauren Bacall look for a while. I sat her down with a cup of coffee and told her about Derek and Maeve. She was less surprised than I thought she might be. Most of her comments were supportive, convincing me that I had done the right thing at every point, as far as she could tell. She was interested to hear that I had gone to Dublin and curious about the parents. I gave her my impressions of them, patiently but quickly. I explained about the expected telephone call.

She said, "So I'll just stay with you until it comes."

"I'm glad you're here." Suddenly the last few days' suspense and anxiety came back redoubled. Corinne and I sat silently, glancing at each other from time to time in an embarrassed, sympathetic way. She took my hand and held it for a while. Outside, whoever it always is was playing heavy metal rock music in a car parked curbside, the bass notes thundering through the air like a giant's heartbeat. We sat on the sofa and sighed.

At five minutes after eleven the telephone rang. As calmly as I could manage, I picked it up and said, "Yes?"

"Avery, it's me. I'm all right." A tropically warm wave of feeling broke over me, and my eyes closed. "Maeve's OK. We're safe."

"Derek, thank God. Where are you?"

"In the south again. I've just talked to Da. I told him we shouldn't stay here and he agrees."

"You're coming back to London?"

"No, it's too risky right now."

Hopes deflated. "Where are you going?"

"We think we might try New York—at least for a while."

"Oh." The implications of this rocked through my nervous system. "So, when will you go there?"

"In a day or so."

"Was this your plan or your—advisers'?"

"We worked it out together."

"Do they have contacts in New York?"

"Not really, nobody directly involved."

"Well, then, I'll go to meet you there."

"I was wondering if you would."

"Of course I will. I'll just pack up everything and go home. We'll live in New York for a while, see how you like it."

"Maeve knows a couple of people there."

"Oh, you'll make lots of friends. All right. It's settled. It'll probably take me a day to get things together. I'll expect you when?"

"Thursday, maybe. Or Friday. Saturday at the latest. We have to be careful." I gave him my telephone number in New York, which he copied and repeated to me. Then he asked if I would like to say hello to Maeve.

"Hello, Avery," a faintly hoarse voice said.

"Maeve, I'm so glad you're all right. Is everything OK?"

"I could use some sleep. It's been tense. I'm really glad to be talking to you. And—will I see you in a few days?"

"Yes. Please be careful. I'm so glad you're safe."

"Yes. Till soon." Derek came back on and said he shouldn't talk much longer. In a few days we would be back together.

And then I did something I would never under normal circumstances do. I blurted, "Derek, I got tested. It's not good news."

The briefest silence. Then, "Avery, I'm really sorry. I wish I were with you. I will be soon. I love you. We'll take care of it together." His voice broke, and then he said, "Avery, they won't let me talk. I'll be there in New York." Then, using a phrase I think he got from his NA meetings, he said, "I'll be there for you."

I put down the telephone and turned to Corinne who was looking at me, shaking her head. "Oh, Avery," she said. We held each other tightly but without saying anything. We sat down.

Corinne said, "It's good news about Derek, but bad news for you." With her longish hair and orange sweater she suddenly looked like someone I'd just met, her gaze traveling over my face, a sort of sad smile or wince flickering across hers. As we got our breath back I went over the details, first about Derek, then about me.

She listened carefully and then, in an efficient tone said, "All right let's both go back together. Call the airline this minute."

As soon as we had our reservations (for Wednesday noon), Corinne jumped up and said, "OK, we both have a lot to do. Talk to you tonight." She grabbed her coat and waved as she went out the door.

I telephoned Adele, and, without explaining very much, told her I'd be home in two days.

"Avery, I'm so glad you're coming home. Now what's the flight number, I'll meet the plane."

"No, I'll call you as soon as we pass customs, and you can go over to the apartment and meet me there."

"This is the most thrilling news. I've missed you so much."

Next there was the follow-through: I began going through my closets and drawers throwing out everything I could possibly do without. Not the photograph of Hypnos, though, which had become a sort of talisman. A good many old clothes went straight into the dustbin, including a beat-up old jacket that dated back to the days before—. A controlled frenzy of practical efficiency mixed in with adrenaline-powered feelings difficult to name. After I had packed two of my suitcases and one for Derek, I suddenly had to sit down, overcome by an enormous fatigue, a delayed reaction from the tensions of the past week—but really extreme, so that I could do nothing more than sit still and stare out the window and breathe. I'd never felt anything like this exhaustion in my life. Eventually, though, I dragged myself to my feet and called a taxi. It occurred to me that Derek's landlady needed to be told. I went down to Earl's Court and rang her bell. She recognized me immediately and didn't question the story I came up with, especially after I gave her a month's advance rent.

"What about 'is things?" I said I didn't know. "Well, if you'll 'elp me we can pack 'em up and put 'em in storage."

We went up to his room, which was dim and musty. Neither of us made much effort to be neat, simply threw clothes and knickknacks into the cartons Mrs. Finchley had brought up. At one point she stopped to scrutinize the issue of *Playgirl* with the black athlete on the cover, shook her head and tossed it in. The rubber plant looked dry and neglected so I took it upon myself to offer it to her. She said she thought she could get it in good shape again. As we were finishing up, I paused and rested my hand on the metal bedstead, thinking back over ... everything. On the wall above, still there, in reposeful anguish, was the painted-over crucifix. I suddenly remembered I would be with Derek in something less than a hundred hours, and a shiver of anticipation ran through me.

"If 'e don't come to collect this in three months, it's going on the street," Mrs. Finchley said, blinking a little at the social indecorum but still a practical-minded proprietress. I thanked her and said she would hear from us soon.

A restless night and another morning of frenzied activity that included trips to the bank, to my landlady, some more packing, and a telephone call to Max Wiesner (who, however, had already heard about everything). Also, a telephone call from Corinne to say that Susannah had insisted on driving us to Heathrow. That would be so much nicer, and a chance to say goodbye

Since Derek's call yesterday, there's been this welcome sense of things falling into place and cooperating. So that, as I sit here next to my luggage, waiting for Corinne and Susannah, the suddenly bare-looking rooms breathe an almost family air of understanding and complicity. They know me very well now, are sorry to see me go, but don't question that I have other obligations that will keep us apart until some future date. They are also conscious of being representatives of the City of London himself, a worthy old alderman who has sheltered so many transient strangers over the centuries—before sending them on their way, most of us glad to have been, for a month or a year or a decade, part of his story....

There is Corinne at the door, and, parked at the curb, Susannah in her Peugeot.

The drive out is a chance for me to say a goodbye that has already been settled between the two of them. Obviously Corinne means more to me than Susannah, but this clear-eyed sophisticate has a level head, doesn't pretend to more emotion than she actually feels, and has her own arguments. She says she'll be in touch, which suggests that she'll make a trip to New York at some point. We have our goodbye hug just in front of the security check. Skimming a slender hand through her curls, she waves and turns away.

As Corinne and I are welcomed into the front of the plane by a brisk, blue-clad stewardess, an image of Adele floats into my mind. I think of her waiting for me in Chelsea, even though the meeting won't take place for seven or eight hours yet. Corinne and I settle into our seats and slip into silent daydreams as preflight briefing about emergencies and oxygen masks begins over the microphone. She quietly takes my hand and squeezes it during the taxi out onto the runway. The plane turns and accelerates for takeoff. Up we go, over the fields and towns, the crisscrossing hedges and roads. The stewardess offers us newspapers. More talks about Northern Ireland, more violence in South Africa. Never have I felt this tired before, a bone-deep tiredness, suffused through every limb.... Please God help Derek find his way to New York with no slip-ups. Corinne sees something in my expression and reaches over to rest a hand on my arm. A certain damp cold seems to emanate from our little porthole, or is it simply that things look frigid outside as we begin passing through the clouds, the sight of the sea just visible far ahead. And we go up through the cottony layers, gray and white, a formless stratum of mist and monochrome uncertainty. On through all of that until, suddenly, there is a glimmer and then another. Surrealistically bright, the realm above the cloud cover begins to flare through our windows. I suddenly have a mental picture of Derek, framed by the porthole and based on a remembered image of him before the window onto Gloucester Crescent: backlit, shirtless, in Roman-coin profile, a curved line leading up from the nape to the crown of his nicely shaped head, his lips parted slightly, eyes gazing off into space. The tug of feeling toward this picture tells me that he has made me his—though not quite how and certainly not why. Oh look, the brilliant, snowy surface of cloud below us....

As icy brilliance floods over the transfixed passengers, a child in the seat behind me half whispers and half speaks: "Look, mommy, the sun came out." I glance down at photographic light and shadow on my hands, the veins developed in high contrast, with just the tiniest vibration visible as each heartbeat pumps and pumps dark blood, my blood, guarantor of this one day, through them.